TRUE DEVOTION

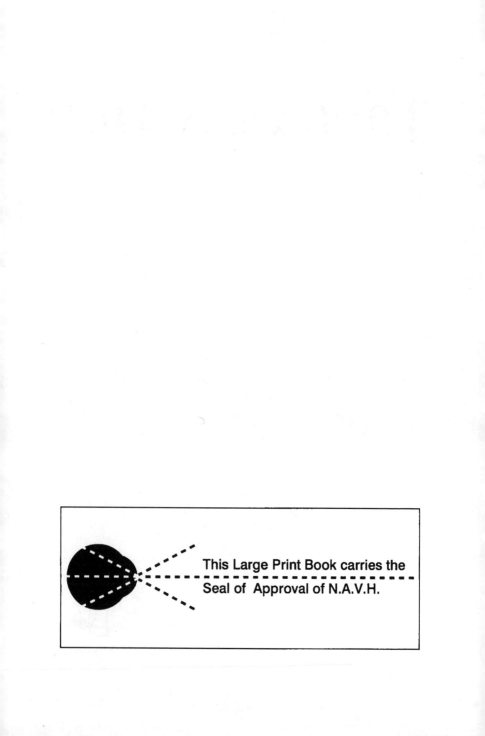

This Large Print Book carries the
Seal of Approval of N.A.V.H.

BOOK ONE
THE UNCOMMON HEROES

TRUE DEVOTION

★ ★ ★

Dee Henderson

Thorndike Press • Waterville, Maine

Published in 2004 by arrangement with
Multnomah Publishers, Inc.

Thorndike Press® Large Print Christian Fiction.

The tree indicium is a trademark of Thorndike Press.

The text of this Large Print edition is unabridged.
Other aspects of the book may vary from the original edition.

Set in 16 pt. Plantin by Elena Picard.

Printed in the United States on permanent paper.

Library of Congress Cataloging-in-Publication Data

Henderson, Dee.
    True devotion / Dee Henderson.
        p. cm. — (The uncommon heroes series ; bk. 1)
    ISBN 0-7862-6317-2 (lg. print : hc : alk. paper)
    ISBN 1-59415-035-4 (lg. print : sc : alk. paper)
    1. United States. Navy. SEALs — Fiction. 2. Widows
— Fiction. 3. Large type books. I. Title.
PS3558.E4829T78 2004
  813′.54—dc22   2003071169

This story is dedicated to the military heroes of my immediate family:

my Grandfather Johnson who rests at Arlington National Cemetery,

my Grandfather Hammer decorated for campaigns through France,

my uncles who served in the Army and Navy,

and my brother who served in the Air Force.

I'm proud of you.

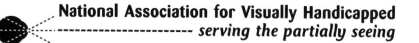

National Association for Visually Handicapped
serving the partially seeing

As the Founder/CEO of NAVH, the only national health agency solely devoted to those who, although not totally blind, have an eye disease which could lead to serious visual impairment, I am pleased to recognize Thorndike Press★ as one of the leading publishers in the large print field.

Founded in 1954 in San Francisco to prepare large print textbooks for partially seeing children, NAVH became the pioneer and standard setting agency in the preparation of large type.

Today, those publishers who meet our standards carry the prestigious "Seal of Approval" indicating high quality large print. We are delighted that Thorndike Press is one of the publishers whose titles meet these standards. We are also pleased to recognize the significant contribution Thorndike Press is making in this important and growing field.

Lorraine H. Marchi, L.H.D.
Founder/CEO
NAVH

★ Thorndike Press encompasses the following imprints: Thorndike, Wheeler, Walker and Large Print Press.

★ ★ ★

Navy SEAL Team Nine is a fictional entity with a few differences from an actual SEAL Team. A real Team would not deploy with the geographic diversity as shown in this story, nor would they serve together for such an extended period of time. These changes were made to accommodate a work of fiction. I have, however, endeavored to be accurate in both the terminology and tactics of an actual SEAL Team. To that end, former Navy SEAL Steve Watkins did me the honor of reviewing this manuscript. All remaining errors are mine.

*"God is our refuge and strength,
a very present help in trouble."*

PSALM 46:1

GLOSSARY

AOIC: Assistant Officer In Charge.

ATTACK BOARD: Underwater guidance board used for long swims. The board has a bubble compass and a depth gauge on it.

AWACS: Airborne Warning And Control System. Special aircraft with powerful radars to scan for planes at any altitude. Controls air-to-air engagements with enemy forces.

BROKEN ARROW: Any accident with nuclear weapons or nuclear material lost, shot down, crashed, stolen, or hijacked.

BUD/S: Basic Underwater Demolition/SEAL. The name for the initial six-month training program at the facility in Coronado, California, which all men hoping to be SEALs must pass.

C-130: Cargo plane.

CHOCOLATE MOUNTAIN: Land training center for SEALs in the California desert.

DRAEGAR LAR V: Rebreather units that suppress bubbles under water.

GPS: Global Positioning System. Satellite guidance around earth used to precisely pinpoint aircraft, ships, vehicles, and ground troops.

HELO: Helicopter.

L-T: Lieutenant.

MP: Military Police.

NAB: U.S. Naval Amphibious Base, Coronado, California.

NATO PHONETIC ALPHABET: Alpha, Bravo, Charlie, Delta, Echo, Foxtrot, Golf, Hotel, India, Juliet, Kilo, Lima, Mike, November, Oscar, Papa, Quebec, Romeo, Sierra, Tango, Uniform, Victor, Whiskey, X-ray, Yankee, Zulu.

NEST: Nuclear Energy Search Team. Nonmilitary unit that reports at once to any spill, problem, or Broken Arrow to determine the extent of the radiation problem.

NEWBIES: A new man in an established military unit.

NVGs: Night Vision Goggles give good night vision in the dark with a greenish view.

SEAL: One of the elite branches of the U.S. Special Forces operating from the sea, air, or land.

SNAKED: Slang for stepping through stuff you don't want to identify.

SNEAK AND PEEK: Slang for stealthy reconnaissance.

TANGO(S): Terrorist.

TRIDENT: SEALs emblem. An eagle with talons clutching a Revolutionary War pistol, and Neptune's trident superimposed on the Navy's traditional anchor.

XO: Executive Officer.

One

★ ★ ★

They were going to drown.

Kelly Jacobs could already see the headline on the front page of the weekly *Coronado Eagle* newspaper: "Riptide Kills Teen and Lifeguard." The cold water had her by the throat. Six minutes had passed since she'd last seen the boy bobbing in the swells, and they were being pulled out to sea at a horrifying clip.

She had a lifetime of experience in the Pacific waters off San Diego, numerous rescues, but nothing like this. The water in early May, warmer than usual from La Niña, was still only sixty-seven degrees, cold enough to induce hypothermia. The swells dropped her four feet down in the troughs. If she didn't find the boy soon she wouldn't have the ability to get them back to shore. And this was a big ocean for a search party to cover in the dark — to her left the sun had already set and the twilight was fading fast.

The riptide created by the conflux of ocean currents and the outgoing tide had formed late in the day with an explosive suddenness. When conditions changed, the riptide would fade as abruptly as it had formed, but whether it lasted a few hours or a day would not matter in the end. It was already on the verge of becoming deadly.

The fear of what was coming overwhelmed her. This fight to reach the boy was turning into a personal life-and-death struggle. The saltwater burned her throat and sent her gasping as another wave caught her in midbreath. To give up the attempted rescue to save herself, to let the boy drown — It had been years since she had cared about something this much. She wasn't going to give up, and she wasn't going to fail.

Kelly strained to find a way to work with the waves rather than against them. The boy was out here, somewhere near, and she was going to reach him. She thought about her husband as she fought the cold of the sea. *Nick, did you die because you drowned?* The Navy had never told her.

She would have said it was impossible for her husband, a Navy SEAL, to drown. With all his training, with all his confidence and courage, she had dismissed it as even a consideration, but she was suddenly not sure anymore and the thought was agonizing.

Three years ago she had said good-bye to her husband at the gates of the U.S. Naval Amphibious Base, half a mile down Highway 75 from their home in the Coronado Shores subdivision. It was a typical good-bye — loving but rushed. Nick had been slipping away from her ever since his pager went off forty minutes before, his attention already on the upcoming mission.

She stole one last hug, burying her face against his uniform, wishing he wasn't leaving but unwilling to put that wish into words. She never wanted to hold him back or give him reason to hesitate. She loved him and she would keep everything on the home front together and ready for his return. Nick lifted Kelly off her feet for his kiss good-bye and then strode with purpose through security to join the other members of SEAL Team Nine gathering to hear why they had been paged to assemble at 8 p.m.

A confident man, her husband, serving in one of the elite branches of the U.S. special forces — a Navy SEAL: from sea, air,

13

or land, they would get the job done. Fluent in three languages, a competent backup medic, he was accustomed to being sent to deal with crises around the world where force had to be brought to bear rapidly. They called him Eagle because he saw everything. A useful trait since he walked point for one of the two squads in Golf Platoon.

Kelly dropped him off at the base and returned home, knowing neither where he was going nor how long he would be gone. She trusted his confidence in himself, in the men around him, in their training. They were the best and the best didn't fail.

There had been no welcome home.

A training accident. That was what the Navy officially said as it buried her husband with full military honors and handed her the folded flag.

She knew they were lying. A training accident didn't bring her husband home in a sealed coffin and bring Nick's commanding officer, Lieutenant Joe Baker, home nursing a bullet wound through his shoulder. She never tried to break the understood code of silence to learn the truth. They were SEALs, and she had been a SEAL's wife. The truth was classified.

She nearly dropped the flag when they

handed it to her. She had not been able to see her husband; the coffin remained sealed. They handed her the flag he had fought to defend, folded neat and tight with no red showing. It had been prepared by the men in uniform with a solemnness of ritual that would allow no slackness in the fabric or imperfection in a fold. They gave her his flag because they could not give her back the man; they gave her his flag to stand in his place. Their salute honored the man, the flag his service, the taps his passing. And it hit her in that instant, the fact Nick was gone for good.

Looking into the eyes of the hurting men of SEAL Team Nine as the funeral concluded, looking into the solemn eyes of men who grieved with her, she was assured that her husband had done his job and not let them down. They were not able to share it in words, but they all shared that truth in their expressions. She clung to the fact Nick died doing what he loved. Under her own grief she was grateful for that.

And yet the pain that had come in the passing days and months ripped deeper than anything she had ever felt. Her life had changed forever. She missed Nick more than words could express. The men of SEAL Team Nine had replaced him because his was a profession that required another to stand in the gap of one fallen. They went on while they always remembered. But no one could replace him for her.

The medallion she wore, Nick's eagle, slapped against her in the waves. She reached for it with one hand, grabbing hold, grateful now she had secured the chain so she could wear it in the water. It had traveled with Nick through five years of missions. Now it was her closest reminder of him.

"People drown because they panic."

She clung to the words Nick had so often said. During SEAL training the instructors tied his hands and feet and dropped him into the deep end of the pool for thirty minutes doing various tasks — the drown-proof test. Nick knew what he was talking about. He just hadn't told her how hard it was not to panic.

Relax. Do your job.

Nick would wonder why she was panicking when she'd been trained for hard tasks such as this. She put her energy into judging the swells, riding them up to scan the surrounding water. The boy had been south of her the last time she had seen him.

There!

She surged toward him with a hard crawl, willing to use the last of her energy, knowing this might be her last chance before darkness fell.

The teenager had been surfing with a friend; both boys got into trouble in the heavy surf. She went into the water to back up her partner. Alex reached them first, securing a hold on one boy bleeding from a gash on the forehead and pushing his float board to the other boy. As Alex headed toward the shore towing the injured boy, she went for the other teen, not surprised when in his panic he fought her. At the same instant she got hit in the eye, they hit the riptide. The sea tore them apart.

The sea helped her this time, tossing her the last few feet. She snagged the boy's arm as she slammed past him, spun into him, the wave breaking over her head and into her face. She coughed hard, struggling to clear her lungs as she held on for all she was worth. She was not going to lose him again.

The fight had gone out of the teen. The straps of the float board that had been pushed to him were around his left wrist, his right arm hugging it. Even though she desperately needed a few brief moments of rest, she was careful not to put any of her weight onto the float board. It had kept his head above water during the last long separation and been a factor in keeping him alive. It would never support them both.

Sandy blond hair, blue eyes, slim, younger than she originally thought, fourteen or fifteen, long, skinny arms and lanky, still trying to fit into his sudden growth spurt. Both his fear and fatigue were obvious in his face. The waves sent them up and down and rocked them back and forth in a never-ending sensation of movement that made *seasickness* too calm a word for the reality. "What's your name?" She leaned close to him to be heard.

He was swallowing water, coughing, and his voice rasped. "Ryan."

"I'm Kelly." Fighting fingers that were stiff, that did not want to do as she asked, she unwrapped the nylon rope at her waist and maneuvered the buddy line around his waist, securely tying the line. She wasn't going to take a chance on the sea once again tearing them apart. She put her hands on his face, smiling at him, even as she studied his eyes and assessed his condition. "That was a pretty impressive wipeout you did on the surfboard."

He gave a glimmer of a smile back. "My dad is going to kill me. I wasn't supposed to be surfing."

Hypothermia. She could hear it in the dragging words and see it in his swollen eyes as he struggled to keep them open against the sting of the saltwater and the cold-induced fatigue. She wasn't in much better shape herself.

She looked to the east. The twilight was almost gone; the shoreline appeared only by reflected lights on the horizon. The distance was distorted by the dim twilight, but even by optimistic assessments it was far away. Getting them back to shore was no longer possible. Even if she had the strength, she would not be able to judge the location of the beach and the dangerous rocks in the descending darkness. There was little she could do but keep the boy talking and hope help arrived soon. She knew the rescue crews would be out looking. As soon as Alex had reached shore, the call for help would have gone out.

"Who's your dad?" The conversation was as much to distract her as to distract him. Waiting was almost harder than searching. She had to figure out some way to get them through the coming ordeal while she still had the clarity to plan. The cold water was a deadly foe for it ruined the ability to think clearly.

"Charles Raines."

"You live here in Coronado?"

"Across the water on the Point Loma peninsula. Dad bought a place on Hill Street."

A wealthy man's son. The homes on Hill Street bordered Sunset Cliffs National Park. That stretch of shoreline had the most beautiful rock formations carved out by the sea she had ever seen. "Those are beautiful homes."

"The house is okay."

"Just okay?" she asked, amused at the perspective of youth.

"Our home in Hong Kong was more exotic, but we had to leave three years ago when the lease expired."

"On the house or the country?"

He laughed; it was weak but there. "The country actually. Dad's British. He had to move his company headquarters to San Diego when Hong Kong reverted back to China."

Having never traveled outside of California, Kelly felt a little envious. Hong Kong sounded intriguing. "That must have been fun for your mom."

"It's just Dad and me."

"I'm sorry."

"It's okay. I barely remember my mom, Amy. She died when I was little."

Even though his words were matter-of-fact, she heard the wistfulness in his voice. He missed not having a mom. And in that simple brief exchange, Kelly felt like she took a step toward understanding him. He would hide the depth of his grief, hang out with friends, and wonder why they thought their moms were the worst when he thought their moms were pretty great. Kelly knew it was after the loss that you missed what had been taken for granted. "My mom died about five years ago. It's rough."

Ryan looked toward her. "Did she —" His hand slipped from the float, momentarily dropping his head below the surface. His panic was instantaneous.

Kelly suddenly found herself pulled down as Ryan tried to claw his way back to the surface using her, his hand pressing down painfully into the nerve in her shoulder, his knee catching her in the calf. She broke to the surface, grabbing him from behind and wrapping her forearm under his chin. "Easy!"

"We're going to drown out here!"

She yanked the float board back by its rope. "Hug it across your chest and stop moving," she ordered, treading water for both of them, knowing just how precarious their situation was.

Ryan went still but he was crying now, the sound of his sobs carrying across the water, the fear overwhelming him. Kelly's heart broke at the sound, knowing for a boy his age, tears would be the last thing he wanted someone to see. She smoothed her hand over his hair trying to comfort without embarrassing him. "It's going to be okay. Just relax. I won't let you drown."

His grip on her arm finally eased enough so circulation could return. "How can they find us in the dark?"

She looked around, deciphering in the flickering moonlight that the waves were increasing in size. There had been a low front coming through this evening and its front edge of wind was already reaching them. "Spotlights. Searchlights. The boats will be out, even helicopters." She didn't add what she knew and feared. Even with the resources, finding them before morning would be difficult if not impossible.

No. She couldn't let herself doubt.

Joe would find them.

"Kelly, I would like you to meet my new boss, Lieutenant Joe Baker."

She turned at the touch of her husband's hand on her shoulder. Standing beside Nick, Joe seemed dwarfed, a good four inches shorter, the same powerful muscles but less bulky. But then at six feet four Nick broke the rules for what made a good SEAL physique. Joe could have been the prototype. He was a triathlete if she'd ever seen one. He had the warm copper tan of a man who spent most of his days outside.

Joe had nice eyes. She always looked there first because nothing told her more about a soldier than his eyes. Joe's were blue, like the sea she enjoyed watching at dawn, and they were calm. He held her gaze as she looked at him, doing his own study. She knew the man was brave. He was known in the SEAL community as one of the best, and that said a lot among men who didn't give accolades until they were earned. He also looked kind. The fact he was taking time to come and meet the families of his men said a lot. She offered her hand with a smile. Her husband would be in good hands.

"Lieutenant. Thanks for coming to the cookout." She felt the warmth as his hand closed around hers and could feel the texture of calluses, the strength of a man who could fight hard and yet still touch with tenderness.

"I never turn down an invitation to good cooking, Mrs. Jacobs."

Kelly was very happily married, but she wasn't immune to the man; she felt the impact

23

of being the focus of his smile and the warmth in those eyes. Her single friends in Coronado would certainly take notice of the new boss. She was going to enjoy introducing him around. "Please, it's Kelly."

"If you'll make it Joe."

"I'll be glad to. No handle?"

The eyes she liked twinkled with his smile. "Occasionally I get called Bear, but that's only if I'm in a bad mood."

A grizzly bear — oh, it was perfect. She laughed at the image. "I like it. Nick goes by Eagle, unless he doesn't see something, then the guys call him Buzzard."

"Kelly . . ." Nick winced, but Joe just laughed.

Joe had been her husband's commanding officer, but he had also become her husband's best friend. The men had clicked that first afternoon, sharing a common bond that went deeper than work. They had similar perspectives and priorities in life. Nick had led Joe to Christ. She had often thought of Nick and Joe as her example of a modern-day David and Jonathan. Best friends. Warriors. Men passionate about their God.

Joe's grief over the loss of Nick was different than hers, but just as deep. The men had spent a lot of time together; now Joe spent large portions of his time alone. He'd lost a best friend and those were not easy to replace.

Since Nick's death Joe had been watching out for her.

He would find them.

The sea, for years his friend, was tonight his enemy.

Joe checked the compass on his wrist and then the GPS readout. The longitude reading as marked by the global positioning satellites made him frown; this current was moving him rapidly out to sea.

Almost an hour had passed since word had come that Kelly was in trouble. Neither he nor the other members of SEAL Team Nine's Golf Platoon had felt like leaving the search up to just the Coast Guard. Normally the Coast Guard asked for help, but in this case, who asked and who offered would get blurred in the reports. The Navy understood what made good public relations — and it didn't look good if a civilian lifeguard and a teen drowned within the immediate vicinity of one of the largest naval bases in the country.

But even if there had been no formal protocol for the help, the military brass would still have backed their involvement. They understood taking care of their own. Not to help the widow of a SEAL who had gone down in combat would insult the honor of an entire SEAL community. For Joe it was much more personal. He had to find Kelly.

He had elected to become a human buoy, to find out firsthand where the riptide began and which way it moved. It had been easy to find and it was vicious. He had felt the sudden pull of the water about forty feet from shore.

Once in the riptide a swimmer could struggle to swim back into shore until his strength was gone and he would never get any closer. If he stopped to tread water he would be pulled out to sea at a rapid clip. The only way to break free was to turn and swim parallel to the shore until clear of the unpredictable current.

Finding the boy, pulling him with her — Kelly would never have been able to get out of this current. Joe prayed she had been smart enough not to try. If she had already burned through her energy . . .

Joe activated the waterproof microphone. "Boomer, I'm getting pulled into grid six." Boomer, given name Chet Walker, was the AOIC — Assistant Officer

In Charge — of Golf Platoon.

"The riptide is still holding together?"

"It's still intact. They've been pulled out much farther than we assumed."

"I'll redirect the boats and come pick you up."

Joe saw the spotlight of the search helicopter veer west, moving farther out to sea. Fifty minutes. It was an eternity. The search area expanded with every minute that passed. Kelly was out in this somewhere, unprotected from the cold, trying to save her life and the boy's. They had to find them soon. The cold was already reaching through his wet suit, and he trained for these conditions. He could only imagine what it was doing to Kelly and the teen.

He heard the Zodiac slow as it approached his coordinates. The boat appeared abruptly from the darkness. He reached up with his right hand and was pulled aboard by Boomer. Joe perched on the side of the craft, the taut, thick rubber familiar to his touch. There were no lights on board the six-by-fifteen-foot Zodiac. They were accustomed to working in the darkness, and a light would only destroy the distance they could see naturally and with the aid of their night vision goggles.

"Take me to grid nine." The SEAL manning the muffled outboard motor nodded and turned the craft west.

Boomer handed over a pair of NVGs. "We'll find them."

Joe accepted the night vision goggles and simply nodded. Sixteen volunteer SEALs plus the Coast Guard — not finding them was inconceivable. Whether they would find them in time remained to be seen. They could already be too late.

It was his job that was supposed to be life-threatening, not hers. He had to force himself to relax and unclench his jaw — something he didn't have to do in combat. He was lousy at accepting a civilian in danger, especially a friend. Feeling helpless was an emotion he worked hard to avoid and getting it flung at him tonight was hard to take.

Kelly was going to be embarrassed when they found her. It would sting her pride a bit, knowing Alex had been able to get back to shore with one of the surfers and she had not. Joe held on to that image of the small laugh and the flushed cheeks that were hallmarks of Kelly when she was the center of the attention; it was better than the alternative.

He prayed she lived long enough to be embarrassed.

"Ryan?" Kelly grabbed for the float board as it slipped from Ryan's hand.

He didn't answer.

"Ryan, wake up." She shook him hard, trying to rouse him. "Ryan!"

She couldn't bring him around. The cold had finally won. She felt for his pulse and found it slow but steady. How long before that changed? Twenty minutes? Thirty? She struggled to secure the float board against his chest with the straps, using it to ensure Ryan would float on his back.

His slow, steady kicks had been helping in the fight to keep them steady against the current. The effort to keep treading water for them both was exhausting. The muscles in her legs burned from the strain, adding a painful agony to the mix as her skin grew icy. It felt like she was trying to kick through thick cement; there was nothing gentle about the water now. She wanted so desperately to take a break.

How had Nick ever made it through Hell Week? She had always known her husband downplayed the effort required by his job. She had never realized how much he downplayed it.

Anyone who wanted to be a SEAL had

to first get through six months of training known as BUD/S, and the basic underwater demolition/SEAL training routinely eliminated most of the candidates. The fifth week had earned being called Hell Week. After four weeks of pushing the men in intense physical training, the instructors for those who would be SEALs set out to find out who in the class *intended* to be a SEAL and who only *wanted* to be one.

For five days and nights, with only four hours of sleep, the men were pushed to the limits — cold ocean swims, constantly lugging a telephone pole or carrying their rubber boats over their heads, conducting explosive ordinance drills, night landings in the pounding surf through the rocks off the historic Hotel del Coronado — all the while the instructors pushing, encouraging them to quit.

By the end of Hell Week, 70 percent of Nick's class had voluntarily withdrawn.

Nick had made it. Kelly could still vividly remember him walking through the door that Friday, given forty-eight hours of liberty. He had collapsed on the bed — sand, grit, grime, and all, and had not moved for twenty-two hours. Blisters, torn muscles, sunburn, exhaustion — her husband had survived the first step to becoming an elite warrior. She had been so proud of him.

She wished she had better understood then what it felt like to be pushed to the limits of your endurance. Her appreciation for what Nick had accomplished had just escalated, and she would never be able to tell him. She was hitting the wall of what she could endure. *Nick, how did you do it?*

SEALs never give up. There is no secret. SEALs simply never quit.

She would love to give up. Closing her eyes, taking a deep breath, Kelly forced herself to find a rhythm for her kicks. SEALs trained to be able to take this kind of physical punishment. That had to be part of their secret. All the mornings she had blown off running, all the days she had ignored her normal exercise routine, were delivering their revenge without mercy. She would never tease a SEAL again about the constant workouts.

"I thought you were going shopping with Liz."

Kelly looked up from the clothes she was putting away to see Nick leaning against the doorjamb to the master bedroom. She smiled. "We're going later. I thought you and Joe were going running."

Nick didn't move out of the doorway as she

joined him. She slid under his arm and wrapped hers around his waist, taking him with her, enjoying the closeness. She loved this man. It wasn't often he got a few free hours on a weekday. The guys were going out to the Chocolate Mountain Test Range later in the day for a nighttime training op. Nick didn't have to report until 1300 hours.

Her husband chuckled. "Honey, we've already been. I left two hours ago." His arm dropped across her shoulders as they headed toward the kitchen.

"I can tell. You're wet." She said it with a grin, for it was more saltwater than sweat. Joe and Nick must have been doing their five-mile run on the beach down at the surf line — SEALs trained, played, and lived in the sand and sea like it was their second home. From the lifeguard tower she would often see the men in the early morning silently challenging each other, racing up the sand, turning everything into a competition — the best friends among them were the worst. "Who won?" She picked up a clean T-shirt from the laundry basket of folded clothes on the counter and tossed it to him.

Nick's grin was quick. "I let him." Nick stripped off the wet shirt, then took one step back into the hall and tossed it into the laundry room. He pulled on the clean one.

"We're heading to the gym to work the weights. You want to come spot for me?"

It was an appealing offer, for her husband working out was a sight to enjoy. He tended to show off just a bit if only with a wink before he lifted a loaded barbell off the bar. She could appreciate later the results as he easily swept her off her feet, but she couldn't totally forget the reason he was so diligent about the workouts. They were preparations for battle.

It wasn't something to tease him about on a day when he had just lost in a footrace at the beach to Joe. There were priorities, and then there were priorities. "Thanks, but I'd be invading a guy's domain." She joined him and rested her hands against his biceps, leaning into him to share a kiss. "Go get back to work. And don't come home till you out-rep him or something."

He grinned. "Yes, ma'am."

Kelly forced herself back to the present. She couldn't afford to let herself drift down memory lane; hypothermia-induced sleep would overtake her too. And it did her no good to remember, for the memories were too bittersweet to enjoy. Nick would never again be around to flirt with, to tease, and that realization cut inside every time she had to face that fact.

Taking a deep breath, she forced herself

to get a stronger grip on Ryan. If she timed the swells, she could make two strong kicks and ride a crest down, giving herself a pause before she needed to make the third kick. It helped, but not enough; she could feel her kicks growing weaker, no matter how hard she tried to keep them steady. She needed help to come soon.

She didn't realize at first that it was a rescue light. It came from the east, traveling west toward her, so slow it appeared almost not to move. Then the sound of the helicopter rotors reached her, forming a deep heartbeat that grew and pounded the air in a welcome beat. She frantically searched for something to signal with. She had nothing shiny. She untied the float board and took on Ryan's full weight, keeping him out of the water with one arm while doing her best to wave the float board with her free hand, using all the strength she had left in a desperate attempt to get noticed.

She watched the light trace over the water.

They were drifting away from where the light would pass over.

With that realization came fear. If the helicopter crew didn't see them, it could be hours before this grid was searched again. Ryan would never make it, and it was doubtful she would either. She struggled to swim against the current into the path of the light, pulling Ryan with her. The spotlight passed five yards beyond them, the helicopter moving steadily on. Kelly lowered the float board when it became obvious they had not been seen. The sound faded.

She started crying.

Two

Joe went back into the water at the east edge of grid nine, absorbing the shock of the cold water, then ignoring it. The rubber of his wet suit sealed a layer of water against his skin where it warmed, creating a blanket of protection around him, but it could not prevent his fingers from turning to ice or his face from feeling the sting of the waves. The equipment vest and gear felt heavy now, but comfortable, for they were familiar weights. In an odd way it was better to be in the water than the boat, for it clarified matters, added urgency. Kelly was going to freeze.

He let himself drift, watching the GPS and calculating his speed.

The riptide had ended. "Boomer, head north. The current has changed."

"It will put us out of radio range." The answer came back through broken static. Joe had sent the boat on to cover the western edge of the grid.

"I'll use a flare if I need you. Come back

on a parallel track to these coordinates in thirty minutes."

He began a steady swim with the current, pausing often to scan the ocean. Kelly was comfortable in the water, wasn't the type to panic, but he could feel the pressing reality. Anything could happen in this cold sea.

Lord, where is she?

He had never learned to pray as eloquently as Nick or as knowledgeably as Kelly. They had both been Christians a long time. They had a comfortable knowledge of God, and it showed in their actions and their prayers. His own prayers were heartfelt but short.

He wished he had been a Christian longer. After Nick died he hadn't been much help to Kelly when the grief hit, and that still troubled him. Other than Liz she hadn't let many people near her, had put up a protective front, and it had left him struggling to help her out. He'd failed at that somewhere along the way, for she had gone quiet, noticeably quiet in the last few months, when normally she talked easily about God.

Now this. She needed him and the idea that he would let her down at a time like this . . . he'd never be able to live with himself if they didn't find her in time.

Please, Jesus. Keep her safe. Help us find her. She's the most important person I have left in my life. I can't face the idea of losing her.

The stars were bright overhead. In the dark ocean expanse, no city lights anywhere nearby, the stars shone in their full glory. *"The heavens declare the glory of God . . ."* Kelly knew she ought to be praying. The words were not there. She was so tired now. Three years of wandering away — a prodigal, a hypocrite, she could think of numerous labels that applied — had diminished a vital relationship to one with few words. However she looked at her life in the last three years, God had not been in the center of it. It made her ashamed.

Oh, people who met her didn't know. She had been more active in the church than ever, almost frantic in keeping herself busy with all her good works. But her Bible had only been opened in public; her trust in God had changed to doing for herself. She hated people who pretended yet she had done it beautifully. God had taken away Nick and she had walked away from Him, blaming Him for her pain.

38

She had already apologized.

There was peace now but not words. Prayer had once been as easy as breathing, now she didn't know how to begin. It made her want to cry to realize what she had lost.

A wave slammed over her face and she tried to shake off the water without releasing her hold on Ryan.

It's not too late to change.

It was a reassuring, profound reminder. If she survived and had a chance to try again, to restore what she had allowed to decay and pick up her dreams again. She had never been happier than when she was a wife dreaming about being a mother.

For years she'd let herself drift rather than accept that she was going to have to fight for a future again, that she would have to pour herself back into life if she wanted something more than the grief.

She'd given up for years. It was time to stop giving up.

Finding energy she didn't have, Kelly strengthened her kick.

She was swallowing too much water. Kelly knew it in a clinically detached kind of way. Part of her mind was screaming for her to kick harder, to keep her head farther out of the water, but she couldn't. The cold had crept deep into her muscles.

She was going to die of hypothermia. She knew it, could feel her heart rate slowing down, could feel herself drifting off to sleep, and couldn't rouse herself to fight, even for Ryan's sake. At least it didn't hurt. Her eyes closed as she sighed.

Don't.

She got shoved by a wave and rolled over. She blinked and tightened her arm around Ryan, instinctively righting herself, the panic startling her body back into motion.

Of all the stupid . . . she wanted to swear at herself as she realized what had happened. She forced her hands to lock together, gritted her teeth, and strained to rhythmically kick her legs again.

How she would die was now painfully clear. Hers wouldn't be a peaceful ending, but rather a series of adrenaline-induced scares until she finally didn't recover in time and she drowned.

Her breathing slowly came back to normal. For the moment she was awake, wide-awake. *Lord, thanks for the shove.* She would have chuckled if she could have done it without swallowing more saltwater. It had been quite an effective wake-up order.

She was not going to die in the middle of the ocean.

The decision settled firmly inside, and it resonated the same way the decision *I'm going to marry Nick* had once resonated. No matter how cold she got, how tired she became, she was going to survive.

It was going to be a long night.

She blocked out the cold and thought about the future, determined to keep her mind active. When she got out of this mess, what in her life was she going to change first? Where did she start rebuilding?

It wasn't a simple question or an easy one. She knew what she wanted most to change. She missed being a wife, being part of someone's life. She had married Nick when she was nineteen and she didn't enjoy being alone.

There was no longer any reason to wake at the crack of dawn. In the past she had groused good-naturedly at Nick's cheerfulness as she fixed him breakfast. But she missed the few minutes of beauty that had been the compensation: sitting with Nick on the front stoop watching the dawn come up, leaning against his shoulder as she covered a yawn and sipped her coffee.

She missed watching soccer games with

him, fixing him chocolate chip cookies, going whale watching — Nick's one intense hobby. She really missed the way the house felt alive when he was home. Now it was just a place to stay. She had not yet found ways to fill the voids in her days in more than piecemeal ways. Being alone was the pits.

When she had been the wife of a military man on deployment, she had been part of a close-knit club. The wives of men who were deployed had common things to talk about and practical help to offer each other. Military widows didn't have a comfortable home anywhere. Not in the civilian world, which didn't understand that *training accident* probably didn't mean what it implied, or in the military family gatherings, where her presence was a painful reminder of the risks.

Out of a sense of kindness her friends avoided talking about their husbands coming home, about the way they were counting down the days, and about the welcome home celebrations that were being planned.

Kelly knew her friends worried more about their husbands now. Nick's death had robbed the entire unit of a sense of safety. The risks hadn't changed, but the false sense of confidence had been stripped away. She had shed tears about the loneliness in private.

Joe's been there.

The reminder made her smile. Yes, Joe had been there. He came by because he was a good friend. When she wanted to remember and reminisce, he was one of the few people in her life who was comfortable listening. He had almost as many stories about Nick as she did — and the shared laughter had deepened their friendship.

They had always been friends through Nick; without him it had been distinctly awkward at first.

"Come on, Joe, five more to go. You can do it."

His arms were quivering, sweat rolling off him as he lay on his back on the weight bench. Kelly hurt with every grimace, every flinch of pain, he gave. His healing shoulder was fighting every step of this recovery. She was spotting for him on the weights because she was one of the few people he didn't have the heart to throw out of the rehab center. It had been six weeks since Nick's death and Joe's injury, and she had pushed aside her own pain to make sure Joe recovered. She wasn't going to let him quit, even though in the early days she had read in his eyes the reality that he

43

wanted to do just that.

He had come back shot, with his best friend dead. She didn't need details of what had happened to know Joe felt responsible for Nick's death and was pretty depressed. It would pass.

Already she could see the fight coming back in his eyes — another couple weeks and he wouldn't need her badgering him anymore. She was going to feel the loss when that day came. She needed someone else to focus on, to divert her from her own pain.

"Ten more reps instead of five."

Too much, *she thought, but she only nodded. She had watched Nick push himself beyond what was possible too: It was the SEAL way of facing an obstacle.*

Joe didn't need her now. She began to understand that as she spotted him through another set of reps. He was letting her be part of this because it gave her something else to think about, gave him an excuse to see her while he was trapped in this hospital rehab.

"What's wrong?"

"Nothing." She rested her hands on the bar, burying the sadness. "Ready for me to change the weights?"

He nodded, breathing heavily. "Five pounds lighter." He cautiously rubbed his injured shoulder as he watched her slide a platter from each end of the bar. *When the change was complete, he lifted his hands up to grasp the bar but didn't lift it free of the stand. He studied her face as she stood over him. "You didn't sleep again."*

It was a quiet observation, but still she looked away, shrugged one shoulder.

Joe drew a deep breath and lifted the bar free from the stand. "How did you handle it back when Nick did six-month deployments aboard the USS Constellation?*"*

The question drew an instinctive laugh, for it brought a wealth of memories. "Badly."

He smiled. "Seriously. What worked?"

"Surely you've heard all the tricks Navy wives use to mark time."

"Like buying a six-pack of soda and drinking one a month?"

"That and a few more elaborate ones."

"Tell me. What did you do?"

Joe's injured shoulder weakened momentarily and she steadied the bar as it swayed. "I had a hug bear."

He fought for breath. "I haven't heard of that one."

"Before he deployed, Nick would buy me a new stuffed bear and give it a hug. Whenever I missed him, I would hug the bear."

"That's pretty good."

"I thought so —" the first glimmer of a

smile in weeks came and went — "especially since I collect bears."

He chuckled and pushed the bar up again. "What else?"

Her amusement faded as she thought about how she had handled those long months trying to sleep while Nick was away. It was that way again, only this deployment would never end.

"What?"

"The Navy wives have a saying — you either lie in bed and listen to the dog snore or you go sleep on the couch."

He looked at her. "Change to the couch, Kelly. Get some sleep."

Joe had been there. He had been determined to help her make the adjustment. She had resented it at times, but no matter how hard she tried to push him away, he had never left. They had stumbled their way through the anniversary of Nick's death the first year.

He was a stubborn man. A good friend. Kelly could appreciate that now with the perspective of time. Three years had given her something with him that was special. *Lord, You're right. He's been a good friend. One I didn't always deserve.*

She had blamed him. She might never have come out and said it, but in the darkest days she'd blamed him. Not because she thought he had been responsible, but because he was around, because he was there. He knew it, but he'd still refused to leave her alone.

While she had been focused on her own pain, Joe had dealt with his. In the last three years he'd faced it and moved on. And he'd made a choice to stick with her even as she fought that moving on; he'd stayed and made himself a good friend.

Kelly, it's more than that.

She frowned at the thought. Joe was protective of her, around a lot, stepping in when something needed to be done around the house or yard that Nick would have handled in the past. He waved aside her comments that he did too much for her, and she had come to accept it as necessary for now. She did what she could to help him out in return — took care of his dog when he was away, got his mail, and on his last four-month deployment she paid his bills. The friendship was strong enough to handle the lopsided investment of time and energy, and Kelly suspected more than part of his involvement could be attributed to Nick and the guilt of being the one who had come home.

Was it more than a friendship? Joe had come to dinner last Friday, something he did frequently. It wasn't anything formal, nothing like a date; they simply enjoyed the time together. Or was that just what she wanted to see?

Kelly closed her eyes. Joe.

How could she have been so blind?

Another grid was covered with no sign of them. Joe could feel despair creeping in. He wasn't sure which grid to check next. The currents showed this was the most likely place to find them, but a helicopter and two boats had both covered the area and found nothing. Maybe farther north. Or should he go west? He turned, scanning the waters, knowing the currents could not answer the most difficult question. Were they still alive? It felt like someone was ripping out his heart.

He saw them on a wave crest. It was only for an instant, a dark shadow in the sea, and then they disappeared — but he saw them for a second. He held his breath as he waited, forcing himself to be patient. There! Distant, moving away, but definitely two people in the water. He surged forward, closing the distance.

Closer to them, he was forced to pause and locate them again. Straight west, maybe thirty feet.

Joe pulled one of the pencil flares he carried from the center pouch of the equipment vest he wore. Pulling the safety cap, he took a firm hold and looked away, firing it into the sky. The flare shot above him, marking the location for Boomer and the others, calling in help.

He cut through the water toward Kelly and the boy with every ounce of speed he had. There had been no change in their movements to the sound and light of the flare, a fact that made him fear the worst.

He came in behind Kelly, and the first thing he saw was her hair streaming out in the water behind her, lit by the fading light of the overhead flare. She had the boy in front on her, holding his head above water, treading water for both of them. Joe slid his arm under her shoulders, finding the lack of reaction to his touch alarming. "Kelly."

She turned her head slowly toward him and her swollen eyes opened. "Joe." Her smile was beautiful to see. And a ripple of fear shook him, for it was the smile of someone drifting on a dream . . .

"Kelly, I've got him. Release your grip. Let me take him."

He had to ask her twice before she blinked and removed her arm. The boy

49

looked so pale Joe was afraid he might already be gone. He had to search to find a pulse at the boy's throat. The only thing that would help now was getting the boy warm. One hand gripping the boy, the other Kelly, Joe used his kick to keep them afloat. "Take a break for a minute. Relax." He would get vests on them both in a minute; right now he just wanted the reassurance of holding her.

She limply rested her chin on his shoulder, her forehead striking his cheekbone as a wave hit her back. He tightened his hold on her, doing his best to secure her to his side as he held the boy with his other hand. Joe felt more than heard her sigh of relief. "I did my five-mile night-sea swim. Did I earn a baby Trident?"

He smiled, glad to hear the humor under her fatigue, relieved she was coming alert. The Trident pin — with its eagle for air, Revolutionary War pistol for land, and Neptune's trident for sea, all fit across the Navy's anchor — defined the SEALs and the men who wore it. "Maybe a tadpole pin." She felt like ice to his touch, and she was no longer shivering. He had to get her out of this water.

"I thought you would never get here."

Not anyone, *him*. It was an incredible in-

50

dication of trust. "I'm sorry I was late."

"You're forgiven. I knew you would come." She reached out a hand toward the boy. "This is my buddy Ryan; he's a pretty brave kid."

She's pretty brave herself. Joe hugged her, overwhelmed at the sudden emotion. "He owes you his life. Hold on to me while I get him in a vest." She nodded and her hands closed around his upper arm.

With the boy unconscious, the maneuver was awkward at best.

Joe felt Kelly's hands slide off his arm; he looked over and lunged out to grab her upper arm as she sank. His heart pounding, he pulled her back to his side. She looked dazed, and he wasn't sure if she realized what had happened.

Ryan still wasn't secure in the vest — Joe desperately needed just a couple more moments with a free hand. His options were few. "Kelly, can you put your arms around my neck?" He turned in the water, still holding her, offering her his back. He felt the slick remnants of the sunscreen lotion she had worn that day as her arms brushed his cheek. Her fingers interlaced and then slipped apart, unable to grip.

"Sorry."

Firmly holding her wrist, he swung her

around his body, back in front of him. His arm settled like steel around her waist. "I've got you."

Her head dropped against his shoulder again. "I have to sleep."

He shook her until she looked back up at him. "Not yet. I'll have you home and warm soon. Then you can sleep as long as you want."

The fact it took her time to understand what he said was obvious. She nodded and began kicking again wearily.

Joe worked with one hand to tighten the vest straps around the boy — it wasn't on fully, but it would have to do. Despite the fact she was trying to kick, Kelly felt limp against his arm. She was dangerously close to a permanent crash. She'd drop unconscious as deep as the boy and he wouldn't be able to wake her again. Where was Boomer? He cradled Kelly's head against his shoulder, trying to figure out how to hold onto the boy while he maneuvered her into a vest.

"I love you."

He froze. They slipped down in the water before he recovered their equilibrium. With her head resting on his shoulder he couldn't see her face. Frustrated at her timing for such a revelation,

Joe had to settle for brushing a kiss across her hair. His heart had just leaped in his throat with an emotion so deep it was choking him. He fought it down even as he wondered if she knew what she was saying. "Tell me that again when you're not frozen."

"Okay," she whispered.

Three

★ ★ ★

The arrival of the Coast Guard helicopter overhead was heralded by a bright searchlight that turned the night into day. The rotor wash created a ministorm of flying water around them. Kelly was no longer responding to any attempt to wake her and the boy was barely breathing. Joe watched as a Coast Guard swimmer dropped from fifteen feet into the swells.

The swimmer had just reached them when two Zodiacs appeared from different directions into the circle of light. Boomer and Cougar sliced into the water beside him. "Take the boy!"

As soon as he was handed off, Joe turned his full attention to Kelly, getting her hands out of the water and onto his shoulders. With his hands cradling the back of her neck, he lifted her head higher from the water. In the bright light he could see what he had only suspected before — her eyes were swollen closed, her lips were bleeding, her skin had turned translucent with the cold, and blood vessels were showing starkly blue through her skin. The sight was terrifying.

A stretcher was lowered from the hovering helicopter. Wolf and Cougar worked with the Coast Guard swimmer to get the boy secured in it. The guardsman clipped onto the line and went up with the stretcher. As soon as the Coast Guard chopper had them aboard, its nose dropped and the helicopter took off toward the coast at full throttle.

A second helicopter came in immediately after it. A secure line came down. Boomer grabbed it, quickly forming a buddy harness and keeping it steady as Joe secured the harness around himself and Kelly. The waves were buffeting her, sending her slamming into him and then yanking her back. There was no way to stop the added bruises being inflicted just by the attempts to help her. He flung out his hand to block her head as the line whipped around. This was one of the most dangerous points in a rescue. The pilot was fighting to keep a hover.

"It's locked," Wolf yelled as the metal locking ring clicked. Joe immediately waved, and the winch began to lift them from the water. He had rappelled out of and been lifted into one of these Navy helicopters numerous times before, but never with such precious cargo.

The wind spun them around as they rose. Joe ducked his head in close to Kelly's, trying to shield her face from the stinging spray.

He was pulled inside by two Navy corpsmen. They lowered Kelly into a waiting stretcher and smothered her in a thermal blanket. They immediately turned their focus to how she was breathing.

"Take us to Sharp," the doctor ordered over the intercom.

"No way! She's going to North Island." Sharp was good, but it was civilian and Joe wanted Kelly someplace where Nick's reputation would make a difference. The second helicopter was Navy, not Coast Guard, and could divert to Naval Air Station North Island where it had originated from with one word from the doctor.

"She's a civilian."

"She's a SEAL dependent. She's going to North Island." If the corpsman weren't in his way, Joe might have made his point with more than words.

A slap on the back paused him midargument. "Bear, quit your growling.

Craig Scott is waiting for us on the pad at Sharp."

Joe turned to see Lincoln in the copilot seat. His boss bore the handle of a legendary president because he delivered that same kind of leadership. The fact he had come out to help with the rescue said a lot, as did the name Craig Scott. The doctor had been one of those who helped put Joe's shoulder back together. Joe swallowed his protests. His boss nodded. "Let's beat that coastie to Sharp," Lincoln ordered the pilot.

Joe settled down beside the door as he watched the doctor and the corpsmen work, ignoring the towel thrust into his hand and the blanket pushed on him.

He hadn't gotten there in time.

He watched Kelly's face during the short flight, watched the doctor swear under his breath at the vital sign readings he was getting, and had to live with the reality he had not been in time. She was so pale she looked dead. Joe had seen that pallor before, on her husband's face, right before Nick died.

THREE YEARS EARLIER

Loose nukes.

They were called loose rather than lost

because there was hope they could be recovered before someone had to admit that
a rogue nation or terrorist group had managed to purchase one. They were leaking
out of the former republics of the Soviet
Union like they were kept in a sieve.
Lately, the SEALs had been chasing them
all over the world.

The intel on this one said it was heading
to Hong Kong, buyer unknown. While the
Middle East rogue nations prowling the
black market were frequently in the press
spotlight, the countries in East Asia
wanting to add a nuclear weapon to their
arsenal were just as numerous. North
Korea had been willing to risk a nation-
wide famine to divert resources to build
one. South Vietnam might be a democracy,
but it felt threatened. And Taiwan . . .

Joe had been on the ground during that
tense 1996 missile exchange as China
flexed its muscles in an exercise to intimi-
date Taiwan. The U.S. had responded by
sending a carrier into the Taiwan straits.
Taiwan needed protection more than it
needed words. Israel had achieved that
kind of sway by becoming a nuclear power,
albeit an undeclared one. Taiwan was
moving more and more toward that same
frightening posture.

But this reality was different; Taiwan acquiring the weapon would lead to war. China already had them, and they would never allow the breakaway province to acquire one. It was in the United States' interest to stop this transfer by any means needed.

The water was icy around Joe, dark, for they had lucked into a night of the month with barely a sliver of moon. It was disorienting not to have light reflecting off the surface of the water above to provide a sense of up and down in the murky blackness. Joe followed the gleaming fluorescent numbers on the attack board GPS, relying on technology to replace his senses. The mission had begun.

Odessa, Ukraine, known as the Pearl of the Black Sea, was an eastern European city trying to assimilate to Western commerce while still bearing the government bureaucracy of the past. The seaport authority had expanded the oil terminal with reservoirs for storage of both light and crude oil products. The passenger terminal now had six major berths for luxury liners. A new cold storage facility had been built.

It was an active port, with three break walls creating seven thousand meters of protected waters, and that activity could hide a lot of unwelcome commerce. Smugglers willing to part with some cash could find ways around the rules that "any cargo may be stored with the exception of ecologically harmful, poisonous, or explosive ones." Joe didn't imagine the port authority would be too pleased to learn they had outside help to enforce that mandate.

Cougar had jokingly asked how the seaport authorities would classify a nuclear warhead since it was a clear violation of all three exceptions — it was definitely explosive, poisonous, and ecologically harmful. It was a good thing they were going to recover it before anyone knew it was around, or some Ukrainian bureaucrat would have to change his forms.

Joe had found the humor a useful indication that Golf Platoon was ready for the mission. Like most missions, it was dangerous, deadly, and now — his platoon had taken the assignment in stride and dug into the planning. Six hours after getting paged, they had been on a C-130 transport plane bound for Italy.

The numbers wavered as he came to a stop, the numbers reading coordinates decided upon during the planning session. A glance at his watch showed they had arrived within the expected margin of time.

He let his body drift, getting a better sense of the current.

Boomer, who had gotten engaged two months before, managed to get a fast call in to cancel dinner with his fiancée the next evening as they packed and headed for their ride, using the tried but true "training exercise, I'm sorry" wording.

Joe couldn't blame the man. Not many engagements, let alone marriages, survived the transition to the reality of a SEAL's life. It was a glamorous life until the inconvenience of deployments began to rub the wrong way, the required silence rankled, the danger created fear. Boomer and Christi might make it — Joe hoped they did — but they were fighting long odds. He had seen too many SEAL marriages get in trouble and fail despite all the best intentions.

Nick and Kelly made it work. Joe wondered briefly how they did it. He had been friends with Nick for four years, watched them together, and knew they had something special. Kelly adapted, maybe that was the secret. Neither the pages that interrupted life nor the danger of her husband's job appeared to ruffle her. She didn't particularly like the injuries from training, but she understood the sweat-now-or-bleed-later reality. Kelly understood the job, and that was unique.

The clock on the attack board gleamed 0212 hours. The wait was over. They never moved on the hour or at any other predictable time — it was a rookie mistake.

Reaching for the rope at his waist, Joe tugged the buddy line to signal Nick. They floated to the surface, sixty meters outside the original and oldest break wall at the Odessa port. In the dark of a moonless night — black wet suits, faces painted, weapons secure at their backs — they were barely visible to each other only meters apart.

No orders were needed. Every member of the eight-man squad knew the mission inside and out. They were heading to the container terminal, a joint Ukraine–American venture just south of the lighthouse and the connecting jetty. The warhead was being smuggled by rail to the harbor, where it was to be loaded aboard a grain transport ship stopping here and then bound for Hong Kong.

The water was cold and its surface marred by a film of diesel fuel left by the numerous ships coming through the port. The air smelled dank, the tons of cargo and oil and the crush of a city built to the shoreline combining to replace fresh air with the smell of an industrial world. It was enough to make Joe's eyes water and his nose burn.

This mission was the type SEALs liked best. Simple. Silently slip into port, locate the cargo, move it to their own secure transport, then take it out to sea. Having the blueprints for the American-designed cargo area had helped them decide where to strike. They considered hitting the train on its way to the harbor, but that would put them too far away from the water, which every SEAL considers his safe home. Hitting the ship once it put to sea was very attractive, and Joe had tasked the second eight-man squad of the platoon to be prepared to do just that if necessary. But it was here, in Odessa, where the real prize lay. The smugglers.

One of them had to know the identity of the man arranging these sales. The intelligence community wanted him identified, desperately. He'd been nicknamed Raider as years passed and his handiwork frustrated the military time and again. He had the habit of swiping military hardware from supposedly secure sites.

He was a thief; it was that simple. One who had graduated from shoulder-fired missiles back in the days of Afghanistan to the big leagues — nuclear components and now warheads. At times Joe thought it was almost like a game with him. Until they stopped him, missions like this one were going to continue.

The fact Raider focused on military weapons . . . He was stealing them at the behest of others, but his buyers' lists were allusive. The variety of items stolen and the years it had been happening had the intelligence community searching for an arms dealer who was filling out his portfolio with stolen goods for sale, but that link had never appeared. These weapons were stolen to fill specific requests. And that suggested the weapons would be used as soon as they were delivered.

Given the years spent searching for a name without anyone coming close to identifying him, the man was probably in the loop somewhere, reviewing the intel on himself. He had stayed hidden too long for that to be accidental or simply good luck. Capturing one of the smugglers was high on the mission priorities — right after "secure the warhead" and "don't get killed."

Joe searched the north side of the break wall while Nick searched the south. Clear. Nick nodded, slipped off the buddy line, and disappeared below the water's surface. He reappeared eight minutes later at the end of the break wall, visible in Joe's NVGs — night vision goggles. Nick left the water, weapon in hand, to disappear among the rocks.

What made stealth was patience. Joe waited. Nick had to check out the jetty before they made the move into the port waters.

The all-clear signal came by infrared light.

Cougar and Boomer appeared beside him in the water. A silent touch to each man's shoulder and they dropped below the surface as one. Wearing Draegar LAR V rebreather units to suppress bubbles marking their passage, they swam fifteen feet below the surface, following the GPS past the break wall to the first container cargo berth. The U.S. registered *St. Juanita* had berthed there late in the afternoon. The three of them surfaced in the shadow of its hull at 0223 hours local time. Anyone moving around would be less than alert; 0300 was the body's natural lowest point. Nick slipped back into the water and crossed from the break wall to join them.

The change from water to land warfare took only moments. They were the front line four. Their task was straightforward — enter the cargo area and secure the warhead. If possible, they would capture one of the smugglers. Once Joe signaled success, the second wave of four SEALs would come in behind them and secure the transport area.

A crew from the Special Boat Unit was idling at sea. They had a forty-two-foot Fountain high-speed boat, with its one-thousand-horsepower engines, waiting for word to come in and pick up the cargo. Snatch the warhead and get out of Dodge. It generally worked like a charm.

Nick went up the ladder to the terminal first, taking point. He disappeared and they waited. A single click over the headset signaled it was clear.

Joe went up next with Cougar behind him. A concrete ledge about two feet wide ran along the edge of the pier, and they dropped over it to the walkway. As the satellite photos and blueprints had shown, the walkway was designed for forklifts carrying wide cargo loads. Joe darted across to the cover provided by massive cable spools stacked side by side. Having destroyed enough of the stuff during his demolition forays with Boomer, Joe instantly recognized the thick cable as power line. The *St.*

Juanita must have been off-loading the spools.

A glance to his left confirmed Cougar was secure. Joe clicked his microphone and Boomer appeared a moment later. Two clicks and Nick appeared as a glowing silhouette on the NVGs, a good hundred meters down the walkway. The black thermal tape across the back of his wet suit glowed like a beacon, a visual reminder that he was a friendly. They each wore unique tape patterns to make it instantly apparent who was where in the dead of night. The guys on the team didn't give him a choice; he was double-striped. It was one of the banns of being the lieutenant.

They headed into the cargo terminal proper, where massive metal containers in all colors, some big enough to hold a luxury car, were stacked in rows waiting to be moved by forklift and crane. The area felt claustrophobic despite how big the terminal was — over a quarter of a million square meters in size, dwarfing several football fields — but there would be no need to search its expanse. Cargo arriving by rail within the last eight hours eliminated the guesswork. For the smugglers to bring the warhead in, keep it concealed, and move it to a ship the size of the grain transport, they only had one option. Berth three.

Nick held up his hand in warning and they instantly, silently, dispersed. Joe watched from the shadows of a container carrying Russian truck brake bearings as a dockworker moved past his location, head down, trying to use a flashlight to read a page on a clipboard.

The sound of the man's footsteps faded. A click over the microphone and they were moving again.

When Nick gestured forty seconds later, it was to indicate they were on target. Joe moved forward to join him while Cougar and Boomer disappeared into the darkness to either side.

Nick had taken up a perch beside a stacked column of steel girders. They were at the foot of the rail yard, and two loco-motives, boxcars attached, were on the tracks before them.

Joe settled beside Nick, next to what had once been an oil drum and was now a catchall for broken pallet wood, providing good concealment. The metal of the drum was cold to Joe's touch, the sea air creating a sheen of moisture on its surface.

He had to marvel at the intel. Even the boxcar numbers were right. Missions never went as planned, and intel was always wrong. For once the axioms they lived by were proving wrong. The warhead had arrived, right on schedule.

Joe turned his attention toward the water. The enormous docking berth three was empty. It would be dawn before the grain transport ship arrived; it was still outside the Black Sea. There had been concern the smugglers would be able to get a ship here early and have it waiting, for the warhead was vulnerable when it stopped moving. But it turned out not to be that easy to find ships able to carry such cargo with legitimate reasons to be in both Odessa and Hong Kong. The smugglers were playing it cautious. But they didn't know they had a mole passing on their travel arrangements.

"There."

The word was a whisper over his headset from Nick.

Someone had just stepped down from between the third and fourth railcar. A second and then a third man appeared, and over the distance there was the sound of men laughing as one slapped another on the back. They were all armed. Joe studied their movements, trying to identify the leader.

Two more men appeared. Joe immediately picked up the way one man turned up his coat collar and pushed his hands into his pockets — he didn't seem to be enjoying the cold air. "Shift change."

Nick nodded. "Five tangos here. Who else?"

Tangos — terrorists — and the smugglers were certainly that. The SEALs had come prepared to handle four times that many, but to do it silently meant taking each step with care. Joe touched his mike. "Cougar, sneak and peek. The rail station house." There was smoke coming from the stovepipe of the small building. There might be a couple more still inside, trying to ward off the chill of the night.

"Sniper. Caboose roof," Nick said calmly. Two clicks came over the mike. Boomer had him. If it came down to shooting, Boomer was carrying a suppressed sniper rifle with a starlight scope. He could drop the man with a whisper, but his fall off the caboose roof would attract attention.

Nick kept scanning. Joe had never met anyone more relaxed in combat than Nick. He didn't appear to have a stressed bone in his body. Any moment now Joe expected Nick to crack his jaw on a yawn.

Joe saw Nick smile. "Cougar snaked." It was team shorthand for slipping through stuff you would not want to name later. Joe spotted Cougar now back at his secure perch wiping his hand off on his wet suit, clearly disgusted. Cougar reached to touch his mike. "One, L-T."

Joe clicked an acknowledgment.

Seven tangos. They had the players; now they needed the best arrangement.

In a matter of minutes, the three men originally by the railcars moved toward the station house. The two that remained looked around briefly and then swung themselves up onto the perch between the cars.

Only three tangos in the open, unheard of odds. "Cougar, quietly jam that front door of the station house closed; then take down the sniper. Eagle and I will take the two by the car. Boomer, anyone interrupts, deal with them."

Everyone acknowledged.

"Go." Joe felt the twinge he always did as he issued the single word that put men into battle. The enemy wasn't showing much foresight, but the element of surprise was always tenuous.

Cougar disappeared. Joe followed Nick around to the back of the railcar. Nick indicated the man on the left, and Joe moved to take the man on the right.

They hit together, bringing the men down. Joe saw a knife coming around and turned it back on his man.

Nick had been able to take his man down alive. At least one of them had been successful. Joe let the annoyance fade away; he had given his man a choice, and that in itself rarely happened. It wasn't like they were smuggling fireworks. Flexible cuffs came out, duct tape, fast security steps to keep the man quiet and under control.

Joe opened the railcar door and lifted the man inside. A quick glance confirmed that they had what they were after. "Boomer, we've got the package and one guest. Signal Wolf to secure the transport area."

A click acknowledged the request.

Cougar joined them and set to work on the case while Nick took up position at the door.

As expected, the warhead had been disassembled and packed in molded foam. Joe looked at the sleek circuit boards that formed the nerves of the timing mechanism and thought them beautiful like a cobra was beautiful — even apart they looked deadly. The warhead casing had been taken out and sandblasted clean of writing. He rubbed his fingers over the oddly chalky white surface and found his fingers covered with the rough powder. Raider was taking extreme measures to hide his tracks if he was trying to conceal any indication of which device had actually been stolen from even the buyer of the warhead.

In the center of the case, held in foam, was another box. Cougar backed out the screws, ignoring the lock. The department of energy frowned on sending its people onto foreign soil in the middle of the night, so they didn't have a NEST guy on-site to tell them what shape this warhead core was in. It was just as well. Joe had worked with enough of the Nuclear Energy Search Team guys to know they were too cautious for the time constraints demanded by a live op. Besides, if it was radioactive, they were dead. Broken arrows — these lost, shot down, stolen, and otherwise missing nukes — didn't tend to be forgiving.

Cougar dismantled the lid and lifted it carefully over the lock.

Joe sucked in a deep breath. No wonder Raider had sandblasted the casing. He'd swiped a K-42, Russia's most advanced compact warhead, only six known to be deployed. The plutonium core was formed in two layers, like a baseball around a golf ball. Joe had seen pictures, but never in his worst nightmare had he envisioned dealing with one. Certainly not in a railcar in Odessa. "Boomer. Send a flash. We've got a K-42."

"Repeat." Nothing rattled Boomer — that had just changed.

"K-42. Flash it."

The Air Force had an AWACS up over Italy so Boomer could get the message off without going to the satellite link. Even if he had to break out the dish, this news had to get out. Every asset in the area would be used to stop this shipment if necessary.

"Pack it, Cougar. Let's move."

Joe joined Nick at the door, watching the rail station house. These guys didn't know what they were smuggling — not the details. Raider was compartmentalizing, and that was his greatest strength but also his greatest weakness. Joe smiled grimly. This little gem would create enough heat in intelligence services around the globe to make Raider's life unpleasant in the upcoming months, to say the least. Get enough people comparing notes and something would click. They would find the guy. You couldn't arrange to swipe and sell one of these without leaving some serious footprints.

"Transport area is secure."

Joe looked at Cougar and got a nod. "We're moving, Wolf."

The case was lead and weighed more than the warhead itself. A forklift would be great but would give away their presence. Nick and Cougar took the case out while Joe escorted their guest, and Boomer took up the rear guard.

Wolf and the three SEALs with him had secured berth three. Nick and Cougar carried the case to the crane being rigged to lower it down to the water.

The eight-man squad was back together. It relieved the pressure Joe felt upon discovering what they had. He had options now. He handed off their guest and moved to join Wolf. "Transport?"

"On the way in."

"We've got four tangos who don't know we stopped by."

Wolf grinned. "They've got about three minutes to wake up before we're cruising."

Gunfire sounded, shattering the night. "They just woke up," Joe replied. "Let me know when that crane is ready."

He moved forward to join Cougar. Four tangos were not a problem. It was the others the gunfire would attract that created the problem. Joe touched his mike. "Take them down."

A series of single shots sounded from where Boomer and Nick had taken up positions, and the night went quiet again.

"L-T, come take a look." At Nick's quiet words, Joe moved to join him.

Trouble. There was no other way to define it. Two police cars had just entered the gate by the rail line. "Wolf, we need to move."

"The cargo is on its way down now."

The two cars stopped by the station house. Five men got out. It would only be a matter of moments before the first casualties were found.

The crane moving behind them was like a bullhorn advertising their presence. Joe didn't like this kind of close encounter. Shouts arose as the first casualty was discovered.

"It's going to get busy," Nick commented, tracking the policemen.

"Very." It was definitely time to get out of Dodge. His team would get very creative before they would fire on a civilian cop. Movement was their preferred way to deal with such a situation, and they were pinned by their cargo to remain at this location. "Feel like making a diversion?"

"I thought you would never ask."

Joe nodded. It was the best option they had. If they could get the police focused into the heart of the cargo area, they would be able to disengage and slip away unseen. But if they were going to do it, they had to move now. "Boomer, Cougar, we're going to try to divert them east into the cargo area. Come up and take the front door."

They had an unfair advantage with the night vision goggles. They could watch the five very nervous cops now coming their way and easily skirt around them.

Nick led the way through the cargo containers, weaving them deep into the terminal. They were three hundred meters into the maze in a matter of moments. Joe had his waterproof pouches already open. "A line of charge with a couple smoke grenades?"

"Sounds like a good diversion to me." Nick slung his weapon on his shoulder and leaped up onto one of the stacked containers. Joe handed up the moldable plastic explosive strip. It was a cutting charge, easy to handle, able to cut through steel, fast burning. Boomer did most of their explosives work, but this task didn't require neatness. Nick slapped it in place and used the duct tape that went everywhere with them to pin down the two smokers. A loop of fishing twine went around the pins. "Set." He dropped back down to the pavement. "Care to do the honors?"

Joe grinned. "Do it."

Nick pulled the pins. They were around the end of the cargo aisle when the diversion went off. The strip exploded bright, white-hot, and the smoke roiled into the air, visible even in the night.

"That got their attention, L-T." Cougar's voice sounded muffled; Joe's ears were still ringing.

"Are they all moving this way?"

"Confirm five coming your way."

The sounds of more police sirens were heard over the fading noise of falling metal. "You've got another eight cops coming into the area," Cougar warned.

"Are you still clear?"

"They are all coming your way."

Joe touched Nick's shoulder. "Dump the silencer and lay down gunfire into the top of that far container wall. Let's give the guys a reason to stay cautious."

Nick nodded, and soon the sound of the Heckler and Koch MP-5 submachine gun came in short bursts.

The police began returning fire randomly, wildly, into the cargo area. If they weren't careful, they were going to hit one of their own men.

"The cargo is secure, L-T. Come on home."

Joe glanced at Nick and got a swift negative reply. Joe concurred. No use risking the cargo. "Go. We'll take to the water and meet you at pickup point Bravo."

"Roger, L-T."

Nick disengaged and they began silently working their way back through the maze of cargo containers, leaving the firefight between the police and the "ghosts" behind.

At the edge of the cargo area, Joe paused and looked across the walkway to the edge of berth three. Fifteen feet to freedom. Get down the ladder and into the water and it would be a nice, easy swim to the pickup point. They both scanned the area.

"Clear."

Joe nodded. "Go."

Nick cut across the walkway and disappeared from sight around a forklift. A single click, and Joe scanned the area one last time then moved to join him. There was a shout from somewhere to his left.

Joe felt the bullet tear into the back of his left shoulder. He stumbled forward but instinctively didn't go down. Nick returned fire, dealing with the threat, then ran back to meet him. Joe had been hit worse in the past, but he didn't feel like remembering it. "Let's get in the water."

"Definitely."

Joe moved down the ladder with one hand. It took focus, but he didn't let himself wonder if they would get clear. The water was in sight; that was all he needed to know. Getting shot when the mission was essentially over was a fluke he was going to have to spend months living down. SEALs had a simple perspective. As soon as they knew he would survive, the humor would begin, and they had long memories. They might not be able to tell the story beyond Team Nine, but it would still be part of their history.

Joe dropped the last five feet into the water, clearing the way for Nick, who slid down the ladder rather than climb down, dropping into the water beside him. Within seconds they were away from the concrete wall of the berth.

Swimming with one arm was possible but slow, and they needed speed. Joe also needed to pause as soon as possible to get a pressure bandage in place to stop the bleeding. One of the first casualties of a mission gone wrong was time.

The shouts above them were loud and becoming clear. "Company," Nick warned.

Joe secured his rebreather and Nick took them below the surface.

The bullets entering the water slowed immediately, but their presence made it clear they were still definitely in the threat arena. Joe and Nick put power into their kicks, heading down and away, Nick guiding them both.

Joe felt Nick get hit, felt him jerk backward and stop moving.

Joe clamped his good hand on Nick's rebreather and kept it secure as he did his best to power them forward. This had just become the worst of all missions. Joe forced himself to keep them down until they were far enough out they would be lost in the darkness of the sea.

Once on the surface, Joe activated the emergency beacon, willing to risk that help could arrive long before the harbor patrol could identify the military frequency being used.

Nick had been hit in the back and the bullet had come through; he was bleeding profusely from the chest. Joe had to use his knife to get the wet suit cut free so he could get a pressure bandage in place.

"Hanging in there, buddy?"

Nick gave a painful smile. "What a pair we are."

Joe was not losing his best friend in some overseas place, worthwhile mission or not. He couldn't see the injury as much as he could see Nick's struggle to stay conscious. "Someone needs to pay Raider a visit."

"Soon," Nick choked.

Nick was struggling to breathe as the sound of a speeding boat reached them.

Joe broke out the light stick and waved it; the boat immediately turned toward them. It was one of the Special Boats Unit's black-as-night workhorses, held in reserve for just this need. Several Golf Platoon members were on board, guns ready for battle.

Cougar and Boomer both sliced into the water beside him to help.

"Keep him steady." Joe watched as Nick was lifted carefully aboard. With the help of Boomer, Joe was pulled aboard after Nick. "Is the nuke secure?"

"Yes."

It was the last thought Joe gave to the mission. He grabbed Nick's hand as the medic went to work. Joe watched his face, his eyes. The entire team was silent, faces grim. The pallor in Nick's face broadcasted the fact he was losing the fight. Tears burned Joe's eyes. "Hang tough, Nick. Kelly is expecting you home."

"Take care of her."

"You'll be there."

Nick's grip nearly broke bones in Joe's hand. "Promise."

"My word."

Joe forced himself to put aside the memory as the helicopter flared to set down at Sharp Hospital. Nick had not made it home, and Raider had slipped into the shadows, still out there somewhere, inactive but free. Joe had been waiting three years to settle the score, for the day to come when Raider reappeared.

He'd been forced to face Kelly, unable to tell her the truth . . . and for that reason alone, he prayed nightly for a chance to settle the score once and for all. He needed Raider to be found, stopped, and brought to justice.

The door slid open and wind rushed in. Craig Scott was waiting with a trauma team. Wanting to help and knowing there was so little he could do, Joe stayed out of the way as Kelly was moved.

He hadn't been in time . . .

Four

$\star \; \star \; \star$

She was so *cold.*

Kelly had never known anything like it before. She cried as something was draped over her legs, for it was burning her. She couldn't move to escape.

The heat was flowing into her bloodstream as well, and she could feel her heart pounding as if it would explode. She couldn't swallow against the tube in her throat, and the taste of blood and Vaseline on her cracked lips made her nauseous. If only she could stop these bone-racking shivers! Her hand cramped in a powerful spasm around the hand holding hers.

"Easy, Kelly."

Joe was here. She forced her eyes open and he wavered in and out of focus in her teary gaze. *Stop them, Joe. It hurts.*

He couldn't hear her silent plea. He wiped at her tears, his own face showing his sympathy. "Just hang in there; you'll be warm again soon."

It was a promise she wanted desperately to believe in, and yet that reality seemed an eternity away.

Her brow furrowed. Joe had found them. *Ryan?* She had no way to ask. The commotion going on in the emergency room frightened her, and she clung to Joe's hand with what strength she had.

The lights were bright and increased the headache that stabbed behind her eyes. The conversations of the doctors and nurses layered on top of each other in an assault of sound. She knew they were there to help her, but she just wanted them to go away so she could cry in peace.

How long had she been here? Where was Ryan?

Cramps in her left leg hit so viciously they choked off her breath. She tried to reach for her leg but found herself hampered by IVs and heavy blankets. Her toes curled up and the calf muscle tightened and began to spasm. The cramp was spreading up her leg, twisting it beneath the covers. She tried to draw a breath against the pain but couldn't. The machine was breathing against her.

She gagged against the breathing tube and began to struggle in earnest to get free. Joe grabbed her hands. "Don't, Kelly."

Her struggle turned to desperation. She couldn't breathe! Three nurses and two doctors swarmed around her. She saw the sheer agony in Joe's eyes as he helped pin her down. She couldn't move against his weight, she couldn't breathe, and she wept as her spirit broke.

Whatever the doctor put into her IV, it eventually eased the cramp in her leg. As soon as she stopped fighting, the machine took over and her lungs filled. She closed her eyes, tears streaming from them as she greedily breathed again.

"Okay. You're okay." She felt Joe's calloused hands tremble as they cupped her face, his thumbs stroking across her jawline. He sounded scared, and Joe was never scared. She cried because it hurt and she was so tired and she just wanted it all to go away. If only Joe wasn't seeing this weepy side of her. The fact she couldn't stop the tears only made her cry all the harder. She had jealously guarded her tears from him for the last three years, and now, when she couldn't even wipe her own nose, he was seeing them flow unchecked.

Her hair was brushed back, a tissue wiped her nose, and a handkerchief carefully dried her eyes. She opened them and blinked at the hand blocking her vision. A tough hand with long fingers, calloused, the palm covered in fine scars from years of climbing ropes. Powerful. Joe's hand. The white handkerchief looked out of place.

Joe smiled at her, his eyes holding emotions she didn't know how to decipher. "Cry, Kelly. As long as you need to. I'll be right here."

It was such an incongruent visual, this man who led soldiers into battle sitting at her bedside wiping away her tears. She could only smile with her eyes.

"Of course, any time you would like to stop —" His words were the first spot of humor in the midst of the pain.

Thank you, Joe.

She stopped crying eventually, and the people around faded into the background as she kept her focus on Joe. He sat beside her and held her hand. Finally the shivers eased enough that the exhaustion took over and swallowed her into a quiet darkness.

What had she meant by *I love you?* Joe's steepled fingers were under his chin as he watched Kelly sleep. It was three in the morning and sleep would not come. He sat in the chair beside Kelly's bed in the private hospital room and watched her and wondered. Having grown accustomed to the dim light, he could see her clearly. She had turned onto her left side and snuggled her hands up under her chin.

The breathing tube, so critical in those first few hours when warming her up had put her at high risk of a shock-induced heart attack, had been removed before she was brought upstairs. It was comforting simply to listen to her breathe. He never wanted to see her in that kind of pain ever again. The memories of her tears haunted him.

He couldn't shake the expression in her eyes as he had been forced to hold her down, that moment of clarity and brightness just before she had given up. It shook him to know she had reached that point inside. She couldn't breathe and she had been willing to accept it and give up, let go. The monitoring equipment alarms going off around her blared that she was at that point. Had the doctors not been able to intervene at that moment, she would have started to slip away from him.

How had she meant her words? I love you as a friend — someone I can count on — or I'm afraid I'm dying and I wish we had become more than friends? He didn't know. And if he reached the wrong conclusion he risked not only hurting her, but also putting their friendship in jeopardy.

He thrust his hands into his hair, weary, struggling to sort out the emotions. He could move on from the events, do the practical things like call her friends, stop by her house and pack for her, make sure she had anything she needed. He could do all those things and still not cope with the emotion her words evoked.

If she really meant them . . .

There had never been any indication she thought or hoped for something more. He had sometimes fleetingly considered it — at the end of a long day, when he faced an empty house, when they walked the beach together enjoying a sunset, when she would spontaneously give him a hug as she said thanks — but then reality would intrude and he would force the idea away. She had been his best friend's wife, and he never planned to marry until he was out of the SEALs. He had seen what Nick's death had done to her. He was thirty-eight; Kelly was thirty-one. Both of them were cautious about change.

He tried to pay attention to the details of how she was moving on so as not to say or do the wrong thing. Kelly would laugh at Liz's attempts to get her to go on a date, always turning them down. Joe had seen her wistfulness when she held Liz's infant son Christopher, but that was the only time he ever wondered if Kelly thought about getting married again. She seemed content to let her life drift by as it was. He didn't think that was good for her long term, but he had been reluctant to add his voice to Elizabeth's. He sensed a fragility that had yet to fade, and he didn't want Kelly making major changes until she recovered some of the self-confidence that had been there in the past.

It wasn't going to be easy to ask her what she had meant. He wasn't even sure which answer he hoped for. He knew the danger that his emotions toward Kelly could be survivor's guilt — Nick had died saving his life — but when his emotions had grown over the years instead of fading, he recognized they were based on something much deeper.

Kelly was a wonderful lady, a great friend, and his emotions were already at the fine line of wanting more. He knew what kind of wife she made, and his life would only be better for having her in it. But he had to think about what was best for Kelly; he owed her that. And for her to get involved with a SEAL, for it to be the man her husband had died to save — She didn't even know the truth of what had happened. He didn't know how to make this work out.

Regardless of the complication her words had created, he wanted to give her a solid hug for having said them. Down in the depths of his heart it had felt so good to hear those words. Those three words had the power to cut right through to his heart.

She had likely known that too. The words made her vulnerable, yet she still went ahead and said them. A gift. She had given him so many over the years: birthday parties she never let him ignore, Christmas gifts, and more than once he had come home from a mission to find a note on the kitchen counter and a home-cooked meal waiting in the refrigerator.

It wasn't just him; she made the lives of the entire SEAL team easier. In a platoon of sixteen men, she knew the wives, the girlfriends, and what had been happening when his men were away. And when something needed to make its way to his or Boomer's attention, it did so quietly through Kelly. It was her nature to look out for the best interests of the people around her. Joe smiled. She also looked out for him.

Lord, don't let me make a mistake with how I handle this situation. She's one of my best friends, and if I hurt her, I'll never forgive myself. But if I let myself dream, I wish there were a way to make this work.

Joe sighed as he stretched out his legs. The cold water had sapped his strength and he was tired, but overriding that was his worry. For three years there had been slow, steady progress as he fought to keep his word to Nick and watch out for Kelly. Tonight everything had changed, and he didn't know how it was going to turn out.

Five

★ ★ ★

"You're awake." Joe sounded pleased. Kelly wanted to pull the covers over her head and hide.

She looked over at the doorway of her hospital room and saw him standing there — needing a shave, his fatigues wrinkled, holding a military mug of coffee. There was something uniquely fascinating about looking at a military man when he was relaxed and at ease. He looked wonderful and she knew she looked her worst. "Hi, Joe."

"Hey, why the frown?" He moved to the bedside chair and grasped her hand in a reassuring grip. His other hand brushed her hair back from her face. "Feeling rocky? You had a rough night."

She felt like her skin was burnt. Her voice rasped. Her hair felt matted. She hadn't been awake long enough to figure out what else was wrong. "I gather I look pretty ugly," she said, feeling out the truth.

He rejected that idea with a small shake

of his head and a warmth in his eyes that melted into tenderness. "You're beautiful."

When he didn't qualify it, she squeezed his hand. "Thanks. That was kind."

"You'll need it when you see a mirror."

His reply drew a grin. "Warning taken. I'll avoid one for a while."

"Probably a good idea."

"How's Ryan?"

"Eating breakfast. He's fine. I missed seeing his dad; the nurse said he was talking to the doctor."

It felt like a weight had been lifted off her chest. "And the other boy?"

"A couple stitches above his eyebrow. He was treated and released." Joe sat back in the chair, picking up his coffee mug. "I like Ryan. He's a good kid, despite the bad judgment of when to go surfing. He was disappointed about not being awake for his first helicopter ride."

She tried to laugh and it came out as a croak; her throat felt raw. "That I can believe. Most teens are pretty resilient." Kelly looked around at the newspaper discarded by the chair and the breakfast dishes on the tray. "You were here all night?"

"Most of it. I left briefly to feed and water Misha, then stopped by your place and got you a few things." Joe leaned down

94

to reach for a sack by his chair. "I brought one of your bears."

"Bo-Bo." Kelly smiled as she reached for it, finding her swollen hands stiff and painfully awkward. "What a great choice."

Joe watched as she fluffed up the fur crushed in transit. "I got it right and I didn't even realize it."

"Bo-Bo found me in the recovery room when I broke my wrist surfing."

"Found you?"

"I woke up from the anesthetic and he was sitting on my chest watching me."

Joe's amusement only made his eyes laugh; his voice stayed serious. "Got it."

Kelly appreciated the fact he had it in him to be indulgent about her bears. They were important to her if only because they gave her something familiar to have around, and there was comfort in that connection to the past. They brought with them good memories.

She reached up with her left hand to straighten the bear's ears and noticed what was missing. "Joe —"

He barely reached for the bear in time to stop it from tumbling off the bed. "What's wrong?"

"My ring. I lost my wedding ring." She frantically searched through the bedcovers.

It was the most precious thing Nick had ever given her. She never took it off and it was gone. The realization was a knife through her heart. Her wedding ring . . .

"No." His hand caught her arm in a gentle grip to still her movements. "They had to take off your ring because your hand was swelling. Your ring is in the hospital safe."

"You're sure?"

"Positive, Kelly. It's safe."

Her eyes closed in relief. "The medallion I was wearing? Nick's eagle?"

"Also in the safe."

He reached over her to straighten the blankets she had massacred when she sat up. "Lie back and be quiet for a while. You're going to lose your voice."

Kelly complied, grateful for the help getting the blankets straightened. Joe was right; her voice was already becoming strained. The order was more like the Joe she knew and had come to love. Memories of what she had said in the water flooded back and she froze. It had to be a dream. She couldn't have said that. *Lord, please just let me drop through the floor and disappear.* "You're staying?"

He met her gaze, his expression puzzled. "I planned to."

She didn't want to talk about what she had said until she had more time to think about it, and if Joe brought it up. . . . She bit her lower lip and yelped with pain as her cracked lip split open again.

"Careful." Joe reached for a tissue and wiped away the blood. "You're going to be off coffee a miserably long time if you don't let that heal."

The idea was appalling. She could already feel the edge of a caffeine headache setting in.

He brushed her chin with the back of his knuckles, his smile sympathetic. "I bought you a Coke from the machine. You should be able to manage it with a straw." He found it and cracked open the tab for her, rummaging for the straw.

Grateful, Kelly let him hold the can while her hand rested against his; she lifted her head slightly to drink. The cold soda felt good against her sore throat. "Thanks." She studied his face, so close to her own, searching to find any sign of his thoughts and reaction to her words at sea and found only the clear gaze of a friend. That was very much like him. He had an ability to bury what he thought until he decided it was the right time to discuss it. But he would want to discuss it. How could she have ever made the mistake of saying those words?

"Sure."

She couldn't let the conversation drift the wrong way. She watched him set down the soda on the nightstand and curled her hand around the bear to give herself courage. "The cold water was brutal." The sea had tried to kill her last night, had come pretty close to succeeding.

He looked back at her, studied her face for a moment. This time when he moved, he rested his chin on his steepled fingers. "I know."

"Is it like that on your missions? The sea so cold it takes your breath away?"

"Occasionally."

She dropped her gaze, plucking at the threads of the blanket. "I nearly gave up."

"But you didn't."

"I wanted to."

"You didn't."

She studied his face. He, at least, seemed confident she wouldn't have. "I'm glad you got there when you did."

He stilled her hand, turned it over, and laced his fingers with hers. She wasn't ready for the contact and felt a sharp tug that what was a casual gesture on his part suddenly had a different meaning for her.

"Do you want to go sailing with me Sunday?" Joe asked.

She jolted at the topic, taken off guard by the request. "Sailing?" The idea was not a welcome one. She had fought the disorienting up-and-down and side-to-side motion for hours last night. Just the thought of being on the pitching deck of a boat made her fight a sense of queasiness.

"The weather is going to be nice, and you need to get back out on the water."

He was going straight for the jugular. "Joe, this didn't make me afraid. I've done rescues before."

"Then you'll have no problem saying yes."

Her eyes narrowed. He was putting her in a box and doing it deliberately. There were times when his kind of leadership made her cringe. She didn't want to get back on the horse that had just thrown her. "Are you sure your new boat — and I'm being generous with that word — won't sink and dump me back in the sea?" Joe liked to restore sailboats from decrepit wrecks back to things of beauty. His latest find, which was partially restored, had only recently been out on the calm waters of San Diego Bay.

"You'll just have to risk it with me."

She understood why Joe was doing this, but it only intensified her nervousness. She didn't know how she was going to react to the water, and she wasn't sure she wanted Joe to see that reaction. On the other hand, if she was going to be scared being back on the open waters, at least she would have the comfort of being with him. He would above all keep her safe. She squeezed his hand, accepting what he was offering. "I'll come sailing."

"Good."

She desperately wanted to change the subject. Sunday. That was soon. "Have they said when they're going to release me?"

"Maybe tomorrow. It depends on if your temperature stays steady."

"Tomorrow?"

Joe chuckled. "The hospital food isn't that bad."

"I don't want to stay."

"Tough."

She was exhausted, but that was no reason to keep her here another day. She wanted her own bed. It was appalling to realize she wanted to pout. "When you stopped by my house and got Bo-Bo, did you think to get my toothbrush?"

Joe reached for a small suitcase against the wall. "Toothbrush, hairbrush, and anything else I thought you might need in the next few days." He set the case on the bed beside her, opened it, and turned it for her to look through.

He picked up a pair of socks and got up. "Let's have those cold feet."

"What?"

"You've been trying to tug the covers tighter around them for the last several minutes, and that's not going to get them warm. Thick socks might." He tapped a blanket-covered foot.

"I can do it."

"Kelly."

Her bare feet were ticklish. She tried not to laugh as Joe slipped on the first sock, but when his hand brushed over her instep, it was simply beyond her control. Her toes curled and she giggled.

He looked up at her sharply, then paused, still holding her now covered foot. He grinned. "I'll have to remember this." He squeezed her foot before tucking it back under the covers.

"Joe —"

He slipped on the other sock and wiggled her toes. "Where else are you ticklish?"

She felt her face flame. "None of your business."

"I have to use my imagination?" he asked when he sat back down, his speculative gaze frank and unrepentant. Kelly wanted to hit him for making her blush.

She turned her attention back to the suitcase. He had done a neat job of packing for her. She remembered the state of her bedroom, her house, and winced. He had not seen her in her best light.

She had become an insomniac in the last few years, and she had a pretty good idea what he had found in her bedroom. There was an empty half-gallon carton of ice cream with a long spoon in it sitting on the floor by the unmade bed. Two magazines were open on the spare pillow; books were in a haphazard pile on the floor where they had been tossed rather than put back on the shelves. She had been working on a Sunday school craft project in bed, and not all the colorful construction paper punch holes and trimmed edges had hit the wastebasket. Neat the room was not. At least the laundry had been done, if not yet put away.

She pulled out the long sweater he had packed. "I'm cold down to my bones."

Her shoulders and upper arms ached with her careful movements. Joe reached over and freed her hair from the sweater collar. Kelly was grateful she didn't have to try to reach back to do it. She felt like an old lady.

Joe had thought to pack the novel that had been on her bedside table and also her Bible. She closed her hand around the cool leather cover of her Bible and wondered with some guilt where in the house he had found it. She didn't remember seeing it since she came home from church Sunday. Daily devotions, such a regular part of her life before Nick's death, had become sporadic over the last few years.

He knew. She could see it in his eyes. He didn't say anything as she placed her Bible on the nightstand. She couldn't change the last three years, but she could still change today and tomorrow.

"Liz said she would be here about nine."

"I thought she and Tom were in San Jose until Monday."

"Kelly, the best I could do was talk her out of catching a flight back last night."

Knowing her friend, that in itself would have been a challenge. "If I'm about to have more company, then I'm going to brave looking in that mirror." She eased herself to the edge of the bed.

"Take your hairbrush."

"I didn't see any makeup."

"You don't need it."

She sent him an amused, knowing look.

103

"Right. You didn't want to figure out what to bring."

"Guilty. You'll have to borrow from Liz."

"Since I can't put on lipstick, I probably shouldn't care."

She turned on the light in the bathroom and froze. "Joe! Why didn't you tell me I have a nice black eye?"

"You haven't had breakfast yet," he replied, holding back laughter. "Bad news before you eat isn't fair."

She gingerly touched the black ring under her left eye. "The last one of these I had was when Nick beaned me with that line drive hit." She had been playing third base in the Coronado charity softball game; her husband was on the opposing team. The game was tied, and a cheer went up when Nick made contact with the second pitch. It had shot down the third baseline right at her. With no time to get her glove up, she tried to twist out of the way but was hit instead. She dropped like a rock. She had never seen her husband so rattled. It took her days to shake off the concussion. "How'd I get this one?"

"You don't remember?"

"No."

She washed her face, then looked with resignation at her matted hair. Long, thick, black, and wavy, her hair was prone to tangle, and saltwater severely aggravated the problem. She had always wished the sun would lighten it to at least a glowing sable, but it just stayed a light-absorbing dark.

Her eyes watered as she tried to work the brush through her hair. She soon realized the task was going to be nearly impossible. She lowered her arms, feeling the strain of simply keeping them raised. "I need a pair of scissors."

"What's wrong?"

She smiled. He was going to love this complaint. "My hair."

"It's not that bad."

She leaned around the doorway. "There speaks a guy with a military haircut."

"True." He pulled over the other chair. "Come sit down; I'll do it for you."

"You?"

"Hey, my dog doesn't have any complaints."

"Joe —" She smiled as she chided him for the teasing. She looked back in the mirror and lifted a matted strand of hair. It looked about like Misha's on a bad day.

"I'll go easy."

She remembered Nick brushing her hair occasionally, how intimate the action could be when it was meant as more than an impersonal touch. "I need the help." She took the seat he had pulled over and held the brush out.

Joe turned her slightly away from him and gathered her hair back. "You've been letting it grow."

"Yes." Her voice had gone husky.

"I like it long."

He didn't say anything else, and after a few moments Kelly relaxed her initial stiffness and closed her eyes to simply enjoy the sensation. It took patience to brush it out section by section like Joe was doing, pausing to work out each tangle. It was a soothing feeling.

Her thoughts drifted as the silence lengthened.

Why had she said I love you? She didn't intend to say the words. She probably embarrassed him — she knew him long enough to know that. He'd handle it tactfully, but he wouldn't ignore it — she was also certain about that.

She loved who Joe was. Everything about him: his character, his absolute honesty, his tact, his self-discipline, his leadership. She had been comfortable with him since the day Nick introduced them. She trusted him. When he had shown up in the water and slid his arm around her, held her tight, she knew she was finally safe. She knew he would come. Years of depending on him and he never let her down. He was a wonderful friend.

But she wanted something more. She was glad her head was bent and her expression hidden because she had the awful suspicion that she was blushing. Her emotions were confusing. This was Joe, and she'd just managed to throw her ability to think about him as her friend totally off. She was incredibly aware of him at the moment, every move he made as he brushed her hair. Having his arms wrap around her again, by choice . . . She sighed, admitting the obvious. It would be wonderful — and the idea scared her to death.

Joe had a romantic streak. He'd brought a few dates to the platoon gatherings over the years and she had seen how he treated his dates. When Joe chose to focus on a woman, he made her life very special. And he wasn't dating anyone now, hadn't since Nick was killed —

She stopped herself abruptly. This was Joe. Her best friend.

Her emotions had said I love you. He was a great-looking guy, with all the right personal qualities to make her want to hold onto him and not let go. She did want something more with him.

But her logic was having fits. Joe would never want to date her. She was Nick's wife. And she didn't want to marry an active duty SEAL again. She didn't have the courage to pace the floor and wonder if Joe was going to come home. She needed to marry a civilian. If the intervening years had taught her anything, it was that she didn't have the courage to face possibly losing a husband again.

It felt like two sides of her were locked in a tug-of-war.

Could it even work for them to be more than just friends? Between friendship and marriage there was only room to get hurt. And she was getting the jitters even thinking about it.

She gave up trying to decide what she wanted. In the end it would not be her decision to make. It would be Joe's. Everything was a moot point unless he wanted to change their present relationship.

Lord, please don't let what I said ruin a good friendship. Please.

She let her head drop forward a little more as Joe worked out a tangle in the ends of her hair. The brush caught. "Sorry."

"It's okay," she whispered. She didn't dare say more.

His hands settled on her drooping shoulders. "Come here." She gave a start from her wandering thoughts to hear the amusement in his voice. He turned her toward him and she didn't even hesitate. She leaned her head forward against his shoulder and relaxed. His arms encircled her. "I'm only half done."

"Fine." She would love to curl up in the warmth she could feel coming through his shirt. She could go back to sleep right here. He felt like a grizzly bear, so wide was the expanse of his chest.

She felt his quiet laughter. "Not fine. Now only half of you looks like a rag mop." He rubbed her upper arms. "Five more minutes."

"Later."

He held her for a few minutes, his head leaning down against hers. Not quite asleep, not quite awake, Kelly found it to be a tranquil place, safe. And better than she had ever imagined it would be. She didn't get held very often anymore, and Joe . . . She would savor this memory. "Bear?"

The hand idly rubbing her back paused. "Hmm?"

"Thanks."

She smiled when he kissed her hair. "Come on. Back to bed."

Six

★ ★ ★

"Go home, Joe." Kelly could tell he was tired, even he couldn't cover up the fatigue of two days with broken sleep. And watching him sit there — reclining in the hospital chair, his hands folded across his chest — was very distracting. She noticed everything about him, unfortunately couldn't help but notice, and it was driving her crazy. A day ago he had been contained in a box called friend. Now it was impossible to put him back into it.

It had been a long day with a steady stream of visitors. After Liz had come, the guys from Golf Platoon and then friends from work and church had stopped by. She was exhausted.

"You sure?"

"I'm going to read for a while then call it a night."

He hesitated for a moment, showing a reluctance she found endearing. He nodded. "I'll be back in the morning."

"After your run."

"After my run." He tweaked the edge of her pillow as he got to his feet. "You just want to sleep in."

"You got it." When he leaned over, his hands resting on the edge of the mattress, Kelly moved her head back a few inches on the pillow to look at him. He really was an attractive man, and it wasn't just her biased opinion. Ruggedly handsome. Fine lines around his eyes, and that tan — The places her thoughts went when she was tired.

"You did a good job, Kelly, but let's not do this again, okay? You scared a few years off my life."

She let out a soft breath, the emotions in his eyes delivering a pounding. She had really shaken him. "Okay." She was crossing a line that was dangerous, but she couldn't stop herself. Her fingers trembled a bit as she reached up and brushed his cheek, smiling as she deliberately lightened her voice. "But don't worry, on you early gray hair will look distinguished."

She had surprised him. She saw it in his eyes as they flared with warmth and he smiled. He captured her fingers and squeezed them. "I don't want to lose you."

His words were manna to her heart. "I'll

be more careful in the future."

"Thank you." Joe eased back, breaking eye contact, letting her breathe again. He reached over and knuckled her stuffed animal. "Good night, Bo-Bo." He looked back at her. "G'night, Kelly," he said softly.

" 'Night, Joe."

The balloon tied to the bouquet of flowers her partner Alex had brought fluttered as Joe left. *Be still my heart.* . . . What had she gotten herself into? It stretched like a tantalizing promise ahead of her, whispering hope.

Kelly leaned her head back against the pillow. Intense emotions were exhausting. She definitely needed to sleep on this new turn of events.

She reached over and picked up her Bible, wanting at the end of what had been a life-changing twenty-four hours to spend it as she hoped to go on. She wasn't sure if anything would have an impact on the first day back into reading God's Word, but she was determined to make it a habit again.

Her bookmark was in John 5, left there from weeks before. "Do you want to be healed?" The question Jesus asked the man who had been ill for thirty-eight years stopped her cold, and she knew she would have to face that question herself. Did she really want to change? Was her resolve going to last once she was back in her daily routine?

I do, Lord. I want regular devotions back, regular prayer. I didn't intend to let a separation happen, and I want to change that. It's going to be hard to leave behind the lingering anger over what I lost, the grief when I think about what could have been with Nick, but I am determined to try. And what's going on with Joe . . . Lord, I'm going to need a lot of wisdom in the next few days. Would You —

A tap on the door interrupted her.

"Ryan! Come in. It's good to see you."

He came into the room on crutches, tall, lanky, moving with the awkward grace of a teen. "Hi, Mrs. Jacobs."

She found his formality endearing. "Try Kelly, you'll make me feel old with that Mrs. Jacobs." She closed her Bible with a slight tinge of guilt, but the interruption was unavoidable. "Joe didn't tell me you banged up your ankle."

"Twisted it when the surfboard crashed me into the face of that last wave."

"How long will they stick you on crutches?"

"Maybe a couple of days. It was either

crutches or a wheelchair in the hospital." He settled into the chair Joe had occupied most of the day. "My dad is behind me — he got caught by a page he had to answer."

Kelly nodded and wondered if she had time to move from the bed to a chair before the man arrived. "Did he give you a tough time?"

"He was too glad to see that I was awake and okay. Listen, Kelly — before he gets here — my dad is probably going to want to say thanks in a tangible way."

"Ryan, thank you is all I want. I'm not expecting a gift."

Ryan appeared embarrassed by what he wanted to say. "No, you don't understand. Dad isn't the type to give just any gift. It tends to be extravagant. Would you please just accept it, whatever it is? It would mean a lot to me."

Kelly was puzzled by the plea. "Ryan —"

A tap on the door interrupted them.

Ryan was dressed casually in jeans and a sweatshirt, but his father was not. It was rare to see a dress shirt, dress slacks, and a silk tie in a hospital, even if the tie was loose and the shirt cuffs were rolled up. Ryan's dad must have come from work yesterday and never been home. He was carrying a wrapped package.

Her hand instinctively straightened her sweater.

"Kelly, this is my dad, Charles Raines."

She returned his smile and held out her hand, trying to ignore the embarrassment of having to meet him from a hospital bed. "Mr. Raines."

Her hand was enveloped in his and held in a comfortable grip. "It's a pleasure, Mrs. Jacobs." She liked the gentle tone of his voice, his smile, although his gray eyes were hard to read, the color unusual, not cold but cloudy gray. "I've been hearing all about your adventure." He took the second chair.

Adventure. Kelly approved of his word choice. It had almost been a tragic accident, but it *had* been an accident. If he had overreacted, Ryan might never surf again.

She could see the toll last night had taken on Charles; the man didn't look like he had had much sleep. For a father to face the possible loss of his son . . . There were few things more tragic. Even the loss of a spouse did not equate with the loss of a child. She had struggled to hold onto the boy; Charles had struggled to hold onto hope. If Ryan was not in the room, she would have apologized for the duration of the rescue.

"Please, it's Kelly. Ryan slept through the fun parts."

He acknowledged the quiet message with a gaze that held hers and a slight nod. Ryan wouldn't have memories of what had happened last night. The man deliberately relaxed and smiled back at her, taking her by surprise as she was enveloped in the warmth of his eyes. "So he told me. He's begging for a repeat helicopter ride." There was laughter in his words as he glanced with affection at his son.

"Dad said maybe. That means yes."

Kelly had to laugh at the boy's confidence. She remembered Ryan saying it was only him and his dad. It was pretty obvious the two of them were close.

"We meant to come down earlier. I would have enjoyed meeting your husband, but we got tied up with visitors."

Her husband . . . She struggled not to blush as the comment flustered her. "Oh — no, that was Joe. He's a good friend. He was the one who found us last night."

"Lieutenant Baker? Now I'm really bothered we didn't get down here earlier."

"He'll be back in the morning. I told him to go home and get some sleep."

"Your husband?"

116

"He passed away a few years ago."

"I'm sorry. I know what that is like." She saw in his eyes that he did, and it made him infinitely more approachable. She had never been comfortable around the very wealthy, and right or wrong, she had pegged Charles as that with Ryan's casual words about where they lived. He was slipping under that caution by creating a common ground between them.

She turned her attention to Ryan. "No problems from our swim besides the ankle? Not even a sniffle?"

"No. Did I give you that black eye?"

"Would you believe I don't remember?"

"It looks like it hurts."

She didn't want to leave that impression. "Only when I forget and rub my eyes." Charles was not quite so willing to accept her words. "No double vision?"

She glanced back at him and she shook her head. "My eyesight's fine."

"I'm grateful you were there, but I hate seeing you pay this kind of price for having helped."

"Relax. It's not my first ocean swim. I may end up with a cold, but that's about it."

"Is there anything you need? Anything we can bring you?" Charles offered.

"Joe stopped by my place and packed for me."

"The bear looks old."

She looked at it and felt childish now about having it with her. "Yes. My husband bought him for me ages ago."

Charles picked it up. "It's certainly more practical than flowers." The expression on his face became distant. "My wife used to buy me little carved figures of jade lions, bears, pandas — so there would be something to put on the hotel dresser when I traveled that would remind me of home." He smiled at her as he put the bear down. "Jade isn't as huggable."

"No." He was lonely. She could hear it in his voice, and she wondered why he hadn't remarried long ago. A good-looking, wealthy man with a teenage son? It couldn't have been for lack of candidates.

"We brought you something." Charles held out the box.

Kelly saw Ryan's silent plea as she accepted the gift, not sure what to expect. It had always been easier to give gifts than receive them. Her hands fumbled with the tape, her fingers not cooperating, making a lie to what she had said about being fine. Her body wasn't quite as resilient as that of a teenager. Charles stilled her hands and broke the tape for her. She glanced up, met his gaze, then quickly looked back at the gift.

The lid on the box came off easily and she moved the tissue paper aside. It was a rosebud vase made of fine porcelain. She lifted it from the box with great care and let it rest against her palms. It was absolutely lovely.

"Dad brought it from the Orient."

Charles met her gaze with a smile, without changing his relaxed posture. "Pretty, but not so expensive it should sit on a shelf and not be used," he noted. "We'll bring you a rose for it tomorrow."

Not totally the truth. She had a feeling that the age she sensed in the piece was real, not a good replication. She felt inept in situations like this. She glanced again at the vase, traced the design. "Maybe a pink one to match this rose?"

"Of course." The warmth in his voice grew. "That would be a pleasure." Kelly could see where Ryan got his charm.

They stayed for half an hour. Charles relaxed like Joe did, completely, and his smile was never far away. She liked the fact that when he asked questions, he really listened to the reply. He made her laugh, and that was rare with a stranger.

119

When they left, Kelly settled back against the pillows, still a little over-whelmed. Charles Raines would not have crossed her path under normal circum-stances. She had made an unexpected friend.

Kelly reached for her Bible and opened it again but soon found herself struggling to keep her eyes open. She finally closed it, accepting reality. *Tomorrow, Lord.*

Seven

★ ★ ★

"Charles, it's gorgeous." The rose was a perfect match for the vase. "Thank you." Kelly moved the vase to the middle of the table, pleased with the gift. In anticipation of his visit, she had risen early and was reading the Saturday San Diego newspaper when he arrived. She wasn't surprised he was alone; it was early for Ryan to be allowed up.

Charles indicated the chair across from her. "May I?"

"Please." She moved aside the newspaper inserts. "Did Ryan have a good night?"

"Fine. I left him eating breakfast and watching music videos."

She laughed at his bemused expression. It was obvious he didn't share his son's music tastes. He had brought his own coffee with him, and she relished the aroma as she sipped ice water. "Will he be released today?"

"I expect so. It was incredibly quiet

around the house last night. Are you also able to leave today?"

"As soon as the doctor makes his rounds."

"I'm glad." Charles set down his coffee. "I wanted to ask you, Ryan's going to need to learn how to surf *safely*. He and Tony were supposed to be going to the beach, but not to surf. I'm not willing to risk such an accident again, and I don't think grounding him for life is going to work." He grimaced at that. "Do you know a good instructor?"

"A few. Greg Peterson is good. He does a lot of work with the park district, has classes scheduled for most of the summer."

"What about private lessons? I'd like to get Ryan scheduled for something in the next week, ten days."

"Outside my purview, I'm afraid. Greg would know." Kelly was aware the world was different when money was not a problem. She hesitated. "I could give him a few pointers until you line something up."

"Would you?"

He looked pleased with the offer and she relaxed, for it had been a bit presumptuous to offer. "I'd enjoy it."

"I'll gladly take you up on it. Ryan

thinks you're neat, so he'll listen to you."

Neat. It sounded like a direct quote. "Tell him thanks. I like your son." She sipped at the water and saw him glance at the newspaper. "Would you like the financial page?"

He looked back at her and gave a lazy grin. "I look like an investment banker?"

"Just guessing."

"Nothing so glamorous. My firm is a dealmaker for military hardware between the U.S. Navy and the British Navy."

"Really?"

"I had to do something once they tossed me out of Hong Kong."

"What were you doing before?"

"Keeping my ear to the ground. Hong Kong presented some unique security concerns both for the British government and the British companies based there. My firm helped fill in the gaps when the military needed some civilian expertise."

A civilian who understood the military. Kelly tucked it away to ponder later. She didn't ask about that area of his life, for she had lived with the reality of military secrecy too long to even raise the questions. "Ryan sounds like he misses living abroad."

"We'd go back in an instant if it were

possible. Hong Kong is a fabulous place to live and work."

"What do you miss the most?"

"Besides the food? Almost everything. The people, the pace, the potential around every corner. My wife was born there."

As she listened to Charles talk about Hong Kong, Kelly could hear how much he loved it. She leaned back in her chair, peppering him with questions when he paused.

He stopped midsentence and gave her a rueful look. "Kelly, tell me to shut up. You don't need an encyclopedic tourist guide."

"I'm a little envious; I've never been outside of California."

"Really?"

She smiled at his shock. "It's not that bad. It is a very big state."

"Maybe I'll get a chance to show you Hong Kong sometime in the future."

She started to say something, stopped, and blinked. The guy was serious. She was still trying to formulate how to reply when she caught movement from the corner of her eye. Joe was here. She turned, pleased the men would get a chance to meet.

She had decided one thing early this morning — she was going to get her feelings about Joe back under control. Yesterday had been nothing but unchecked emotion, spurred by events. She was thinking more rationally today. They were friends. She wasn't going to let anything mess that up, didn't dare. His friendship was the best thing she had in her life. It wouldn't work for them to be something more. She was rather proud of the fact she could look at him this morning and not have heart flutters. How long that control lasted was another matter. He *would* have to show up in his summer whites, not his usual desert cammies. He looked sharp and in command.

"Joe, I'd like you to meet Ryan's father, Charles Raines. Charles, Lieutenant Joe Baker."

Charles got to his feet. They were an interesting match — Charles with his smooth charm and easy smile, Joe with his innate confidence and sense of presence.

"It's good to meet you, Lieutenant." Charles held out his hand.

Kelly was startled by the hesitation before Joe offered his and shook hands. "Mr. Raines." His voice was cool and his expression anything but welcoming.

What was his problem? She pushed back her chair. "Charles was just telling me about Hong Kong, where he and Ryan used to live." She could hear herself rushing her words, for the tension in the room was palatable.

"Did you live there for long?" Joe asked, never turning his attention from the man.

"Ten years. Have you ever been?"

"I've visited. How's your son?"

"Doing well. I would like to offer my thanks for your help in a tangible way."

"I'm sure the naval base would appreciate a contribution to the family fund."

Charles nodded, then glanced over at Kelly. "I should let you get packed." He reached for his coffee mug, keeping one eye on Joe even as he spoke to her.

"Thanks for the rose." She hated to see him leave but couldn't blame him given Joe's reaction. She had never known Joe to take such an immediate dislike to someone. She didn't understand it and there was no reason for it.

"It was my pleasure. I'll call you this evening, see how you are doing."

"I'd like that."

She walked with Charles toward the door. "Tell Ryan I said hello."

Charles smiled. "I'm sure he'll want a few minutes on the phone tonight. See you later, Kelly." He turned slightly. "Lieutenant."

Joe nodded tersely.

Kelly made sure the door was closed behind Charles before she turned on Joe. "What was that all about? You were rude."

"Guilty."

Joe was in full grizzly bear mode this morning, but she wasn't going to let him off the hook. "Why?"

"I don't know, Kelly." It wasn't an angry denial as much as a frustrated one. "Call it instinct. The guy put my back up."

"Well, that doesn't give you the right to be impolite."

"What was he doing letting his son go surfing anyway? The sea was churning."

"Joe!"

He strode over to the window, rubbing his hand over the back of his neck. Picking up her sweater, Kelly folded it and placed it in the open suitcase on the bed. Joe acted like he had been up all night. Had he dealt with a page? It would at least explain his surly mood. Great. Now she was worried about him as well as irritated with him.

She sat down on the bed and slapped the mattress beside her. It was time to find out if she could still be that friend. "Sit down."

He gave a rueful smile and then did so. Tentative at first, she dug her hands into the tense muscles of his shoulders, working out the knots. The feel of the tension in him was a bit of a shock. It wasn't like him to react this way. He rolled his neck, silently asking her to tackle where the muscles had tightened the most. She smiled as she complied; it felt good to be able to help him out for a change. She used the heel of her hand to apply pressure between his shoulder blades and wondered how she could ask without stepping across a line she tried to avoid. "Anything happen last night you can't tell me about?"

"No." He rotated his shoulder and he finally began to relax. "I'm sorry I growled."

She wrapped her hands around his waist and hugged him from behind, resting her chin against his shoulder. He was such a solid man, durable. It felt good to have the friendship back on its old footing, if only for the moment. "You're forgiven. But you owe Charles the apology not me."

"I'll think about it."

His reaction puzzled her. "Go find the doctor and help me check out of here. I'm ready to go."

"In a minute." He reached into his pocket. "Hold out your hand."

She moved to sit beside him and did so. He closed her hand around what he held.

"Your wedding ring."

Kelly was relieved the swelling had gone down enough she could wear it again. "Thank you."

"Your hand looked bare without it."

"It felt bare. I've worn this ring for over ten years."

"It belongs there."

She slipped it on. "Yes. Losing the ring would have been a disaster."

Joe squeezed her hand, then set a manila envelope down on her open suitcase. "Nick's eagle medallion. Are you sure you're ready to leave?"

"If I'm going sailing with you tomorrow, I'd better be."

"Seriously."

She still had a low-grade headache, but it was one caused by a lack of caffeine. She was gutting it out, deciding now was probably as good a time as any to cut back. The room felt cold, and the second-day muscle soreness made her grit her teeth, but she was going to bury it rather than admit it. "I'm fine, Joe. Not even a sniffle."

He wasn't totally buying it, but he finally nodded. "I'll go find your doctor."

Kelly watched the door close behind him.

What was Joe going to say when he

brought up those three fateful words she had said? She couldn't contain the jitters in the pit of her stomach. One of the things she liked about him was his willingness to be kind to her after she had made a blunder. And she had blundered by saying those words. They were friends. It was going to be a difficult conversation to have.

Lord, I'm asking a favor. Please don't ask me to deal with this subject today. I've got enough to worry about just thinking about sailing and facing the sea again. And I need some time to sort out with You all my past problems. I lean on Joe; please don't let my words shake that relationship at a time when I need it the most.

She let go of her wedding ring and got up to finish packing. It was time to go home.

Eight

★ ★ ★

Charles took the return call on the encrypted line in his home office. "Your device has been found," he said tersely.

"How soon can it be delivered?"

"Eight days."

"No sooner?"

"Patience," he cautioned. "There is more paperwork with this one." He was already far out on a limb. Arranging to smuggle a nuclear warhead out of a secure Russian weapons lab took the finesse of a negotiator and a deep pocket of cash. He was a thief, a good one, but this was one deal he wished he could walk away from. "Eight days. It's the best I can do." He could see his son in the backyard and fear coiled in his gut.

He still couldn't believe it had evolved to this point. Several years ago, a similar deal had gone bad and men had died. He had gotten out of the stolen arms business after that, retired abruptly, relieved to be able to walk away. Now he was being pressured into coming out of retirement to pull together a similar deal.

The general was using a very effective weapon. Fear. Charles knew he wasn't the only one watching his son.

The device would be ready to move in four days, but the general didn't need to know that. Charles needed the extra time to get precautions in place — he wasn't going to let anything happen to Ryan.

He turned the gold pen in his hand. "My money is ready?" Getting to the warhead was an expensive proposition. He might not be able to refuse the deal, but he was going to make it as costly as possible. The general wasn't in a position to quibble over details. He wanted a nuclear warhead smuggled into Taiwan territory. If it could be done, and Charles had his doubts that the general could maintain the necessary secrecy at his end, it would not be a cheap endeavor. Charles planned to pay enough to insure there was silence among thieves. It wasn't his money he was spending.

"Yes."

"Begin assembling your team. I'll put the shipment in motion as soon as the money appears in my account."

"You are confident this delivery will

not be intercepted?"

His hand tightened on the pen; the threat was less than subtle. They had been having this conversation too often. "I'm inside with more than one resource. I'll know before they move."

He'd been forced to involve his son to make that second contact, and when it had gone bad Charles nearly had a coronary. Ryan was not supposed to be surfing. He was supposed to just hang out at the beach where Kelly worked, playing Frisbee with his friend. Charles had planned to swing by after work, then ask Kelly a couple casual questions as he collected the boys. The door to a later conversation when they just happened to bump into each other at a local bookstore would have happened without her thinking anything about it. Instead there had almost been a tragedy of epic proportions.

It wouldn't have been necessary to try and get that second contact for a means to monitor the SEAL teams if he had made a better original choice. But his first source was becoming too chatty, too . . . attached. He had made that contact too early, kept it too long, chosen poorly — in hindsight all those facts were obvious. He had no choice but to stop seeing her and go with a new source at this late date. While he regretted who he had been forced to select, he accepted it as necessary. He needed a way to keep track of Lieutenant Baker and his men, and Kelly was the only way to accomplish that with any degree of certainty. He'd been pushed into a corner and there wasn't another option. "There are contingencies in place."

"We will need time for the assembly."

"And I'm staying put to give you that time. You're getting a bargain considering the risk involved." When the device was stolen and shipped, he would have a hard time creating an airtight alibi when he couldn't catch a plane and be occupied elsewhere. He wasn't making this deal happen only to get caught and have Ryan pay the price of losing his father.

"Considering our last attempted purchase, you owe us."

If the Americans were good enough to intercept a shipment occasionally, it was inconvenient, but from Charles's perspective not a disaster. It only made the asking price on the black market higher. Before his retirement, he had even been known to help the Americans out on occasion with a nudge in the right direction. This man would not appreciate that insight. "You'll get your device."

"Call when the shipment is ready." The call was abruptly terminated. Charles returned the phone to its cradle.

Eight days.

He would be relieved when this was over.

He had considered going to the authorities early on, but he had secrets to hide that went back three decades. He could handle the general. It was a business deal, a nasty one, but he could deal with it. The threat to his son arose only if he didn't deliver the device, and this was one deal he was going to make certain went off without a hitch. He would deliver.

He had seriously considered sending private security after the shadows watching him, then reluctantly dismissed it. The general would only send others to replace them.

And putting a bodyguard with his son — Charles wanted to wrap Ryan in a cocoon of security, but he knew reality. If the general decided to make good on his threat, a bodyguard would merely be an annoying pause in the hit. And one bodyguard or ten, it would change his son's image of him forever. For the illusion of safety it would offer, it wasn't worth the price. He had managed to get out of the business before without Ryan knowing he had ever been in it. He wouldn't allow this crisis to change that.

He had begun stealing arms to pay for his wife's cancer treatments, so nervous about the first transaction he sweated over the stealing of a single stinger missile. She thought the money was coming from a promotion and a series of good investments. The illness let him cloud the details; the job he held allowed him to cover the travel. His wife had died. And the anger had become a willingness to take risks, to make money and stash it away for his son should anything ever happen to him.

It had been a foolish time in his life, and fools eventually paid the price. He just hoped he gained a little wisdom in the intervening years. He would need it to get himself and his son out of this spot.

He had never been caught because he had infiltrated the network of arms dealers before he stole his first weapon. His clearances and past in-depth security checks had held against the few things that might have otherwise raised interest. The men he had stolen weapons for were the same men who on another day he sold weapons to with his government's blessing.

He had been inside the business long enough to understand the circles and subcircles necessary to protect his identity. His networks evolved and disappeared afresh with each deal. Compartmentalizing information was second nature and served him well.

The problems with this deal were myriad. He had been out of the business too long. His contacts were stale, his resources for information limited. This was not only the most complex deal he'd ever faced; it also carried the highest risk. And he had to find ways to moderate it.

The situation on the ground in Taiwan might work in his favor. The U.S. defense department was acknowledging a gap in what they knew about China's military capabilities regarding Taiwan. He had a copy of the report summary on his desk, pulled from the defense department's own web site.

For the first time the U.S. was admitting in a public document that they couldn't predict what would provoke a conflict between China and Taiwan or how either side would respond. China had always said it would use force to unify Taiwan with the mainland if Taiwan declared its independence. The report noted that China had recently added that it would use force if Taiwan acquired nuclear weapons.

If he could carefully tip off the U.S. military to this deal at the right time . . . maybe there was a way out of this. If he could ensure the right information leaked without jeopardizing his son's safety, maybe the U.S. military could quietly take down the general.

He'd have to pass the information along after the deal was done but before the device was operational. And given the distance to the nearest deployment of U.S. forces, he was either going to have to give them some other reason to move forces into the area early or arrange his leak through safe channels so the general wouldn't realize it had been made.

Joe Baker was going to be key before this was over. Charles was glad Kelly had the man as a friend. If he could somehow figure out how to tip the SEAL to what was happening . . . Charles was under no illusions. Joe was still hunting him, the man he called Raider, hoping to extract revenge for Nick's death.

Joe would deploy the SEALs if there was any indication the man responsible for Nick's death could be caught. Charles had stayed deep underground, moving from

Hong Kong to the SEALs own backyard so he could watch them and make sure his trail stayed closed. It wouldn't be easy to leak the name Raider without it leading back to him, but it was one possible way he could go. He had to find a plan that would work.

He would have to play both sides of the fence and hope he could somehow keep his balance. The general could not be allowed to acquire a working weapon. But Charles was under no illusions. If the general was at all suspicious he was trying to disrupt this deal, the man would kill Ryan. And that risk was unacceptable. If he had to let the deal go through to protect his son . . . Charles opened the bottom drawer of his desk, his keepsake drawer, and with care lifted out Amy's photo and beneath it her diary.

His wife had written the diary while she had cancer, and when reading it he could hear the sound of her voice. She never suspected what he had done in order to arrange the cancer treatments. All the guilt he felt over his activities could not change the fact he still would have done it. For all its promise, the treatment had only been able to buy him some more time with her. Precious time. But not enough of it.

He missed Amy . . . beyond words. He had promised her he would watch out for Ryan. Starting a war would be easier to have on his conscience than breaking his word to his wife.

Nine

Kelly shifted the phone so she could reach for another Kleenex. If she caught a cold to cap off her return home, it would ruin what had been a nice day.

"Did you get my flowers?"

Kelly glanced around at the six dozen roses now occupying every table in her living room and dining room and smiled across the room at her friend Liz. "Yes, Charles, I did. They are . . . exquisite."

Joe had brought her home, then left when Liz arrived. The delivery van had arrived about forty minutes later. Kelly didn't have words to describe her reaction to Charles's latest gift. The first dozen roses in their cut glass vase had been gorgeous, the second dozen stunning, and by the sixth vase Kelly had gone through pleased, stunned, bemused, and had finally settled on laughter. Ryan had been right about his dad — he did say thank you in extravagant ways. Liz was convinced Charles was smitten.

"The vase yesterday was my son's suggestion for thanks; the roses are mine."

"You do have a nice way of showing your appreciation."

"I'm glad you think so."

Her doorbell rang. "I hear the door; I'll let you go," Charles said, then softly chuckled. "Have a good afternoon, Kelly."

Kelly put down the phone and had a sneaking suspicion he had known that the doorbell would ring. She raced to answer the door.

The deliveryman looked startled at the abrupt reception.

"Another gift from him?" Liz asked as Kelly signed for the box and gave the man the last dollars in her purse as a thank-you. This had to be the last delivery today. She was officially broke until next payday.

The box was beautifully wrapped in gold paper; the card bore the logo from one of the exclusive shops in San Diego Kelly had never dared venture into. She took a seat on the couch and set the box in her lap. "He wouldn't have." She looked helplessly from it to Liz.

Her friend shook her head. "I'm not the one he apparently has a crush on." Liz tapped the card with a grin. "Only one way to find out."

"If it is from Charles, I'm returning it," Kelly said firmly, not sure how to stop what felt like a dream afternoon. She was both flattered and flustered with the attention; she couldn't accept something like this. She opened the card.

Thanks doesn't cover it, and roses will eventually fade. Enjoy.

"It's from Charles," she said quietly, handing Liz the card. Intrigued even as she was overwhelmed, she opened the box. "Oh my." A shimmering blue silk dress lay within the folds of tissue paper. Kelly set aside the enclosed envelope to open in a minute and lifted the dress from the box. It was a designer original, of that she was sure — a classic cut, understated elegance in every inch of the dress. She stood, held it up for consideration, and saw he had correctly guessed her size.

"The man has good taste," Liz said.

"He needs a wife to tell him not to spend his money."

Liz burst out laughing, stood up, and hugged her. "You rescued Ryan. It's only fitting that Charles rescue you — he's throwing you a wonderful lifeline back to the world of guys and dating."

Liz had no idea how on target her words were; only it was Joe that Kelly had her eyes on, not Charles. The idea was terrifying no matter what name she used. "What am I supposed to do? Flowers are one thing, this —"

"Why don't you see what he had to say?" Liz offered the envelope that had also been in the box.

Kelly handed Liz the dress, then accepted the envelope. She withdrew a single sheet of paper with Charles Raines III on the letterhead.

In the water, you told Ryan you had a love affair for the ballet. Swan Lake, in these circumstances, sounds appropriate. I hope you have a wonderful evening.

Kelly glanced at the two tickets for next month's performance and recognized some of the best seats in the house. Then she read the last lines of his note: *PS: I hate ballet. If you want company, I've got two tickets to a hockey game.*

She burst out laughing.

Charles . . .

She would keep the dress. From his perspective it was a nice thank-you for saving his son's life. That this gift represented her salary for a couple of months was beside the point. "I don't have his number to call and say thanks. And I bet it's unlisted."

"Smart man. He's not letting you get noble and reasonable."

"He is being unreasonable."

"Romantic is never unreasonable."

"Charles, you really shouldn't have bought me a dress." Kelly was glad he had called back. She pinned the phone against her shoulder as she folded laundry. It was going on 8 p.m., her house was beginning to be less of an embarrassment, and she was enjoying the chance to talk to him.

"I couldn't resist. My business headquarters are across the street from the shop, and I've been passing that dress in the window every day at lunch. I knew it would be perfect for you."

"Would you at least make it the last gift? I'm grateful, but you're overdoing it." She didn't know how to handle this attention. She liked Charles, liked the fact she could have a relaxed conversation with him, and really liked his son Ryan, but she wasn't ready to accept a date with him. Too much had happened recently. She wanted a few days to adjust before saying yes to an invitation from Charles.

How was she ever going to explain that vase, all those roses, and the dress to Joe? Her friends? She set aside the folded towel.

"You gave me back something more precious than money could ever buy. It's the least I could do."

"I was glad I could help. But I'll tell you what — I'll accept the dress if you promise no more gifts."

She heard him sigh. "Are you always this difficult?"

It felt good to be able to give him a hard time; joshing with a guy was fun. "Yes."

"Now you warn me." He paused, and she could well imagine him formulating new tactics in some master plan. "Okay, no more gifts. As long as you promise to enjoy the night out."

"The ballet — I guarantee I will. Are you sure you don't want to go?"

"Please —" she could almost hear his wince — "take Joe."

Kelly had to laugh. Joe hated the ballet. She had a feeling Charles knew that too. "I'll find someone. Maybe my girlfriend Liz. She was impressed with the roses, by the way."

"As long as you were too."

She glanced across at the bouquet on the living room table. "You made an impression."

"I didn't want to miss your favorite color, and if I just sent you a dozen red roses, you would think I was angling for a date."

"You mean you're not?" She bit her tongue, appalled she had asked the question. As the quiet stretched out, she felt her face begin to flame with embarrassment, suddenly mute when she desperately needed words to get her out of this situation.

"You didn't mean to ask that, did you?" Charles asked softly into the silence. "Should I be a gentleman and pretend I didn't hear it or the rascal I am and get you to say when? And in case you were in any doubt, if I thought you would say yes, I would ask in a moment."

Kelly looked up at the ceiling. "I didn't say it."

"Okay. But you owe me one."

He had just proven he was both that gentleman and a rascal. "I can live with that," Kelly replied, liking that image of him.

A phone rang in the background and

Charles said, "I hate to let you go, but I've got an overseas call coming in."

"Thanks for calling. Good night, Charles."

"Good night, Kelly."

She hung up the phone, grateful she had gotten out of that call with no more stumbles. She did love the gifts, even if she needed them to stop.

She carried the laundry basket of folded clothes into the bedroom to put away. The house was almost back in shape. By the time she opened the third drawer in her dresser, Kelly knew she had best pause and work here for a while. Neatness had slowly dwindled in importance, and the chaotic shape of her dresser drawers showed that fact. She found an empty box, sat down on the floor, and started to work.

Nick.

She had forgotten how many pictures and memories she had tucked away in the dresser drawers as it became painful to look at them.

The framed photo of Nick and Joe, both men smiling, standing beside their Zodiac in full gear — black wet suits, fins, breathing apparatuses, weapons slung. It was from a snapshot taken at a competition between dozens of two-men teams. They had placed silver that day and had come home laughing together, Joe razzing Nick for missing by an eighth of an inch the shot that would have given them the gold.

Kelly polished the glass in the frame. Joe didn't laugh like that anymore. He was close to Boomer, but it wasn't the same as it had been with Nick. She missed that laughter, that adventure Joe had always presented whether he was climbing rocks, sailing, or doing his job.

What had happened on that mission that had taken Nick from her? It had changed Joe into a quieter, more intense man. At times she saw him running the beach, lifting weights, pushing himself alone as he had never pushed himself when he and Nick were training together.

Lord, I know he misses his best friend. Should I offer him some of these pictures? They mean a lot to me, but I have a feeling they would mean even more to Joe.

She eventually set aside several she thought he would like and carefully boxed the rest. Kelly found a place in the closet and stored the pictures away. She had delayed letting go of Nick, wanting to hold onto someone, if only a memory. It was time to go on. And maybe, just maybe, it would eventually be with Joe.

Will heaven be this peaceful? Kelly wondered. The night had quieted down to utter stillness. Kelly felt it settle into her body, mind, and heart. Utter peacefulness. She was falling asleep on the back patio lounge chair, but it was a comfortable enough spot she had yet to seriously consider getting up and going in to bed.

Her first day home.

Lord, it was a wonderful day. Laughing with Liz. Charles's gifts. Joe's phone calls just to check up on me. You opened my eyes today, that life without Nick can still contain laughter, joy, and fun. How do I say thanks?

The words of Psalm 16:11 came to mind, and with them a warmth that overwhelmed her. "Thou dost show me the path of life; in thy presence there is fulness of joy, in thy right hand are pleasures for evermore."

Today had been God's gift to her.

Thanks, Lord. You rescued me not only from the sea, but also from the despair I was sinking into. I won't let life tear us apart again. I have missed You so much. Thank You for such a warm welcome home. If nothing else, the last few days have made me appreciate even more the friendship I have with Joe. He's a good man, Lord.

Her thoughts drifted, centered on Joe.

He thought of her as a friend. And even if they could get past the obstacle of her being Nick's widow, two more remained: the fact he was an active duty SEAL walking into harm's way, and children. She had a hard time even thinking about being a SEAL's wife again, and she had no idea if they shared a common outlook on having a family.

Lord, this is going to get complex. But the situation has revealed one thing — I'm ready to move on with my life.

Ten

Early Sunday morning, a pad of paper lay beside Kelly on the bed, an open Bible beside it. She had forgotten what it was like to be hungry for God's Word. She was in the psalms, reading verses she had underlined through the years, hearing arise from the pages a powerful statement of God's character. At Psalm 62, she paused again, impressed, and reached for her pen, writing down a few of the phrases.

"On God rests my deliverance and my honor; my mighty rock, my refuge is God."

"Once God has spoken; twice have I heard this: that power belongs to God."

The words drew her to prayer, and she wrote her prayer in fragments beneath each of the phrases.

On God rests — The responsibility, pressure, and outcome rest on You.

My deliverance — I need to be delivered from the weight of expectations, mine and Joe's, as I talk with him.

My honor — I need to make wise decisions as I rebuild my life.

My mighty rock — You don't move when the hard times hit; I do. Help me hold onto You.

My refuge is God — So many mistakes in the last three years make me hesitate to make decisions. I need this safe place with You no matter what mistake I might make.

Power belongs to God.

Kelly looked at that phrase for a long time before writing beside it — You are the One who makes things happen and gets results. Please do that on my behalf in the coming weeks.

She reread the page, impressed with the depth of the promises in one short psalm. God was everything she needed.

Power belongs to God.

There was a promise in those words, a reassurance. Nothing was beyond Him. She'd left Him in the past as she sought refuge in herself. She had closed herself in her own pain. God had been there patiently waiting for her to seek Him out. She wiped her eyes at the realization. He'd been waiting for her to come back to Him and accept all of this: deliverance, a refuge, the power to deal with the situation that confronted her.

Lord, I'm back. Please be my refuge.

It felt good to pray again. To feel the assurance she was heard. She glanced at the clock and dropped her pen. She was late for church.

She scrambled to dress, grab her Bible, and leave the house. Her first Sunday, and she had blown her plan to get her act back together. She was going to be late. It was embarrassing. Friends would be looking for her arrival and would notice she was late.

The parking lot was full, and she had to park on a side street and walk back to the church. She heard the opening music as she stepped into the foyer. An usher was still at the back handing out bulletins. Kelly accepted one, then moved to the south door of the sanctuary to see if she could slip in unnoticed.

She saw friends, acquaintances, people who would be eager to hear about what had happened this week. The realization of what had just happened made her stop and whisper a thank-you. By not preventing her from being late, God had just handed her a refuge. He had postponed dozens of inquiries about the rescue at sea and let her focus instead remain on Him as the church service began.

Kelly saw Joe five pews from the back just as he turned to scan the doorways. He was watching for her, had saved her a seat. That realization made her feel so good. She quietly walked down the aisle and slid in next to him, then said a soft hi to Boomer and his wife Christi.

"Car trouble?" Joe whispered.

Her old car ran only because Joe bullied it frequently. For once she was glad to be able to say it wasn't that. "Overslept." It was true, not the whole truth but sufficient to allay his worry.

The songs were ones she knew by heart, but they sounded fresh this morning as she absorbed the words. When the song leader concluded the opening part of the service, Kelly reluctantly closed the songbook.

"Nice shiner," Joe commented with a twinkle in his eyes as the choir took their seats and the announcements were read.

"Isn't it though?" She had to smile because there was nothing she could do to cover the black eye, hadn't had time this morning to even try, and it had become a real beauty.

"Sleep okay?"

"It was peaceful."

Joe reached over and squeezed her hand. "I'm glad to hear it."

When he removed his hand, she felt the loss. *Friends,* she reminded herself. *That's all we are at the moment. Just friends.*

Christopher, Liz's son, abruptly shifted his weight in Kelly's arms as he awoke. Kelly settled her hand more firmly across his back as the infant briefly raised his head from her shoulder, wrapped a fist in her hair, then laid his head back down. At three months, he was a wonderful baby. She was going to hate parting with him, but the church crowd was thinning out and her baby-sitting duties while Liz handled the children's worship hour were almost over.

Kelly saw a group of ladies at the end of the hall begin to disperse. She didn't have as long with Christopher as she thought. "Joe, I need to talk to Lucy. Could you take Christopher for a moment?"

"Sure."

If she took Christopher with her, Mrs. Michaels would focus on him and they would never get around to talking about the upcoming Fourth of July festival. Joe accepted the infant with confident hands, putting him against his shoulder with barely a pause in his conversation with Boomer.

156

Joe was good with children, had a natural confidence around them. There were times when Kelly had baby-sat Christopher at her house, and she would rarely get to hold the infant because Joe would stop over and end up holding the boy for his entire visit. Kelly watched him now, saw Christopher poke a finger in Joe's ear, and caught Joe's smile as he eased the infant down a couple inches. This was not the first time she thought he would make a good father. The thought made her feel mushy inside. "I won't be long," she promised.

"Take your time."

Kelly wished she had a picture of this. Christopher was now blowing bubbles at Joe, trying to get his attention.

You're avoiding what you promised to do.

She forced herself to turn and locate Mrs. Michaels again. Kelly crossed the foyer, dreading the reaction to what she needed to ask. "Hi, Mrs. Michaels."

"Kelly, I am so pleased you didn't miss a Sunday and ruin your attendance record."

Kelly smiled, having heard an opening sentence of that form in praise or admonishment since she was in second grade. Lucy was sincere about her relief, and Kelly loved her too much to mind how she expressed it. "Thank you." She hugged her and was enveloped in the smell of peppermint and lavender, both familiar to Kelly. "I was wondering if you might have a substitute who could take my place at the festival this year." It was short notice to ask such a thing, for the Fourth of July festival was only seven weeks away and Kelly was one of the coordinators.

Her friend looked worried and upset. "You're hurt — your eye. It's more than just a shiner?"

"No, I'm fine, really. I just —"

Tell her the truth.

The soft words echoed in her heart. It was so hard to admit the truth to this lady she so admired — the lady who had taught her to name the apostles and the books of the Bible, who had shown her how to stuff a turkey for Thanksgiving, who had ignored her depression after Nick died and pulled her to the flower shows and badgered her into taking care of the flower garden Nick had planted. Kelly sighed. "I just need to cut a few things out of my schedule, and I thought it might be easier to find someone for the festival than for a children's Sunday school class."

"Of course I can find a substitute, but are you sure? You've been a festival coordinator for eight years."

Getting a ten-year plaque from Lucy was a big deal. She taught loyalty by example like no other person Kelly had ever met, and she had a spirit of service that anyone who met her envied.

"Sometimes in showing loyalty to duty, you forget devotion," Kelly said softly, repeating Lucy's own often quoted, favorite admonition. "I've been busy but not devoted. I need to change that." It stung to admit to her teacher such a serious failing.

Mrs. Michaels patted her hand. "Go walk your beach. Jesus spent a lot of time by the seashore. You'll find your balance again." It was blunt, direct, but said kindly. "My grandson loves your Sunday school class. You haven't been doing too badly, judging by those around you."

Her words made Kelly blink back tears. "Thank you."

"You can come and hand out tickets at the festival if you like, keep your service record intact. All you have to do is show up and know blue means adult and green means child. It's amazing how many people are color blind."

Kelly hugged her as she laughed. "Deal."

"Kelly?" Joe had come over to join them.

Mrs. Michaels glanced at Joe, then at

Kelly. "I'm late for lunch. I'll see you two next Sunday." She left them there.

"Are you two okay?" Joe asked. "You're fighting tears and Mrs. Michaels didn't tell me how many Sundays I've been absent so far this year. She's never missed that before."

Kelly had to laugh, for she heard Joe's mix of frustration and worry that he had somehow fallen off Mrs. Michaels' favorites list. "I'm okay, and don't worry, she'll probably drop you a note in the mail. You're still her favorite SEAL."

"Only until Boomer and Christi have the baby, then I'm relegated to the back bench again. What were you two talking about?"

"I asked her to find a substitute to take my place for the festival," Kelly replied.

"Really?"

"My schedule has become chaotic; something has to give. A few less hours at work, a few less hours a month with church events, and it might balance out better."

"It would."

"I know. You told me months ago I should do it."

"It's hard for you to say no," he said gently. "Is Christopher asleep?"

The infant was nestled against his

160

shoulder. Kelly glanced around at his face. "Just content."

"Learn from him. An infant knows relaxed and content."

"I *have* been wound pretty tight lately."

"Then a day on the water should help. What time should I pick you up?" The last thing she wanted was to go sailing and face the water, but on Tuesday she was scheduled to work a six-hour shift at the beach. She had no choice. "Give me an hour to go home and get changed."

Eleven

★ ★ ★

Kelly had to stretch to reach the deck shoe that had somehow become wedged halfway under her bed. The comforter was in her way, making it impossible to see what she was reaching toward. *Lord, I don't want to go sailing. Joe is going to bring up what I said again, and this time there won't be an interruption to save me.*

Kelly got hold of the shoe and wiggled herself back, careful not to lift her head until she was clear of the bed frame. Joe had tried to bring up the subject yesterday when he first brought her home from the hospital.

"Kelly, about what you said in the water . . ."

If Liz hadn't breezed in through the front door at that moment, saving her, she would have been left stuttering her way through some explanation that made her look foolish. She had read in the tone of his voice the words that had tactfully been coming. Why couldn't Joe just pretend he hadn't heard what she said? There were days when his brand of integrity was painful. It was obvious he wasn't interested in changing their relationship beyond a friendship. But rather than let her words die from being ignored, he was going to insist they talk. Just thinking about the conversation was making her so nervous she was sick to her stomach.

Lord, Liz's timing yesterday had the feel of You stepping in to answer my prayer. Would You mind doing that again? Occupy Joe so he doesn't bring up the subject? I don't want to deal with this now. Dealing with the water is going to be tough enough.

The brisk knock on the front door was distinctive and familiar. Kelly scrambled to her feet to see the bedside clock. Either it had been a short hour or Joe was early. He was early; he always was. "I'm coming!"

She tossed the shoe on the bed next to its mate. She kicked the empty laundry basket from the hall to the laundry room as she moved through the house. The door stuck and she groaned. She turned the lock and tried again. "Hi, Joe."

Kelly couldn't see what he was thinking behind his dark sunglasses, and in a mood to be annoyed, she found that irritating.

Joe leaned against the doorjamb, not taking her up on her implicit offer to come in, so she had to stand there while he swept her in an encompassing look from head to toe, then grinned. "You look like you need a few more minutes."

Her bare feet curled against the rug. His teasing grin was not endearing. She sent him a frustrated glance and walked back through to her bedroom. "Find me the aspirin bottle; I'm going to need it."

She heard the front door close. "You sound like you didn't have time for your morning coffee before you left for church."

She knew that tone of voice; he figured to tease her out of her bad mood. She did not want to think about her rushed morning. "I didn't. Could we go sailing some other time?"

She knew when he didn't answer that all the roses had caught his attention. She leaned against the bedroom doorpost and waited for him to ask the obvious question.

Joe joined her but didn't ask whom the roses were from. Why not? Didn't it matter?

"Come on, finish getting ready," he said, and she couldn't tell anything from his voice.

"I really don't want to go."

Joe studied her thoughtfully. "You'll survive. Besides, Ryan is joining us — at least for a sail around the bay."

Changing one of Joe's decisions was like hitting her head against a wall; she didn't have the energy to try. Kelly crossed the bedroom and tossed him the sunscreen she had found. "When did this get arranged?"

"He came down to the docks yesterday when I was replacing the sail covers."

"Charles and Ryan came to the docks?"

"Nope. Ryan was with the teenager he was surfing with. Tony has his driving permit, and they came down to the docks to say hello."

Kelly frowned. In the short conversations she'd had with Charles yesterday and the longer one when he had called back that evening, he said nothing about Ryan going down to the docks. She felt the need to defend Charles against the implied criticism in Joe's voice but didn't have the facts to do so. Joe had obviously made up his mind about Charles, and that made her mad. She liked Ryan's dad. "Ryan's never sailed?"

"Not often. Charles owns a big powerboat. I told Ryan I'd take him around the bay and teach him the basics of sailing if it was okay with his dad."

Joe had probably not made the offer to Ryan simply to cut off her avenue of escape, but the effect was the same. She was going sailing even though she would prefer to do almost anything else.

"You look a little green. Did you also skip breakfast in your rush to get to church?"

"I wasn't hungry."

Joe disappeared before she got a chance to say she was still not hungry. Sighing, she sat down to slip on her deck shoes. She had her swimsuit on under her shorts and T-shirt. She looked around the room. She had found the sunscreen but not her sunglasses.

"Try these." Joe tossed her a package of peanut butter crackers. He knew where her stash was hidden.

Normally they would perk even a tepid interest for they were her favorite comfort food, but today she didn't even want to open them. "I'm really not hungry."

"If you don't eat, you'll just make yourself seasick when we get on the open water."

She pulled a face at him and opened the package. She knew he was right. She dutifully munched on the first one as she scanned the room looking for her sunglasses. "I've got beach towels folded on the dryer. Grab us a couple." She found a book to take along on the vague hope Joe would give her a break today and let her sunbathe rather than actively tack sails.

"Ready?"

Her hair barrettes were still lost, along with her sunglasses. "I guess so." She grinned when she saw the size of the stack of towels he had picked up. "I gather Misha is going with us?" The Labrador loved to be out on the water.

"She's waiting in the car, eager to go."

Kelly picked up her keys. "Did you remember lunch for her? Last time she was sharing mine."

"She knows you're a soft touch. You didn't see me sharing my Oreos." Joe paused on the porch beside her as she locked the front door. "Did you and Liz have a good time yesterday?"

"Yes." She thought about the plans she and Liz had made, before the roses had begun to arrive. "We're going to repaint and wallpaper my kitchen."

"Really?" She'd startled him with that abrupt announcement.

"You'll paint the ceiling for me?"

"I suppose. What brought this on? Not that I don't approve; you just haven't mentioned you were thinking about it."

She shrugged. "It needs to be done. We were sitting at the kitchen table having tea, and we started talking, and before long we had the kitchen redecorated." It was more elaborate than that, but Joe didn't need to know all of it.

Her quest. She was beginning to think about the changes in her life in that way. She liked the word, for it was a journey with a goal. It was the first time in years she was looking forward to something. She had been telling Liz about some of the changes she wanted to make around the house, the excitement obvious in her voice, and was stunned to realize her friend was blinking back tears. Liz laughed, hugged her, and told her it was about time she started living again. The conversation turned to paint colors and wallpaper. They had just gotten started on wallpaper ideas when the doorbell had rung and the roses had arrived.

They reached Joe's Jeep. Misha was sitting in the front passenger seat, her head out the open window. Her tail beat against the seat as Kelly opened the door. "Backseat, Misha. You're not sitting in my lap, no matter how adorable you are."

The dog maneuvered back beside the

cooler and Kelly slipped into the Jeep, barely getting the seat belt fastened before Misha leaned over the seat to pant in her ear. Kelly laughed and reached back to ruffle the dog's head. "Joe, you need to brush her teeth."

"Next thing you'll be telling me is she needs to floss."

She hugged the dog's neck, burying her fingers in her warm fur. "It wouldn't hurt."

Joe started the Jeep and Kelly settled back against the fabric warmed by the sun. The heat felt good, but the sun was already aggravating her headache. She lowered the visor to get a little relief.

"Kelly." Joe slid off his sunglasses and handed them to her.

The action surprised her. "Thanks." She slipped them on.

He tapped her nose. "I want them back."

"I notice you didn't say when."

"Don't worry; I'll let you know."

The trip south to the docks near Joe's home took less than ten minutes even with traffic. When they pulled into the parking lot, Kelly was pleased to see that both Charles and Ryan were already there. They were walking back along the pier toward them, eating ice cream cones. So much for the vague concern Charles didn't know what his son was doing. Kelly slid from the Jeep and waved. She felt more than a little self-conscious about meeting Charles again — talking to him on the phone was one thing; seeing him was another. She didn't exactly want to talk about the gifts in front of Joe.

Ryan, no longer on crutches, came ahead of his father to join them. "Hey, Kelly."

"Hi, Ryan. I hear you want to go sailing."

"I can't wait. It's been a while."

"You're going to love it," she promised, his enthusiasm contagious. She helped Joe unload the cooler. Misha was looking at the ice cream cone Ryan held. Kelly laughed and nudged the dog to move over. "This is Joe's dog, Misha. She's coming with us."

"Really?"

"She loves the water."

Charles joined them. "It's nice to see you again, Kelly."

She did her best not to let his appreciative gaze fluster her. "Hi, Charles. Can you come with us?" she asked, ignoring the fact Joe would probably not make the offer.

"I wish I could, but I've got a meeting with Admiral Stone in about forty minutes." Charles glanced over at Joe. "I appreciate this, Lieutenant. My son was thrilled with the offer."

"It's no problem. I'll enjoy having him aboard. He can take the pressure of being the only crewman off Kelly."

"I can help with the sails?" Ryan asked eagerly.

"You bet."

Kelly relaxed at Joe's easy smile. He might have some reservations about Charles, but it was clear he and Ryan had struck up a friendship.

"Kelly, show me the boat?" Charles asked.

"Sure. Joe, what can I carry down?"

"Take the cushions."

In another few months the sailboat would be a jewel, but at the moment it looked sadly worn out. Joe had been focusing on safety, seaworthiness, and sails, not appearance. "This is it." She expected a comment from Charles, but he held his opinion and stood back, inspecting the boat. She credited him with that foresight, for despite its appearance, the boat was fundamentally sound and would someday make Joe a nice profit when the restoration was finished. She stepped down onto the deck and stored the gear.

"I bet she's a pleasure to sail on a windy day." Charles stepped down beside her.

"Fabulous. Once you've sailed, you never want to go back to a powerboat," Kelly replied, taking a gentle dig at his choice of boat.

"It's easier to fish from a powerboat."

"But not as romantic."

"True."

Aware she was getting in over her head with where the conversation was heading, she turned her attention to removing the bench cover so she could get to the lockers underneath. "Where do you have your boat docked?"

"Down by the Bay Bridge. How long would it take to sail to Catalina Island?"

"Depends on the wind. The round trip makes for a great Saturday." She and Nick had made the trip many times.

"We could have lunch there some afternoon if you don't mind taking my boat."

Kelly glanced up from the locker padlock she was opening. Was he asking for a date? Charles was watching her with a twinkle in his eyes. He had said she would owe him one, and this request might actually be useful to her. "I rarely turn down an invitation for a meal," she finally replied.

"Good."

Thank you, Charles. He had just given her something she was going to need — a way to extricate herself when Joe tactfully said he wanted them to remain only friends. She could at least assure him she wasn't going to make a nuisance of herself, that she already had lunch plans with Charles. It might be enough to keep her friendship with Joe intact and unchanged — that desperately mattered to her.

Misha barked from the pier, her body quivering with excitement as she looked at the boat. Kelly grinned and folded her arms. "Jump, Misha. I'm not going to lift you across. I learned my lesson last time."

"What happened?"

After several false starts, Misha launched herself across, skidding on the deck with her feet going all directions. Kelly laughed. "That, except I was the one doing the skidding."

She glanced over at Ryan, judging his size. "Let's get you in a life vest." She handed him one from the locker. "See how that fits."

Ryan put it on. Charles helped him straighten the straps around the back. "Wear the vest the entire time you are out on the water."

"I will, Dad."

"Listen to Kelly and Joe."

Ryan looked embarrassed. "I already promised."

"Just checking." Charles glanced at his watch. "I've got to head to my meeting. I'll be at the waterfront restaurant next to where we bought the ice cream; come join me when you get back."

Ryan nodded.

Kelly slipped on her own vest. "I'll make sure he has fun."

"Make sure you have fun as well," Charles reminded her. He stepped back up onto the pier. "Thanks, Kelly."

"My pleasure."

She watched him walk back up the pier, pause on the way to speak briefly to Joe, then walk toward the restaurant. He was a nice guy, but she was way out of her league with him.

Twelve

Joe arrived with the last of the gear. Having sailed with Joe frequently over the years, Kelly knew the routine for getting underway. Joe was a great instructor, and she enjoyed listening to him as he walked Ryan through the steps, letting the teen do many of the tasks rather than just observe.

They were soon out on the calm waters of San Diego Bay, and it was time to raise the mainsail. Kelly was relieved to find herself up to the task. It wasn't hard, but it took strength and a steady hand on the ropes and winches. The fabric became taut in the wind and the boat leaped forward.

Ryan laughed. "This is awesome."

It helped having Ryan with them for it kept Joe from focusing on her. The water skimmed by, so near Kelly could almost reach out and touch it. She swallowed hard at the near vertigo she felt when she looked down. This was awful.

The water was calm in the bay, swells

one to two feet. She had only to brace herself against the constant tilt from the wind-filled sails to keep steady, but today she also kept her hand firmly on the railing when not required to be at one of the sails. As time passed, her fingers relaxed their white-knuckle grip. The irrational fear of being flung into the water and held under was fading. She had always loved the water, had been swimming from her earliest memories. Joe had been right to get her back out on the water as soon as possible. Some of her frustration directed at him had been spurred by the dread of facing this. Considering she was due back at work on Tuesday afternoon, it was a good thing she was getting this reaction behind her now.

The wind blew her hair around, making her wish she had taken time to French braid her hair, rather than simply pull it back. She dug out the sunscreen and applied it liberally out of habit. Misha joined her at the bench, and she wiped a bit of it on her muzzle, laughing at the dog.

She spent the first hour tacking sails as Joe sent them around the bay, showing Ryan how to work with the wind. Ryan was hanging on Joe's every word, and Kelly heard the number of SEAL questions mixed in with sailing questions. Joe had another future recruit in the making.

Kelly was very aware of Joe watching her. Finally deciding that keeping her distance was just piquing his interest, she brought Joe and Ryan cold sodas and opened Joe's for him.

"Thanks. Want to take her?"

Normally she would be eager to take the wheel, pit her skill against the water and wind. It was beyond what she wanted to face today. "I'll pass."

He studied her face, then nodded. "You look much better than you did thirty minutes ago."

"I looked that green?"

"White. It's just water. It doesn't mean to be threatening."

She looked forward at Ryan, now in the front of the boat laughing with Misha as she stood with her front legs up on the bench, her face pointed into the wind. "Ryan doesn't seem bothered by it."

"You promised him you wouldn't let him drown. There wasn't anyone there to tell you that."

She blinked. He did understand. He was so confident, so comfortable in the water that she forgot sometimes just how well he could truly empathize. She felt vaguely ashamed that she expected him to criticize her fear. "Have you ever almost drowned?"

He hesitated, and she accepted the disappointment that he couldn't answer. So many things she would like to know about him, even about Nick, but could never be told.

"A mission about a year after I got pinned with my Trident — we were going out a reconfigured submarine missile tube to launch one of the SEAL's underwater delivery vehicles from the submerged deck. It was cold, dark, hard work that gave no room for error. There was an equipment failure on my air pack, and I had to buddy breathe back into the tube. It took them more than a minute to decompress the tube. It wasn't just holding my breath; it was being sealed in what felt like a coffin. It was hard not to panic."

She was surprised he had told her specifics, even if it was almost a decade old. "Thanks."

"We'll go swimming later, and you'll find you can put it behind you." He obviously saw her discomfort. "I'll be right beside you."

"Yes." She grimaced, remembering the taste of the saltwater. "It's going to be cold."

"The ocean is this time of year." He nodded toward Ryan. "He's going to be a good deckhand."

"Yes, he is. Thanks for doing this."

"I like him."

"So do I. He's hitting you up with more questions than just sailing."

"What can I say? Kids just want to be like me." They shared a smile; then he nodded to the clock in the dash. "Unfortunately, it's time we head back in. Charles will be waiting."

"Yes." They had been out on the water almost an hour and an half. Kelly buried the shiver at the knowledge that once they dropped off Ryan, they would head out of the sheltered water of San Diego Bay to the open sea. Joe believed she could handle it, and she had no choice about the matter. The fact one rescue had come dangerously close to ending in tragedy was something she had to deal with. She only hoped she didn't disappoint both Joe and herself.

Joe tossed back his head, flinging the cold water away. "Ready?"

They were anchored off Torrey Pines Reserve near Del Mar, having sailed up the coast. Kelly, sitting on the edge of the sailboat, was worrying the cut on her bottom lip. Her tension was palatable. Joe tried to make his smile reassuring, wishing he could do this for her. She couldn't stop the fear she was feeling. There was a very good reason for it, but she would have to consciously overrule it. At his insistence, she wore a life jacket over her swimsuit; she was likely going to get a nice flashback the first time her head went under the cold water.

"Don't move."

"I'll be right here," he reassured her.

She turned her back to the water as a diver would. He watched her take a deep breath, then force herself to relax and fall back. It wasn't a graceful way to enter the water, but it was easier than jumping in as he had done. She wouldn't go as far down in the water.

He moved fast to make sure his hand was on her arm as she came back to the surface. Her face was sheet white. His hand tightened. "Breathe."

Her eyes closed as she sucked in a deep breath. "Sorry."

"You're doing fine."

She settled her hands on his shoulders. "It's cold."

She was looking at him rather than the water. He pushed her hair back for her as she showed no inclination to relax her grip.

"Thanks."

"Sure." His eyes narrowed. She'd been lying about what happened before he reached her and Ryan, or at least not telling him all of it. There was too much terror mixed in with her fear. He saw these kinds of shakes in SEALs only after they got so close to death they were practically tasting it. His hands firmed their grip. "The hard step is over."

She tried to smile; it rapidly disappeared.

"Relax. Just float for a while. With the vest you don't even have to tread water."

She closed her eyes and did as he told her. He watched and slowly saw the tension fade away.

"I'm okay."

Her fingers were no longer digging into his shoulders. She would be fine. She simply needed to get her confidence back. "Ready to go for a swim?" They would do a lot more than just swim before he was satisfied she was ready to go back to work, but they would take it one step at a time. He knew she could handle anything he tossed at her, but that wasn't the point. She needed to know she could handle it.

"Yes."

He unbuckled the life jacket and she ducked her head as he lifted it free. Her hair tangled briefly on the straps and he had to pull her close while he freed it. It wasn't the first time he had made the realization she felt good in his arms, like she belonged. Easing back, he tossed the vest back up on the boat deck, determined not to let his thoughts go there. "Let's swim."

His words were more abrupt than he intended, and her face showed brief hurt before she nodded and turned away. She headed north, swimming parallel to the shore.

Annoyed with himself for being curt with her, Joe watched her briefly, seeing the full extension of her reach, the strong kick, the disciplined way she turned her head to breathe, all the hallmarks of the competitive swimmer she had been since high school. He had always enjoyed watching her swim; although he didn't necessarily enjoy watching her swim away from him. He moved to catch up with her, using his more powerful kick and longer reach to close the distance.

It had probably been good to make her mad. Her hesitation to be out in the open water had been overcome before she looked around and realized where she was.

They swam side by side for almost ten minutes. Joe let her set the pace and distance she wanted to travel. She finally turned on her back with a flutter kick, lifting her face to the sky. "That was fun."

"You're stopping already?"

The straight edge of her hand plowed water in his face. Caught by surprise, he swallowed some of it. Amused, he considered retaliating but thought better of it. Her grin was back and he had missed it. "Okay, I guess you deserve a lazy day."

"Thanks, I'm glad you agree."

He idly treaded water beside her as she caught her breath. "It's a beautiful day."

"Yes."

Her hair had begun to drift in the water, spread out by the movement of the waves. It felt silky smooth as it brushed against his hand. He wondered if she would mind a compliment.

She turned abruptly to tread water rather than float. "Let's get back. It's cold and I'm hungry now."

He had taken care packing lunch, knowing they needed to talk. "Sounds good to me."

They were close to the boat when he made himself slow and fall behind her. He knew he needed to do this but hated what it could mean. Friendship demanded thinking about what was best for the other person, and sometimes it wasn't always being kind. He hoped she was going to be in a forgiving spirit after this.

He silently dropped down below the surface of the water, kicked hard, and grabbed her ankles, yanking her deep under water. They called it pool harassment when you trained to be an Air Force pararescueman, life saving in the SEALs, water rescue 101 when you trained as a lifeguard. All were designed to test one thing — if you could think clearly under harassment while under water. If you panicked, you failed, and in a real situation you died. Kelly had to be able to cope with this situation.

He expected the violent kick to free herself and he dropped farther below her to avoid it. In a real life rescue, someone panicking at sea would be trying to climb over her to get to the surface, holding her down, but he let her go immediately, hoping she would react as she had been trained to do, not freeze.

He had to admire her form. She didn't flounder around or panic, even though she had probably swallowed water and her lungs had to be burning. Once free of his hold, she let herself settle for an instant to get her bearings before moving. It took her only three powerful strokes to break back to the surface.

What he didn't expect was her almost instantaneous dive back under the water. He was drifting back up to the surface as she made the move. She zeroed in on him. Forced to add a burst of speed to avoid getting caught, he grinned, pleased with her response. Her own speed surprised him — he wasn't going to be able to make the surface without moving her out of the way. His lungs were beginning to burn. If he didn't care about the tactics he used, moving her aside would be simple, but he censored most of the moves.

He froze her with a feint to the left and powered to the right.

She still got her hand on his shoulder, delaying him.

He broke through the surface, having to take her with him. He coughed, amused as well as annoyed with himself.

She slapped his back. "Need help?"

"Cute."

She grinned. "I think I'm fine." Her hands kneaded his shoulders. "Should I dunk you next?"

"You can try."

She laughed and turned to swim the last

few feet to the sailboat.

He wanted more than friendship with her. Her grin didn't just make him want to smile back; it made him want more. He wanted exclusivity. He wanted to watch her bloom back to life as she left the past behind.

Lord, I already decided this question.

He had started to talk to her yesterday, to back them away from this step. Relationships were fragile things. If anything went wrong, he would be the loser. He thought about it, waiting for logic to over-rule the decision, and instead it became more settled. He wanted something more than friendship with Kelly, and he was willing to risk their friendship to see if it could develop. He wanted the right to wrap her in a hug and have her full attention focused on him. She would make his life wonderful, despite all the obstacles that had to be dealt with.

Six dozen roses — he had counted — convinced him that if he didn't act, someone else would.

If this is a mistake, in about five minutes it's going to be irreversible.

He swam toward the boat, his jaw set. *She better have meant what she said.*

Thirteen

★ ★ ★

Life didn't get much better than this. Kelly stretched out on the side bench cushions and closed her eyes behind the sunglasses, enjoying the gentle rocking of the anchored boat. The chill of the water was fading with the warmth of the sun.

She had done it. She took pleasure in the fact she had beaten her fear. It was a private reason to celebrate and she wasn't going to let her critical side dismiss it as trivial — swimming at sea, handling getting dunked, had been a big deal. The day had become one to enjoy.

Maybe Joe would let her take the wheel for the sail back down the coast.

"Kelly." She heard him come up from the galley and take a seat on the opposite bench. He had turned down her offer to help fix lunch, saying something about the galley being equipped for only one. Since she tended to overbake the fish, she hadn't argued.

"Hmm?" Lunch couldn't be ready yet, and she didn't feel like moving.

"We need to talk."

She didn't bother to open her eyes. "No, we don't. Consider it said." She was too relaxed to tense at the introduction of the subject she had known would eventually get raised. He would just have to forget what she had said.

"I really think we do."

Something in his voice . . . she turned her head and saw an expression so tender it made her blink.

"I think we ought to start dating."

She was glad she was wearing his sunglasses — they hid her shock. "You think what?" she asked faintly.

"I think it's time we started dating."

His words caused her to swing her feet around so she could sit up. The pit of her stomach dropped. From his tone yesterday, she had dismissed any hope he would respond in this way. "Why?"

His eyes narrowed, and she could see him cover his annoyance. "Didn't you mean what you said?"

How was she supposed to answer that? She looked away, feeling more vulnerable than she had ever felt in her life. For the last three years she had been doing her best to hide the emotions, protect her heart, and now it was about to be totally exposed. *Don't be a coward.* She took a deep breath and looked back at Joe. "I meant it. But I didn't mean to say it."

"What's *that* supposed to mean?"

She sighed. "It means I don't know if I want you to do anything about it." She reached over for her cold drink and turned the glass in her hands, watching the sweat bead on the outside. "It's been a hard three years, Joe. I miss Nick, I don't like being alone, and frankly I've been leaning heavily on you as a buffer."

"You're lonely."

She nodded, willing to accept the obvious answer. "When you found me in the water, I wanted to wrap my arms around you, to hold on and never let go. Ever." She smiled ruefully. "My emotions around you are going crazy at the moment, and I'm afraid it's because I want someone to rescue me from what is going on in my life."

She could see in his eyes that her answer had disappointed him. "You told me you loved me," he said gently.

She bit her lip.

"The words are said. They can't be ignored. If they were prompted because you need me, do you really think that is so bad?"

"Joe, you've never talked about getting married, having a family." She saw him blink. Kids. He hadn't thought about that, how important it would be to her. "If we start down the road to being more than friends, there is no way back. I spoke out of place, and it's best if you simply forget I said it."

He looked at her a very long time. "I don't want to dismiss it."

"Do you feel the same way?" It was hard to ask that question. Part of her wanted desperately to hear I love you back, yet part of her was petrified at the idea.

He looked at her steadily. "Kelly, I've been trying for months not to risk a good friendship by letting myself speculate." He gave a slow smile. "But it doesn't take much thought to know I would love to go out with you and find out just what might be possible."

She blinked and wished he would tone down that smile a notch. She couldn't think when he was looking at her that way. And she desperately needed to think. There were so many problems inherent in them being more than friends! Not the least of which was the probability she would walk away with a broken heart when it didn't work out.

She wanted it to work out. She could be dating Joe if she said yes. It was so tempting just to ignore the uncertainty and agree. *Jesus, why do I have to be noble about this right now? I want to say yes, and here I am trying to think of ways to talk Joe out of it! But he has to know what he's getting into. He's my friend; I owe him that.* She took a deep breath. "You still think of me as Nick's wife."

"You are."

She dismissed his immediate reply, was annoyed at it. "You know what I mean. It's the first thing you think about me. You feel more guilt, more pity that I'm a widow, than anything else." It felt awful to say those words, but she knew it was a factor. And though it pained her, it had to be put on the table.

"Kelly." He paused as he chose his words. "I'll always regret the fact Nick died and that you lost him. And yes, I am uncomfortably aware you are my best friend's widow. But that is our past. I'm interested in what is in our future."

"I told myself I wouldn't get involved with an active duty SEAL again."

"Understandable. There are numerous

reasons to say no, to say let's just stay friends." He looked at her with an intensity she didn't know how to handle. "But I don't want us to do that. I want to find out if we can be more than friends."

And if it doesn't work out, do I lose our friendship? She was afraid to make the decision. "I don't know, Joe."

"Think about it. You know where I stand." He got to his feet. "Lunch should be ready."

Kelly was grateful for the pause, giving her time to think. He had just gone out on a limb, and she was going to have to be very careful with her answer.

Kelly stared at the clouds drifting by as Joe moved around in the galley getting their lunch. Anyone else would be leaping to say yes. How many ladies had she seen trying to get Joe's attention, to convince him to date, through the years? For Joe to have responded as he did . . . He may have surprised her with his answer, but he was serious.

She was ready to move on, but it still felt disloyal to think about replacing Nick in her life.

"Kelly, if I die, are you going to pull back in your shell, make a saint out of me?"

Nick was stretched out on the blanket beside

her, watching the night sky. They were looking for meteorites from the Pegasus shower. For a while the meteorites had been streaking across the sky one every twenty seconds. They had begun to thin out, had dwindled to one every ten minutes or so. Conversation in the quiet night had drifted through numerous topics.

Kelly, holding the binoculars in one hand, glanced down at him and grinned. "Don't worry. You're no saint. Not when you leave things that smell dead in the clothes hamper."

Nick chuckled. "Joe's the one making up the training schedule. Talk to him about his choice of locations." He tugged her hand. "Seriously, would you let yourself become one of those Navy widows, constantly living in the past? I would hate that."

"Why the question? Is there something I should know? Like why you're wading through sewer tunnels for the fun of it?"

"Not that I could tell you, but no. We've probably been tapped to play the urban terrorists for the citywide drill later this summer. That's Cougar's guess anyway."

Kelly scanned the sky again. "I decided a long time ago that your job was at least safer than a police officer's. You are a whole lot better trained and you've got fifteen other guys covering your back. If something happens, I'll deal with it, but I'm not borrowing trouble by wondering about it. I've watched the other wives, seen them torn apart by worry when you guys get paged, and I'm not going to do that. So I really don't know how I would react if something happened. Get mad at you probably."

"You would." He shifted the jacket folded under his head. "I've never figured out how you do that — simply decide not to worry. I worry about you being a lifeguard."

"Do you? Why?"

"The crowds. Your having to deal with more and more parties that get out of control at the beach, guys that don't have any respect for your job."

"Did you or did you not teach me how to put even you on the ground?" Kelly protested.

"You're too much of a lady to get mean early, take the other guy by surprise."

"If I had to I could. Besides, you know there would just happen to be a SEAL or a SEAL trainee on the beach to help me out. Don't think I haven't noticed that you put the word out. Compliments of you, I've now even got SEAL groupies on my beach, asking me to make introductions."

"The guys have been impressed too. Cougar likes Alisha so much he's taking her home to meet his mom."

"Matchmaking is serious business, and

Cougar definitely needs to settle down."

"*He's young,*" Nick replied.

"*That he is. He can certainly swim. I clocked him to Point Loma and wondered if my stopwatch was broken.*"

"*He'll settle down once he's been shot at a few times,*" Nick said matter-of-factly.

Kelly reached over and squeezed his hand. She didn't have to ask to know the date of the first mission when Nick had come under live fire. He had returned after twelve days away, and he had been different. More intense in his training, a little more quiet. Much more focused on her. His confidence when he walked out the door for a page after that was the confidence of a warrior already proven and comfortable with what he could do. It was one case where she wished he could tell her what had happened.

It wasn't fair to tell Joe yes if she was saying it for the wrong reasons.

She didn't want to be lonely anymore. She had been married, had tasted being single, and she knew how badly she was handling being single. The lack of interaction with someone left her dull. In dozens of ways being married had been the best thing for her. She didn't have ambitions to make her mark in a career; instead she wanted a home, husband, and children. She hated the fact she had delayed having children with Nick, that she had let caution rob her of that joy. She wanted children.

And when she thought about those things, there was one definite name that came to mind. Joe. But did he want those same things in his future?

Joe, what am I supposed to say?

If she said no and he didn't ask her again . . .

"You really like to throw my life into chaos, don't you?"

Joe had to smile at Kelly's comment. It came out of the blue and she sounded truly annoyed. He fed Misha another part of the sugar cookie he was eating for dessert and watched Kelly finish her peach. She was stretched out on her back on the bench cushions, having finished lunch. He had been wondering how long her silence would last. "Because I said I wanted us to date?"

She nodded. "Do you have any idea what our friends would think?"

"Sure. They'd ask how come I waited this long."

She snorted. "Right. Everyone at church would be talking about us."

He tucked another cushion behind his back, glad they had such a gorgeous day to be out on the water. He had a feeling this was not going to be a short conversation. "Your friends want to see you happy," he corrected gently. "It wouldn't be gossip; it would be genuine interest."

"They feel sorry for me."

"Some of them do. You represent what they fear most." As the first military widow in a decade in a church full of military families, there was no way for her to escape that pressure. He knew how isolated she felt at church, a nomad between couples and friends who increasingly didn't know how to relate and the much younger singles who had never been married. He had watched friends drift away, and he had hurt for her.

"If it didn't work out — I don't think I could stand the pity."

He couldn't promise her the future. He knew this idea was risky. "Do they have to know?"

"What?"

"We don't have to tell people right away." It would be hard to pull off, but they could do it for a while if it would help Kelly be more comfortable with the idea of dating him.

"If we're dating, I don't want to be sneaking around pretending we're not. The ladies are too thick around you. They need to be swatted off — I don't share."

He laughed at the image of a mosquito storm that didn't exist. "Kelly, when was the last time I went on a date?"

"Five months ago. You took Boomer's cousin from the naval personnel department to the symphony."

His annoyance was sudden and intense. "I bought the two tickets so I could take you, remember? You said you didn't want to go. In fact, as I recall you turned me down so fast you didn't even bother to give me an explanation."

Emotions flickered across her face he wasn't expecting, and he softened his voice. "Do you want to tell me now what you didn't tell me then?"

She swallowed and didn't look over at him. "It was the anniversary of Nick getting pinned with his Trident. I went out to Sunset Park, found our favorite place, and cried my eyes out."

Joe dropped his gaze to the napkin he had just shredded, wishing he could take back months of simmering irritation with her over that memory. He realized now he had been flirting with asking her to be more than a friend for some months. He looked up. "I'm sorry."

She nodded, her focus still on the furled

sails overhead, and frowned slightly. "Every anniversary, the loss just gets sharper. I should have told you. But frankly —" she turned her head to glance over at him — "I haven't been telling any-body about those kind of secrets."

He narrowed his gaze slightly, studying her eyes. "That's dangerous."

"I know." She sighed and looked back toward the sky. "Grief is a funny beast; it has tentacles all over the place."

"Where else does it show up?"

"Old movies. Some sunrises. Last month it was fireworks at a baseball game."

Joe began to wonder just what else he had missed. She was having crying jags he had no idea about. He had figured out Thursday morning that she had managed to snow him and hide an insomnia problem. That glimpse of her life when he packed for her had been enlightening. What else was going wrong that he had been oblivious to?

"Did you and Nick ever talk about what it would be like if he died?" He had avoided asking her that question in the past. His own emotions concerning Nick's death were complex, tinged as they were with his own grief, frustration, helpless-ness, and guilt.

"We talked about death occasionally," she finally replied.

Her tone of voice suggested it was a private memory. Joe accepted that and changed the subject. "If we did date, could you handle the fact I'm on an operational team?"

She fluttered her hand. "I worry now, Joe."

"I know you do. Is it too big an obstacle?"

He knew how much he was asking her to accept. While Nick had borne the weight of being one of the members of an operational platoon, Joe bore the weight of leading that platoon: Fifteen men depended on him. The stress on Kelly would be greater. He didn't leave his work at the office; that leadership weighed on him twenty-four hours a day. He was often quiet, distant, repeatedly thinking through plans and contingencies for missions the men had not yet even been briefed on. She had accepted that as his friend, but since Nick's death — he knew the worry that shadowed her eyes every time his pager went off.

"You'll be an active SEAL as long as you physically can do the job. I know that."

It wasn't the answer he wanted to hear, but it was apparently all she was going to say.

"Joe, what if something goes wrong? What if we have a big fight or something? I don't want to lose your friendship."

"Worried about my temper?"

"You have the handle Bear for a reason," she pointed out. "But no, you growl more than explode. I was thinking more about your stubbornness."

"*My* stubbornness? You could teach lessons in tenacity."

"Exactly. We're going to clash. And hurt feelings can quickly destroy a friendship."

"Don't borrow trouble. You've been my friend for six years. I'm going to protect that at all costs."

"It's still risky."

He wished he could take away this worry. She'd developed that trait in the last few years rather than praying about a problem, and he wished he'd spotted it earlier before the worry had become ingrained. "Relax. I bet you didn't do all this introspection when Nick asked you out the first time."

"I was sixteen, and I had no idea what I was getting into."

"Then why don't you half close your eyes and just enjoy it again? Dating isn't going to destroy our friendship."

"Joe." She met his eyes and swallowed

hard. "I'm not looking to replace Nick."

He was puzzled by her remark. "Good, because in many ways we are as different as night and day."

"Exactly. But I just want to warn you that it's going to take me a while to realize how many ways I may be doing it subconsciously."

He felt the hit from that answer. He had known he would be competing with the memory of his friend, but he didn't have to like it. He knew better than anyone just how short he fell in that one-on-one comparison. Nick had been a good husband, a solid SEAL, and a Christian since his teens — he would be a hard act to follow. "Kelly, you'll do that comparison with anyone you date. It's not unique to going out with me. The best way to deal with it is to accept it will happen and move on."

"I don't want to hurt you."

"The only way you're going to hurt me at the moment is if you turn me down."

She considered it for a long time. "Then I guess I've really got only one question."

"What's that?"

She smiled. "What do you want to do for our first date?"

Fourteen

★ ★ ★

Dinner and a movie. Tonight. Joe glanced at his watch and smiled. Kelly thought by limiting how much time he had to plan their first date, it would limit what he could arrange. He had seen that smile on her face, and her excuse that she was busy tomorrow evening had been pretty lame.

He was determined to make it a memorable first date. She had forgotten what a SEAL could do in three hours. He nudged Misha aside; the dog joined him in the front of the Jeep after they dropped off Kelly. He picked up his cellular phone and dialed a number from memory.

His second-in-command answered on the first ring. Boomer had a baseball game on TV; Joe could hear it in the background.

"Boomer, buddy, I need a favor."

"Name it."

"I need to borrow your car." A Jeep did

not fit what he wanted to arrange for to-night.

The silence covered two seconds before Boomer laughed. "Sure. Who's the lucky lady?"

Joe smiled. "I'm taking the fifth. Can I swing over and trade vehicles? Say in about an hour?"

"Not a problem. We're not going anywhere tonight."

"Thanks, I appreciate it. Is your wife around? I need to talk to her a minute."

"She's in the kitchen, hold on." Joe heard him muffle the phone. "Christi, can you get the phone? Bear needs to talk to you."

"Coming!"

Joe heard another extension pick up. "Hi, Joe." Christi sounded breathless.

"Sorry to interrupt —"

"I was just fixing iced tea. I'm breathless because junior is kicking up a storm at the moment." Christi was seven months pregnant but looked more like nine months plus. The doctor swore it wasn't twins, but on petite Christi, it sure looked like twins.

"Eight more weeks," Joe said. As god-father to the infant he kept track of such important facts.

"The day won't get here fast enough. What's up?"

"What's your favorite restaurant when you want a classy night out?"

"You've got a date?" She sounded surprised, and more than a little thrilled.

"In less than three hours. And it's got to make an impression." She lapsed into French for a moment as the time frame registered. Joe interrupted her. "I know it's short notice. Why do you think I'm appealing to you for help? Come on, I need some ideas."

"*Really* romantic, or *fun* romantic?"

Joe hesitated. How sharp did he want to make the transition from friendship to something more? He wasn't taking anything about Kelly for granted. Better if he made a statement with tonight and erred on the side of how special she was. "The best Coronado has. I'd prefer not to go into San Diego."

"Prince of Wales Grill," Christi replied immediately. "But you'll never get reservations for tonight."

"Sure I will." He didn't believe in the word *impossible*. "Flowers — it's been a while. Is Marsha still the best?" Marsha, now in her fifties, was the owner of Roses and Lilies. She coordinated the annual flower show and qualified as a town treasure. There was no way he could compete

205

with six dozen roses, but he was not going to abandon that to Charles either.

"Absolutely. Do I get a name?"

"Like I told Boomer, I'm taking the fifth."

"You have to tell me all about it later."

Joe smiled, thinking about Christi, Kelly, and Liz. "Oh, I'm sure you'll hear." He didn't want to spoil Kelly's fun by being the one to break the news. "Thanks, Christi."

He called Marsha about the flowers next, then set out to find a way to get reservations for two at the Prince of Wales Grill. As Christi had warned, they were completely booked. He was talking to his counterpart on Team Three as he unlocked the door to his home and held open the door for Misha — this was his fourth call and he was getting closer. "I know the pianist who is playing there tonight is Heather Wailes. Do you know someone who knows her?"

"Pretty name. How old?"

"Midtwenties."

"Try Victor, Millan, or Paulson. One of them has probably met her."

"Thanks."

"Anytime."

He tried Victor first. The SEAL was a great guitar player and the type of guy who had friends all across the community. "Sure, I know Heather. She plays great jazz."

"I need to get reservations for two tonight at the Grill — they're booked. Think she might be willing to help?"

Victor laughed. "Lieutenant, let me ask. I'll put you on hold and give her a call."

Joe walked back to his bedroom and pulled open his closet door as he looked through options. Black-tie? He knew Kelly would look lovely; she always did. He pulled out his best suit.

The phone clicked and Victor came back on. "Lieutenant, you've got reservations for two at 1900 hours. A quiet table overlooking the water. The reservations are in your name."

"Victor, I owe you."

"No thanks necessary. That call just got me a date with Heather. She liked being asked for the favor."

Joe smiled. "I still owe you."

"I'll collect someday. Have a great evening."

He glanced at his watch. Still plenty of time for one more errand before he came back to shower and change.

Kelly pinned the phone against her shoulder as she sorted through her closet for the third time. "Liz, I don't have anything he hasn't already seen. You know I can't wear the blue silk. It would be incredibly rude to wear something Charles gave me on a date with Joe. Oh, I should have never said yes. I know he's going to make a big deal of tonight. Joe doesn't know how to do something halfway."

"You've still got two hours. Get over here. We can solve this problem."

"Not if I'm going to do something with my hair," Kelly practically wailed, looking at the aftereffects of the saltwater. "I'm going to call Joe and tell him not tonight."

"Don't you dare! Take a shower; throw all your shoes into a bag; then come over. I'll find the perfect dress for you. Come on — you'll have a great time."

"Liz, I can't do this."

"Okay, new plan. I'm on my way to you with several of my favorite dresses. Take that shower and don't you dare call Joe."

Kelly closed her eyes and forced away the growing panic. "I already hate dating."

"By the time tonight is over, you'll change your mind. I promise."

★ ★ ★

Which bear? Joe looked over the selection for the third time, wrestling with which one was best. Kelly had marked every special occasion in her life since eighth grade with a bear of one sort or another, and he was not about to break that tradition tonight. It was kind of childish. She was the first to laugh about that and admit it, but it had taken on a life of its own over the years and he rather liked the continuity of it.

He had no idea which one she would like. Big? Small? White? Brown? Maybe he should take her for a walk tonight through the shops and let her choose the one she wanted.

No, for this occasion, he needed to choose it.

Joe picked up a medium-sized white bear with beautiful brown eyes. It was soft in his hands. If he added a ribbon that matched the flowers — yes, this would be perfect.

He left the shop with the bear in a box. Marsha would be able to help with wrapping paper and a bow. He slipped into his Jeep, prepared to pull out into traffic, and the pager clipped to his belt went off. Pulling it from his belt, he glanced at the numbers.

Lord, please, no. Not tonight.
It was the duty officer at the base.

"What about this one?"

Liz held up the dress for her consideration. Kelly thought about it, then shook her head. She could never pull off that color. "The teal is still my favorite."

"Are you sure? You don't want something more bold?"

Kelly retrieved the teal dress from the bed and held it up to look again in the mirror. "I love the length and the flowing skirt."

Liz set aside the other dresses. "You'll need something striking in jewelry."

"Maybe my pearls?"

"Something gold and heavy would be better. If we pull your hair back like this —" Liz stepped behind her to show her — "with long earrings?"

The image in the mirror was more elegant than what Kelly normally saw. "You think so?"

"Definitely."

For the first time in the last hour she felt like she would be equal to whatever Joe had planned. She looked at Liz in the mirror. "I'm so glad you came over."

"Are you kidding? I'm the one who's

thrilled. You and Joe — I can't believe he finally asked you out or that you actually said yes."

"It's time to go on with life."

Liz hugged her. Kelly felt the stress of what she was doing bleed away in her friend's silent assurance. "Remember what it was like the first time Nick asked me out?"

The question brought laughter instead of tears to her friend's eyes. Liz stepped back. "Do I remember! I don't think there was a clothing store we didn't visit to find you the right dress."

"At least we found a dress here. I remember when Tom asked you out the first time — you had us traipsing around San Diego for days before you found the perfect outfit," Kelly teased, stepping into the bathroom to get her hair dryer. "How are we doing on time?"

"Fine. But if Joe were a few minutes late it would be better."

"That's what I was afraid of. How are you at makeup? Covering this shiner is going to be difficult if not impossible."

"I can do it," Liz said. "What about shoes?"

Joe prayed this wasn't a recall for tonight. His call to the base had been transferred and put on hold for his boss. That fact was a little unusual; normally orders passed through the duty officer. While he was waiting, he scanned the radio news stations looking for something unusual going on that might have triggered the page. It wasn't uncommon to hear about a hijacking or a third-world coup on the news before a decision was made to assign a SEAL team to the problem.

He didn't need this kind of start with Kelly. She had always handled pages interrupting his schedule, but throwing off their first date . . . It left a bad taste.

"Bear."

"Yes, sir."

"Are your men in town?"

Joe briefly closed his eyes. "Yes, sir. We've got a training op scheduled for early tomorrow morning. Everyone was to stay close this weekend."

"Good. I'm deploying platoons Echo and Foxtrot. Put your men back on short notice; you may be recalled next."

His men were going to regret the fact they hadn't been tapped to deploy. As a rule SEALs preferred to be where the action was, but for Joe the news brought relief. He didn't want to be on a plane tonight. "Yes, sir."

Joe headed back to base, dialing Boomer as he did so. Going to short notice status was an administrative headache. It was easier to be asked to jump on a plane than to go on short notice — at least then someone else did the paperwork. He glanced at his watch and winced. Even if he hurried this was going to be tight.

"Boomer, we just got bumped up to short notice status. Echo and Foxtrot are moving now. Can you start clearing the medical and personnel paperwork? And we've got training rotations out to Fort Bragg that will be messed up."

"What are assistant officers good for if not paperwork? I'm on my way in."

Joe cleared through security at the Naval Amphibious Base. With the duty officer taking care of tracking down his men and passing on the short notice order, Joe went to find his counterpart on platoon Echo. Kevin was in the middle of packing and glanced up when Joe tapped on his door. "Bear, I hoped you would get here before I had to cut out." Kevin reached for the red binder on his desk and handed it over. "Updated as of yesterday noon."

"Code word clearance, or can you tell me where you're heading?"

"Okinawa as a stopping off point.

They'll tell us after we get there. I'm thinking South Korea."

"Tough job."

"At least it's not Alaska." He nodded to the red binder. "You won't find many surprises in the list of current hot spots. Available resources are still showing the aftereffects of that deployment to Panama — support staff is just now getting back into their normal rotations. I've updated the latest numbers."

"Thanks."

Kevin smiled. "Don't thank me until you see the hole I'm leaving you to backfill in equipment. Okinawa got stripped for that exercise in the Philippines, and I've got to backfill from here." The phone rang, and Kevin reached for it, shaking his head. "Moving out on a Sunday is a nightmare. It's all newbies on duty."

Joe grinned and left him to it. Okinawa and real action. His men were going to be jealous. Joe turned pages in the notebook as he walked back to his office, reading through the briefing summaries. Boomer had arrived and was on the phone. Joe took a seat as Boomer hung up.

"That was the duty officer; all the men have answered the page."

"Good."

"Not the evening you had planned."

Joe relaxed. "Thirty minutes, Boomer. You've got the paperwork. All I've got to do is read and sign. I'm not about to miss a date just because we're now in the hot seat."

Boomer laughed and slid over a folder. "Start with those."

The office became quiet as they both went through the paperwork.

Joe signed his name a final time and moved the personnel jacket to his outbox. "That's it?"

Boomer nodded. "We won't know equipment status until Echo and Foxtrot get their deployment list finished. That's tomorrow's problem."

"Kevin warned me it would be a mess." Joe glanced at his watch. The flower shop was about to close. Wonderful.

"Kelly will understand."

Joe glanced over at his friend, hearing the amusement.

"Christi figured it out in about five minutes. At least we can swap vehicles here, save you a little time."

Secrets never lasted in this place. "Thanks, Boomer. It is rather important that I not totally blow this evening." That was an understatement.

"Short of something else happening in the world —"

"Please, I don't need to borrow trouble."

A final check with the duty officer, and they both walked out to the parking lot and traded vehicles. "Thanks again, Boomer."

"Anytime."

Joe transferred the box with the bear to Boomer's sedan, then glanced again at his watch. After he passed through base security, he picked up his cellular phone. "Marsha, I'm going to be a few minutes late. Would you *please* stay open for me?"

"Joe —"

"Please."

"You're going to have to tell me who this mystery person is."

"I can't. But you won't regret it. I promise." He turned on the charm and he heard her laugh.

"I'll stay open. But it's only because I adore you."

"Thank you. Five minutes."

He made it in four. Marsha not only found ribbon for the bear to match the roses but also found wrapping paper for the box and a matching bow. "She's going to love this Joe, whoever she is."

Marsha suspected. Did everyone know

Kelly and her collection of bears? "I hope so."

"Just remember: Besides romance, I do apologies, birthdays, and every holiday on the calendar."

"How profitable is the apology business?"

"Better than the romance," Marsha replied with a twinkle in her eyes, handing him the flowers.

On impulse, he leaned across the counter and kissed her cheek. "Thanks."

A fast shower, shave, change — there was no getting around the fact he would be a few minutes late picking up Kelly. But if he called her, there was a slim chance she would try to cancel. He wasn't going to take that risk. Better to apologize than to call.

Lord, do You accept prayers for clear traffic and green lights?

Fifteen

⋆ ⋆ ⋆

Joe hurried to get his tie straight. This was turning out to be the most rushed date in his lifetime, but he was going to make it. *Lord, I'm nervous.*

He laughed softly at the realization. It was easier to step out of an airplane at ten thousand feet in the dead of night than to do this. He slipped the package Marsha had wrapped into a sack, careful not to crush the bow, and checked again that he had his keys and wallet. He gathered up the bouquet of roses.

"Misha —" his dog lay sprawled on the rug by the patio — "don't get into any mischief while I'm gone. I'll be back in a few hours." She whined softly, knowing she was getting left behind. "Sorry, girl, this is a private date."

He bound down the steps to Boomer's car.

He pulled into Kelly's drive only minutes late and took a deep breath before getting out of the car. Knowing Kelly, she had probably been ready early, passing her time reading a book while she waited for him to arrive. He rang the doorbell.

She had been reading; the book was held in one hand when she opened the door. Joe's smile widened when he got a good look at her.

He spun his finger, encouraging her to turn around. She set down the book and did so, and the dress flared around her. "Wow."

Her blush was adorable. "Liz helped."

Her hair was pulled up and back; her jewelry was beautiful. None of it came close to the sparkle in her eyes. "You look wonderful."

"Thank you, sir. You don't look so bad yourself."

"These are for you." He placed the roses in her hands.

"They're beautiful."

"Marsha's best," he confirmed. "And Charles forgot this color."

She blushed, and it made him feel petty for taking a soft shot at a man just because he was using his money to say thanks in an extravagant way. Kelly deserved every last rose in Coronado for what she had done. Joe was relieved when Kelly gestured to the kitchen and thus removed the likelihood of him putting his foot in his mouth again. "Just let me put them in water and I'll be ready to go."

"Sure." Joe followed her, then leaned against the counter as she arranged the bouquet. Her color was still high. That did it. He wasn't going to mention the name Charles again tonight for any reason. "So you told Liz."

She nodded. "Since I raided her closet, I had to."

"You must've made her day."

She laughed softly. "I think you could safely say that." She glanced over at him. "Did you get paged?"

He frowned slightly. "Why do you ask?"

"I've never known you not to be early. I was convinced I wouldn't be ready on time."

Considering he had been running around racing the clock, it felt good to find out she had been too. "Actually, yes. We're back on short notice, so my sailing time has been temporarily curtailed."

"I'm sorry to hear that."

He didn't want to talk about something that serious, not now. He tilted his head, not recognizing the perfume she wore but liking it. "Did you get a chance to glance at the movies playing tonight?"

"I'd already tossed out my newspaper. I don't mind choosing when we get there."

"Really?"

"Really." She finished arranging the roses. "They are gorgeous."

"I'll have to buy you flowers more often. That smile is worth it." She could have so easily and subtly made a comparison between his gift and Charles's, but she hadn't, not even with a glance at the bouquet on her kitchen table. That was more than tact. It was honoring him by not comparing them. He loved her for that.

"Joe —"

He held out his hand. "Come on, let's go eat."

She picked up a small clutch purse and let him lock the door behind them. He settled his hand lightly on her back as he escorted her to the car.

"You traded the Jeep for the night."

"The occasion demanded a nice ride." He held her door for her.

"Where are we going?"

"The Prince of Wales Grill."

"I'm impressed. How did you swing reservations on such short notice?"

"Ingenuity."

"And a friend somewhere?"

Joe glanced over to share a smile. "A

friend of a friend. Coronado is a small place when you get right down to it."

"I knew you would try for extravagant."

"Just wait — I think I pulled it off."

Her laughter was nice to hear.

The restaurant was in an exclusive part of the Hotel del Coronado, overlooking the Pacific Ocean. It had been recently voted most romantic restaurant by *San Diego* magazine for a reason. Joe gave his name and they were escorted to a table with a wonderful view.

Heather did indeed play nice jazz on the piano. Joe caught her attention and gave her a small salute, pleased to see the roses he had sent her as a thank-you had arrived. Heather touched a rose and smiled back at him, sending a silent thanks.

Kelly saw the exchange. "What's her name?"

"Heather."

"Your friend of a friend?"

Joe settled into his chair. "Yes."

"Thanks for sending the roses."

"Not jealous?"

"When you went to the trouble on my behalf? Flattered is a better word."

He handed her the cloth-covered menu, appreciating her reply. "What would you like for dinner?"

★ ★ ★

"Joe, are you sure you want to see a comedy? We've already been laughing most of the evening."

Kelly's hand was clutching his arm, and her weight leaned slightly against him as they stood in front of the theater debating which movie to see. The happiness seemed to sparkle out of her, and Joe wished he could sweep her closer. It was hard to subdue his own pleasure. He had set out to make tonight memorable for her, but instead discovered she had done it for him. She never mentioned Nick or Charles, never touched on a serious subject. Instead she thoroughly enjoyed everything — the food, the music, the ocean view, the short walk from where he parked to the theater — and in doing so, pulled him along to share that happiness. It practically bubbled from her.

"I like laughing with you," he replied, enjoying the merriment in her eyes.

"You laugh at all the wrong places in my jokes."

"You don't know how to tell one. You need more practice."

She giggled. "Probably true." She looked again at the marquee. "Okay, let's see the comedy." She glanced around at the crowd they had joined. "We fit right in."

They were a decade too old and considerably overdressed, but the couples in the crowd were easy to spot. Joe settled his arm comfortably around Kelly's shoulders as they moved into line. "Yes, we do." His satisfaction at having her at his side matched the expressions of numerous others on dates around him.

Mingled in the crowd were a few men who saw him, glanced to Kelly then back to him, and nodded a greeting. It was a good thing Kelly hadn't asked that they keep their dating a secret. By morning most of the base would have the news he had been seen escorting her.

The movie was good. Joe figured it could have been a bomb and it wouldn't have mattered. They simply would have laughed together at how awful it was.

The evening had relaxed the tension and the wonder over what it would be like to change from friends to something more. It had been a smooth transition. Joe hoped it was only going to get better. After the movie was over, he offered his arm as they walked back to where he had parked. Kelly accepted without hesitation. He liked that about her, the way she accepted his statement of belonging together. He offered her one of the last hazelnuts from the bag they had been sharing.

"Do you suppose this is what makes dating so much fun?" She glanced up at him and he gestured toward the people ahead of them also strolling toward their cars, then at the sky. "This sense of time stopping? There's no reason not to stroll along and enjoy the beautiful evening."

"I think it also has something to do with who you are with," she offered.

"I figured that much out. But you and I have spent a lot of time together in six years. I don't think I've ever enjoyed an evening more."

"I've got a theory about nights like these."

"What's your theory?" he asked.

"That you've invested so much into them, they become a moment in time you have to really live in. Most of the time we rush around and never realize what's around us, enjoy the person we are with, because we're too busy to let ourselves live in that moment. Dates are designed to take our full attention."

He paused to glance down at her. "That's really good. I'm impressed."

She leaned against him. "You should be. It's my one profound comment for the night."

"Are you in a hurry to get home? It's getting late."

"Not particularly. I don't work tomorrow."

"Want to walk down along the beach?"

"Could I change first?"

"Sure."

He drove them back to her home. The full moon was bright overhead when he pulled into her driveway. She leaned her head back against the headrest and made no move to open the car door. "Thanks for all of this, Joe. You have no idea how much it means."

"I've enjoyed every minute of it." He left his hands resting atop the steering column, for she looked a little too appealing at the moment. "You've still got a present to unwrap. Before or after we stroll down to the beach?"

"I do?"

He reached around to the backseat and picked up the sack. "It wouldn't be a truly memorable first date without one."

"Joe."

Her protest made him smile. "It will cost you a cup of coffee, though."

"In that case —"

He came around the car and opened her door for her. "I like this about you."

They walked to her front door, and she glanced up at him as she found the right key to unlock the house. "What?"

"You make it nice to give you gifts."

Her blush was incredible. He probably shouldn't tease her about it, but it was too much fun.

Kelly shooed him out of the kitchen while she started the coffee, and Joe moved back to the living room, taking off his tie. When she joined him, she handed him one of the china cups, then slipped off her shoes and curled up on the couch. "A nice restaurant, roses, a present — our second date has a lot to live up to."

Joe took a seat on the chair across from her. "We're painting your kitchen," he replied dryly.

"You're serious?"

"Yes."

She laughed so hard her eyes watered. "Oh, Joe, I needed that."

Joe offered her the box he had set on the table. "A memory for tonight."

Kelly carefully unwrapped the paper and set aside the tissue paper. "Joe — he's beautiful."

He was surprised at the emotions on her face. "Bad move?"

She shook her head. "I love it. Thank

you. I was afraid since Nick bought me so many bears, you would think you shouldn't."

"Kelly," he waited until she looked up, "you collect bears. I think it's the perfect way to mark this occasion. You'll have to come up with a name."

She gently straightened the ribbon the bear wore. "Bear." She smiled. "Just Bear."

"You need one that's brown or black and looks kind of rugged for that name."

She looked over at him. "Insulted?"

"Embarrassed."

Her laughter filled the room. Joe decided it was best to change the subject. He got to his feet and held out his hand. "Come on, let's take that walk."

She let him pull her up. "It won't take me but a minute to change."

"Bring a jacket."

She put the bear in a place of honor before she left the room.

Bear.

When the guys got wind of this — maybe if it lost the ribbon and got pulled through the dirt — a white plush bear with his handle was embarrassing. It also made him smile. Kelly knew how to say a lot without saying it directly.

Kelly slipped her hand into Joe's as they

strolled down to the water's edge then turned north to follow the beach toward the Hotel del Coronado where their evening had begun. Music from the Ocean Terrace restaurant at the hotel drifted toward them, the colorful lanterns lit around the Terrace reflecting off the water. It was a festive mood.

"One of the last memories I had in the water before you found me was from the last time we walked this beach."

"Really?"

She nodded. "Friday night after dinner. You indulged me with a walk down to the Terrace to buy a frozen fruit smoothy. Remember?"

"I remember the smoothy — it gave me an ice cream headache."

"I had forgotten that."

"I haven't."

"What I remember is holding your hand while we walked, deciding how nice it was not to be walking alone."

He squeezed her hand gently. "Thank you. You're welcome to hold my hand anytime you like."

Kelly returned the pressure, and they walked in silence along the shore. This was the best memory maker of the evening. The restaurant, the movie, roses, and the bear — of all the images of the evening, this was the one she treasured most. She had walked this beach with Joe before, but this time it was different. This time in a new way she belonged beside him and it felt special.

The evening was going to end eventually, and she didn't want that to happen. Would he kiss her good night? There were already stars in her eyes; that would certainly cap this evening with the best ending possible.

The moonlight flickered as clouds skimmed over the sky.

Joe stopped.

She looked at him, puzzled, and saw his eyes narrow as he gazed ahead.

There was only the dark shadow of the surf and the resulting white breakers. The sound clued her in, an odd interruption in the withdrawing surf as it pulled back to sea.

They both began to run.

A limp body was rolling in the surf, being thrown by the sea to the shore.

Sixteen

★ ★ ★

"Kelly, go back to the house and call the police." Joe still wore his pager, but he had left his phone with his suit jacket in her living room. He was angry at himself for leaving the phone behind, because he couldn't comfort Kelly and do what needed to be done here. She was not reacting well, was scaring him, in fact.

She had gone up to her knees into the surf with him, having instinctively moved to help get the person out of the water, but now she stood shaking, icy white, not unlike the coloring of the lady they could do nothing to help. In only the few moments it took to lift the lady to the sand, they knew there was nothing they could do to save her life.

Joe carefully closed his hands over Kelly's shaking ones. "Go, honey."

Her horror-filled eyes lifted to his, and she fought to get a breath. Joe nodded. "You're okay. Go get us some help."

When she turned, she ran across the sand like hornets were after her.

Lord, I need someone with Kelly. Liz, Christi, someone she trusts. Please, yank someone out of bed. She's shattering.

Joe turned and knelt beside the young woman lying on the sand. She would never walk on a beach again. Never laugh. She had drowned. Probably tonight. With painful sympathy he reached over and closed her blue eyes.

When he eventually arrived back at the house, Kelly was sitting on the couch, a blanket around her shoulders, still shivering. She looked up as he entered the living room. Her gaze was haunted. A cop was with her, and Joe sent the lady a grateful look at seeing the warmed-up coffee mug Kelly gripped and the fact she had now changed into dry clothes. It was a good answer to his prayer.

"Sorry." Kelly's teeth chattered around the single word.

Joe hid a wince at her apology. "Don't be." He sat down on the couch beside her and reached around to tug the blanket more firmly around her shoulders. He wanted to wrap his arms around her and hold on until her shivers stopped, but she was fighting for control in her own way. He settled for rubbing his hand back and forth across her wrist, feeling the coldness gripping her skin.

"I looked at her, and I saw my own face." She gulped for air. "In my dreams, that's what I looked like when I drowned."

She'd been dreaming about drowning. He should have expected it, but he hadn't. There wasn't much assurance he could offer. "This comes a little too close for comfort."

The officer who had been with him at the beach joined them. He spoke with the officer who had come to meet up with Kelly. Joe heard the quiet debriefing and ignored it. There hadn't been much he could tell the officer, and Kelly knew even less.

"Do you know who she is?" Kelly asked the officer as he came over and sat in the chair across from her.

"Not yet," he said, frowning slightly.

"What happened? Do you know how she drowned?"

He looked at her steadily. "She wasn't swimming or surfing. She wasn't tossed against the rocks. There's no sign of a struggle, and she hasn't been in the water long. The dress slacks, sweater, jacket —

they suggest she was out on a boat, no life jacket, probably slipped, hit her head, and fell overboard. The currents are strong; they may not even know she's missing yet."

Joe felt Kelly shudder. What the cop had described happened several times along the California coast each year. An accident.

"It's also possible it's a suicide, but few would enter the water with their jacket on if that were their intention And it's doubtful she could jump from a cliff and end up on this stretch of beach. If she swam out until she was exhausted, then couldn't swim back — we'll look into it. Until we know something definite, we'll be treating it as a crime scene."

Kelly and Ryan almost drowned, and three days later, someone does. Joe knew the timing was coincidental, but it didn't feel that way.

"I'm okay, Joe. Really." He realized his hand had tightened around hers. She smoothed her free hand over his.

The officer offered Joe his card. "We'll be down at the beach for at least another hour. If you remember anything else, please let us know."

"I'll call."

"I'm sorry your evening ended this way, Mrs. Jacobs." The officer hesitated. "My daughter clipped out your picture from the paper to add to her scrapbook. It would be a real shame if you let what happened Thursday and tonight scare you away from the water, from your job. The kids love you."

"What's your daughter's name?"

"Lynnette."

"Fifteen, gorgeous blue eyes, loves country music?"

"That's Lynn."

Kelly gave a glimmer of a smile. "Please tell her thanks. She is one of the best junior lifeguards we have at the beach."

"I'll do that."

Joe saw both officers out and locked the door behind them. He returned to the living room and hesitated when he saw Kelly had tugged over a pillow, wrapping her arms around it. "Let me call Liz."

She glanced up at him and shook her head. "She has enough broken nights of sleep with Christopher waking up to be fed."

"Christi then."

She pushed her hands through her hair. "No. I appreciate the thought, but I simply need to sleep and forget."

It was a good idea, but Joe knew sleep wouldn't be coming soon for her, not when she looked so haunted by what had happened, was still shivering occasionally. She'd just dream again, and this time it would probably be so vivid it would feel alive. He sighed as he crossed back to join her. He caught the edges of the blanket and tugged the ends around her lap. He'd suggest a hot shower, but water wasn't a good idea at the moment either. "You need someone with you tonight."

She looked up at him. "Just sit and talk to me for a while, please?"

His hesitation had nothing to do with her request. She had no way of knowing that at 0400 hours he was due to leave for the Chocolate Mountain training grounds. If he told her, she would insist he go home, that he call one of her friends. Where was the balance between his job and Kelly supposed to be when she truly needed him?

He took a seat beside her and knew for now it was the right decision. He wouldn't have slept anyway.

She sighed. "That could so easily have been me."

"I know."

Her eyes searched his, looking for something. She finally gave a slight nod, accepting something. "Joe, did Nick drown?" she whispered.

The question sliced into him and the

fact she had asked it — he couldn't tell her, and yet to leave that question unanswered . . . "No," he finally said softly, "Nick didn't drown."

She wrapped her hands more firmly around the blanket and seemed to pull back into herself. "I couldn't handle it if he had drowned." She took a deep breath, then looked over at him with desperate eyes. "When you drown, you know it's happening."

He froze. He was right; a lot more had happened in the water than she had told him. "What happened out there in the water?"

She looked away. He wanted her answer but was afraid of it, and he was afraid of so little. He couldn't fix what had happened that night, and for that reason the emotions were hard to accept. Helplessness was an unnatural state. He thought she was never going to answer him. "I went to sleep."

Went to sleep in the water. *Lord, I'm so glad she didn't tell me before!*

He didn't break the silence. It was easier if she could choose the words to say.

"It was so peaceful," she admitted softly, "and I just didn't want to go on. I knew it was happening, and yet I closed my eyes and let myself go to sleep. The next thing I knew I was shoved by a wave and toppled over, and the adrenaline scare got me moving again. The panic was enormous. For that woman to have drowned —"

He cut her off. "You survived."

"She didn't." Kelly set the blanket aside. "Why did God help save me and not her?"

Kelly didn't need theology at 2330 hours; she needed to set aside a horrific memory and get some sleep. "Even if you could get an answer to the question 'why me,' I doubt you could accept it. The bottom line is still the same. Let it go, Kelly. You don't need survivor's guilt."

She looked hurt at his answer but eventually nodded. "Fine, we won't talk about it. Would you like some decaf coffee?"

"I didn't mean to make you mad."

"I'm not mad."

"Kelly, honey, trust me. I've seen mad. You're mad."

"I'm . . . upset."

No, she was mad, but he would concede the point. "Okay. Then I didn't mean to upset you."

She looked at him, shook her head, and went to get their coffee.

Joe knew the problem. Theology had always been a subject they disagreed on. She loved to ask why, and he preferred to just apply common sense. Some questions were not worth the effort to ask — for some things there were no answers in Scripture besides "I am God."

He had seen her spend three years asking questions, making herself miserable. *Why did Nick die?* had been the first question and it had gone on from there. Kelly thought by asking the questions she would get answers, find peace. She was wrong. What she got was more heartache because she didn't get an answer she could accept. The Bible said God's ways are at times unsearchable. She wasn't going to find an answer to explain Nick's death that she could accept. She needed to set aside trying to understand and instead lean against the character of the One who had made the decision. God was trustworthy.

When she came back with the coffee, her expression had steadied. "This was not the end to our first date I expected."

The subject had been set aside, as she said it would be. That fact made him feel like he'd kicked a puppy. "No, it didn't end as planned."

"Thanks for taking the actions you did. I'm glad I wasn't alone when I found her."

"Don't worry about it. The situation

shook me up too, Kelly."

"You've seen people die before."

He didn't answer that question; he couldn't. The positive answer made him wish he had a different profession. Like David, he served God with a faithful heart, but also like David, he was a warrior with blood on his hands. Tonight he wished his path had been different, that he could tell Kelly no.

"Tonight was my first time."

"You handled it."

It was after midnight before Joe was convinced Kelly would be okay left on her own. When she encouraged him to go home, he reluctantly got to his feet. She walked him to the front door.

"I'll come by tomorrow evening after work." He studied her face one last time in the light that came from the hall behind her.

"I would appreciate it."

"You'll sleep?"

She nodded and smiled slightly. "I'll probably take my new teddy bear to bed with me."

Her reply made him reach out and pull her to him, wrapping her firmly in a hug. "Really? I'm jealous."

She rubbed her chin against his shirt and

laughed softly. "I'll consider changing his name if you really feel strongly about it."

"I can live with Bear." He reluctantly released her and stepped back. "You'll call if you need me? If you have a bad dream?"

"Yes."

She probably wouldn't but he had to hope. "Then good night, Kelly."

He drove home feeling somber. That could have so easily been Kelly found drowned, tossed back to the beach by the surf. She'd been in the water long enough she'd fallen asleep once that she could remember. The odds were good it had happened more often than that. She hadn't been alert when he found her. Had she been in the water much longer she would have been found washed up on the shore somewhere along these miles of beach.

Who was she, the lady who had drowned? She'd been young, pretty, and someone tonight was pacing the floor waiting for her to return home. Instead they would get a phone call and a visit from a police officer.

Joe turned on the radio, wondering how long it would be before the news broke. He hoped Kelly's name stayed out of it. The last thing she needed was more press attention.

Seventeen

★ ★ ★

"What do you think you are doing? You killed my inside source!"

"We know who they're sending. She had become a liability to you. My men said she was talking," the general arrogantly replied.

Charles watched the television coverage as word of the drowning led the morning news. He wanted to curse this man's actions. Yes, platoons Echo and Foxtrot had deployed to Okinawa, and from there his own careful inquiries had revealed they were going on to Seoul. But they were reacting to a diversion he himself had created. He needed the SEALs and their equipment spread thin so this shipment could get through, and the diversion with North Korea and South Korea had been carefully planned. None of it led back to him and this deal.

All of that careful planning was gone because of the general's rash actions.

Charles's own anonymity was shattered — the casualty happened right in his figurative backyard. He had also lost a crucial source of data he might still need. "Why did you decide on your own to kill my contact?"

"She jeopardized this deal."

"She didn't know anything!" Another person was dead. Another innocent person was dead. *This situation is spiraling out of control.* "Back off and let me do what you're paying me to do." There was no way to reason with this man.

"If this shipment is intercepted, you will pay for the mistake."

"It will be delivered. Just don't touch my remaining source. I need her."

"We'll be watching." The phone call ended as abruptly as the last one.

This was the first time Charles truly couldn't live with a shipment being intercepted. He thought about the lady who had died and felt sick. She had been caught in crosscurrents she wasn't even aware of. He paced to the windows, feeling the noose of events tighten around him.

He needed to turn this around, but it was already too late. He could feel his feet sinking down in the quicksand of what was happening. He wanted to pray for help but couldn't gather the courage to say the words. He knew the truth. He was reaping what he had sown from years before and appealing to God to intervene . . . Charles thought it unlikely help would come. Everyone lived with the consequences of their choices and he was living with his.

His wife Amy had died when Ryan was four, and his grief had manifested itself in anger. He had begun to steal again during the last stages of her cancer, at first as a way to get desperately needed cash. Then after Amy died, he stole as a way to lash out at God by intentionally crossing the line, going back to doing what Amy had worked so hard to reform him from.

Mortars had become guns, and guns had become missiles. Diverting shipments had become his specialty. Only it had spiraled out of his ability to control it. Once he'd crossed a line from small things to large, the demands of those he dealt with had become such that he could not step away.

He was in too deep and he hadn't been able to say no when his buyers wanted more unconventional weapons. He had begun tipping the Americans off to the weapons, providing detailed shipping information. It was better to have the weapons intercepted than to say no to the deal and let his buyers get a hold of the devices from someone else.

But then Nick Jacobs had been killed in a recovery mission that should never have gone bad, and Charles had finally been able to get out. Even moving his business from Hong Kong to here had been calculated to help him disengage. It let him keep an eye on the SEALs, make sure his tracks stayed cold.

When this situation was over, he would find a way to ensure that this could never happen again — even if it meant selling his business and cutting all his contacts. If he had done that before, the general would never have been able to pressure him into this situation.

He already owed Kelly; he had Nick's death on his conscience, and now one more debt had been added to that pile. He'd been forced to use her as a way to watch Joe and without intending it had just placed her life in danger.

He would have to use the extra days he had built into the schedule, and not as he had first planned. Any idea of tipping off the SEALs early, before this deal was complete, could be forgotten. The general had made his point. Killing Iris had been a simple reminder that next time it might be his son. Or Kelly.

He would have to make sure the SEALs could not disrupt this shipment. It had been three years since he had been in the business. There were always leaks. If the SEALs picked up through other intelligence assets that the device was moving . . . He needed a decisive way to take the SEALs out of play.

Kelly found the sand warm under her feet. She had slipped off her shoes; they dangled in her left hand. It was a sunny late afternoon, and children were laughing as they built elaborate sandcastles in the smooth sand at the water's edge. Ryan, his dad having a meeting over at the Naval Air Station North Island, had called and asked if he could stop by after school. Kelly was enjoying their walk together, even if the conversation was quite serious. What happened last night had shaken not only her but also Ryan.

"Her picture was on the news. She looks familiar; I think I've seen her."

"Coronado is a small place. I would be surprised if you hadn't seen her around."

"I wish we knew what happened, why she died."

Kelly heard the tension in Ryan's voice and understood it. "So do I." From the morning newscast, Kelly now knew the lady's name: Iris Wells. She had lived in an apartment complex at the south end of the strand. The police were not offering any details of what had happened. That puzzled Kelly. If it had been an accident, the details would be made available by now.

"We almost died the same way she did."

"Yes." It was hard to be the adult, to sound matter-of-fact about it when she felt that same lingering fear.

"The kids at church were asking about what it was like to almost die."

Kelly was surprised at that until she thought about it. She hadn't faced those questions, but only because adults would hesitate to ask. "What did you tell them?"

"Not much."

"I was scared," she offered. *Terrified* was a better word, but scared worked.

"Me too."

She didn't know Ryan well enough to read what he wasn't saying, but she guessed it was probably what he most wanted to talk about. "Were you worried about what would happen if you died? Do you really, in your heart, know Jesus? Or are you going to church because of your dad?"

"I accepted the Lord as my Savior and

was baptized when I was ten. It's not the question of heaven or where I would spend eternity." Ryan glanced at her. "What it made me wish is that I knew Jesus better. Does that make sense?"

The maturity in Ryan impressed her. "I made that same decision," she replied quietly.

"Really?"

"I call it my quest."

"I need to do something like that. I felt . . . I don't know, kind of hollow. That up until now my faith had all been a game. It suddenly became very serious."

"There's a wilderness camp being planned by my church youth group next week. You ought to think about going along."

"Do you think so?"

"I seem to remember that trying to climb a sheer rock face got me pretty close to Jesus," Kelly pointed out.

"That sounds perfect. I'll ask my dad." Ryan hesitated for a moment. "Dad was really shaken up by what happened, the lady who drowned. I've never seen him like he was this morning when he saw the news."

Kelly wrapped her arm around him and gave him a hug — the boy was about as tall as she was. "He's your father; that's to be expected. He nearly had that happen to you." Ryan was embarrassed at the attention but also looked pleased. "Enough serious stuff. Let's talk about you. Do you have plans for the summer?"

"Not many. Dad wants us to travel some — probably to London, Paris, and maybe a visit back to Hong Kong."

"That will be fun."

Ryan shrugged. "I've seen those places before."

They had entered the stretch of beach where the volleyball nets were set up. There were two games going on. Kelly noticed the glances being sent their way by some of the high school girls. She wondered if Ryan had a girlfriend yet. There would be several girls asking her later to make introductions.

Ryan was noticing it too and looked a little embarrassed. "You have a crowded beach."

Kelly nodded. "I like it this way. Listen, your dad said you might be interested in some surfing pointers. Want to come hang out on my beach tomorrow? It's supposed to be a calm day. I'm working, but I'll be free at lunch and on breaks."

"You wouldn't mind?"

"You're a local celebrity around here. You need to get back on a surfboard soon, and I like to teach."

"You're on. Thanks."

Kelly was aware of the whispers now going on among the spectators of the volleyball games. "If you don't mind me asking, do you have a girlfriend?"

"No."

"Would you like a few introductions?"

Ryan glanced at her. "Maybe."

"I know someone you would really like. Her name is Lynnette. Two *n*s, two *t*s, and if you're really sweet, I bet she'll ask for your autograph."

Ryan's face turned red, and his voice slid up part of an octave. "You're serious?"

"She asked me for mine this morning." Kelly was enjoying this immensely. Ryan was a good kid, and she would like to see him go out with Lynnette. He struck Kelly as a little lonely, having been dropped back into the States after so long overseas. "Come on, I'll introduce you as my surfing buddy."

Eighteen

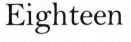

"Bear, your problem is you haven't been running in those boots long enough to get them broken in."

"Boomer, just pass me the ice." He'd run eight miles on the sprained ankle today, and he didn't need his AOIC's humor. They had a sweat now or bleed later attitude toward training in the SEALs, and the last seven hours out at Chocolate Mountain had been intense. He was glad to be back at the base.

Joe probed his swollen ankle, rotating it, ignoring the pain the movement caused. The muscles were tightening as he sat and the ankle was stiffening.

If it had been one of his men who went out on a dangerous training mission with less than four hours of sleep and his mind not fully focused on the task, Joe would have ripped a strip off his hide and seriously considered yanking him from the roster for lack of judgment. He had already

251

given himself the verbal dressing down; the question now was what else he was going to do to rectify the situation. It could never be allowed to happen again. He had let a situation in his personal life be a distraction at work. It wasn't just bad form; it was what got SEALs killed.

The lack of sleep had been unavoidable. There was no way he could have left Kelly rather than stay and talk until she was over the shock. But today, losing his concentration during the op as he wondered how Kelly was doing — he was lucky it had cost him only a sprained ankle and not a broken one. Only a first-jump rookie took his concentration off the landing site during a parachute jump, and Joe had been jumping with a full load in the dark. He had managed to land on rocks. Joe scowled as he wrapped the ice in place with a bandanna. He had spent the rest of the day paying for that mistake.

"You were the one who decided the extraction helicopter was grounded due to mechanical problems," Boomer reminded him.

"Don't laugh too hard; next time the sprain might be yours," Bear growled back.

The training mission had gone well otherwise, re-creating a hostage rescue mission the Israelis had executed a year before.

After the low altitude jump into the target area, Cougar had done a good job of leading them through the rugged terrain in the dark. The assault at the close quarters battle house, rescuing a hostage affectionately known as Elma, had taken five minutes too long to execute in the first pass. The second pass had gone better.

Joe had decided just before they left the base that on this mission their extraction helicopter was going to be grounded by mechanical failure and they would have to get out of the hostile area by their alternate route. Hence the last long hike on a sprained ankle to end the day.

Working, he could ignore the pain. Now his ankle was barking. He reached for his soda and two ibuprofen. "The guys are improving."

"Not only the mission, but they handled that curve you threw them without complaint," Boomer agreed.

Joe grunted. "What they did was set out to run me into the ground, and you know it."

Boomer laughed. "I noticed you didn't let them."

The squad medic, a young guy from

Kansas, who shouldn't even have been able to swim let alone practically run his L-T into the ground, had just about done it. Joe had ignored the glances among the men when the pace picked up and simply let them try. Authority came from more than words. The entire platoon had been struggling for wind by the time they reached the alternate recovery site. The old-timers had looked at him and just grinned while the newbies had shaken their heads, not sure how he had done it.

It felt good. Very good. At least the sprain had been worth something.

The day he couldn't answer a challenge like that was the day he needed to consider letting a younger man have his job. At thirty-eight his body was not as forgiving as it had been at twenty-eight. He smiled. It was one of the best treks his men had made under full gear this year. It was good to be back on short notice. There had been an extra sharpness to their assault.

"Anything on the board I need to know about?"

"It was a quiet night around the world, no new hot spots."

"Good. Let's hope it stays that way. What time is the debriefing?"

Boomer glanced at his watch. "Twenty

minutes. Did you hear they identified the lady who drowned?"

"Oh? Who?"

"Iris Wells, civilian, but she's one of ours. She worked in the personnel department."

The news was a shock. While a large percentage of people in Coronado and San Diego worked for the Navy, most of the civilians were with Naval Air Station North Island, not here at NAB. "Who's on it from Naval security?"

"I heard they assigned two investigators, but I didn't get names. Was there any indication of foul play?"

Last night he would have said no, but now? "There was nothing obvious, but I hope these guys are thorough."

"You'll probably see them soon, as you two found the body."

"They had better go easy on Kelly. She doesn't need another round of this. Last night was tough on her."

"Tough on you as well."

Bear glanced over at Boomer and nodded. "That could have been Kelly's body washing ashore."

"You're going to spoil me," Joe accepted the coffee refill and one of the still warm chocolate chip cookies Kelly offered and leaned his head back against the lounge chair as she settled into the seat beside him. She had taken one good look at him when he arrived, pointed him to the chair, and had not let him help with dinner.

"You deserve it." Misha was staying in step with her, hoping to mooch part of her cookie. "Are you eventually going to tell me anything about today? Like how badly you're hurt?" There was a gentle scold in her voice.

He smiled. "I'm not hurt."

"Joe —"

He shrugged. "A sprained ankle hardly counts. It was a long day out at Chocolate Mountain."

"Was anybody else injured?"

"No. But there are a few who will be doubling up on the daily runs so they don't get embarrassed again."

"I've seen that wolfish smile in the past. How much ground did you cover?"

Joe thought about those miles and still felt every one of them. "Far enough that they got the point. You'll see them on the beach kicking up that loose sand."

"The SEAL groupies will thank you for that."

Joe laughed. "Hey, I aim to please. That

256

was my day. How was yours?"

"Shopping, housework. I found paint and wallpaper for the kitchen." She'd kept herself busy; he was grateful for that.

Joe sipped his coffee, aware of the subtle change — Kelly had bought his favorite brand. She was studying him, adapting, like he had seen her do with Nick. He wasn't sure yet what he thought about the change in how she was approaching him. He felt an equal amount of unease and appreciation.

"Could I go running with you tomorrow morning?"

Even knowing what she was doing, he was surprised at the request. "Sure, if you'd like to. I hit the beach at 0530."

"Run this way and pick me up. I only plan to do a couple miles."

"Not going back into training?"

"Once in my lifetime was plenty."

She had once braved entering the ten-mile Bay Bridge run. He and Nick had taken it as a personal challenge to get her ready for it. "I rather enjoyed being your training coach." He remembered those days with great fondness. She looked great in shorts and sweat.

"You and Nick ran me into the ground."

"I'll go easy on you tomorrow," Joe

promised, already looking forward to her company. He knew Kelly preferred to swim competitively rather than run. She had taken up running because it let her join Nick of a morning. He had always admired that, the deliberate focus she had on her husband, the way she put her energy into her marriage.

Now Kelly was dating him. Joe was beginning to realize exactly what that meant. He hadn't fully appreciated the difference that would happen.

He thought for a moment and knew one way he could return the favor. "If you've found the paint and wallpaper you want for the kitchen, do you want to work on the project tomorrow evening?"

"Sure, if you have time."

"I'll make time. Leave the ceiling for me."

"It's all yours." She fed the last bite of her cookie to Misha. "I saw the evening news. I can't believe no one has come forward with information about Iris Wells. If she were on a boat and fell overboard . . . But no one called for help. And no one reported seeing her on the docks Sunday. The last time someone reported seeing her was 3 p.m."

"The investigation has just started. Give

them another few days. They probably know a great deal more than they're making public." He didn't mention the fact he had spent over an hour talking with the investigators late that afternoon, going over the details about finding her on the beach and also the details on paperwork his platoon would have sent to personnel recently. The investigators were developing a list of everything she could have seen in the last few months. Since she handled scheduling for training classes around the country, most platoons had contact with Miss Wells. If there was any suspicion of foul play, the investigators would find it. When the time came they needed to talk to Kelly, they agreed to notify him first.

"Did you talk to Christi about Boomer's birthday party?" he said.

"We were thinking about doing something at the park. Rent the pavilion, have a cookout. Christi will try to do too much if we throw the party at someone's home. Maybe if we did it on the third Saturday? That would give us five weeks to plan it."

"I could take him fishing that morning, then deliver him back to the party."

"That would be great."

"The guys have been talking about getting him a new set of free weights."

"He'd love them."

Joe heard her real opinion in the tone of her voice and glanced over at her. "I'm dead if I ever get you something that practical."

"Absolutely."

"Just for the record, I like practical. I could use a new sander."

"There is a rule about buying a guy tools. If you give me brand, model, and accessories, I'll consider it. Otherwise, forget it."

"Is that why Nick was always pestering me before Christmas? He was doing your investigative work?"

"You had better believe it."

"I'll remember."

"If you do, I promise never to buy you a tie."

"I've already got a drawer full of them from my mother, never worn. The last thing I need is a tie."

Kelly swatted at a mosquito. "I think they like this perfume."

He grinned. "I know I do."

"Well remember it, because in another minute I'm going to smell like mosquito repellent. Need anything while I'm inside?"

"I'm fine."

"Be back in a minute."

He was relieved Kelly had stepped back inside for a moment. He would love to tug her down on his lap and figure out where she had touched that perfume to her skin. It was a problem, the aching awareness of her he had. She moved; he noticed. It was becoming an interesting — and increasingly difficult — challenge to keep his concentration on the conversation and the meal when he also had the pleasure of looking at her.

He gave a comfortable sigh. Evenings like this were nice. He enjoyed crashing on her back deck after a hard day and spending time with her. It would be so nice to be married; he wouldn't have to get kicked out of a comfortable chair to go back to a solitary home anymore. Having to call it a night, walk home, and spend it alone — it was getting old very quickly.

He leaned his head back as he heard the patio door open and Kelly came back outside. "Come sit with me." He caught hold of her hand and tumbled her onto his lap.

"Joe!"

She felt so good in his arms. He considered kissing her — had been considering nothing else for the last few days — but decided it might spook her. He doubted she'd kissed anyone since Nick, and he wasn't eager to rush that comparison. But that didn't mean he wasn't going to take advantage of the situation. He slowly smiled. "I seem to remember you're ticklish."

Her helpless peals of laughter filled the evening as he proved his memory correct.

Nineteen

★ ★ ★

"Now this is a sight I could get used to." Joe came to a stop beside Kelly's back patio. It was a quiet morning, slightly foggy, a perfect morning to run. Kelly was stretching. Her shorts had shrunk since the last time he had seen them; either that or her legs had grown longer. She always had great legs. He tried to temper his appreciative gaze by remembering he had seen Kelly in shorts before, but in truth he didn't try very hard. He was dating her; it would be rude not to notice.

She glanced up and it was obvious she had no idea what he was thinking or that openness in her greeting would have never survived. Kelly had a blush that could rival a red rose. "Good morning."

She must have just rolled out of bed; she still looked half asleep. He felt the sucker punch of what it would be like if they were married to see her tussled hair and sleepy eyes, arms curled around a pillow, lying beside him in bed, just stirring to wake up.

"We can wait until you've had your coffee, Kelly."

She yawned and covered it with the back of her hand. "No, it's okay. I'll be fine once I'm moving." She got to her feet. "Can I set the pace?"

"Sure."

He followed her down the path to the beach. The water was calm this morning, the waves rolling in with gentle swells. Kelly started in the soft sand and soon moved closer to the water where the sand was packed by earlier tides. Joe pulled back his pace to match her stride, staying higher on the beach where the sand was softer and the workout harder.

They passed SEALs running in small groups along the beach, the cadres of men putting in their two and three miles to loosen up before going to work, where they would do the serious physical training for another two and a half hours.

"Are you normally a loner in the mornings?" Kelly glanced back at a group they had just passed. "They're certainly surprised to see you running with someone."

"You're prettier than Boomer."

"Got it. Let's hope I don't embarrass you."

"Not possible."

"Gallant of you."

He smiled at that. She lengthened her stride.

They ran the first mile in silence. Joe watched her from the corner of his eye and began to get concerned. Her pace was too fast and she was breathing rapidly. Rather than settle back into the natural pace her body needed, any time they were passed by other SEALs she actually increased their pace.

She glanced over at him. "How's the ankle?"

"Fine." He had been ignoring it.

"Seriously."

"Fine. How's the stitch in your side?"

"As good as your ankle."

"You're stubborn." Her muscles had to be quivering like Jell-O; running on sand increased the effort required. "Slow down a notch; you don't have to prove anything to me."

"Maybe I do to myself," she replied, but did ease her pace.

That sensible act lasted only until they were passed again, this time by two teens who had to be in high school, probably on the track team. Her pace picked up again.

Joe decided to remain silent. She moved past two miles and started on three. Stubbornness had to meet common sense eventually. She suddenly stumbled.

He grabbed her arm, afraid she had twisted her ankle. "Kelly?"

"That was stupid of me."

She leaned over, resting her hands against her knees, sucking in air. Not her ankle — she had lost her balance when her legs gave out.

"Sit down." He was angry at himself for letting her run too far, at the wrong pace, when he knew she should have started slowly over several days.

She waved the suggestion away.

"Need some help, Lieutenant?"

Joe glanced over and saw Cougar thirty feet away, pausing in his own run, obviously concerned. "Could you get me a water jug from by the obstacle course?" The base and its expansive training grounds were just ahead, adjoining the public beach.

"Joe! Cougar, I'm fine."

Kelly looked mortified that he was pulling someone else into this, but Joe refused to let her change his decision this time. He glanced at the man waiting. "Go."

Cougar nodded and set a pace that ate up sand.

Kelly took a deep breath and glanced up at him. "That wasn't necessary."

"I disagree."

"I only need to catch my breath."

"Accept a little common sense. You won't win this debate."

She walked away from him, circling, fighting leg muscles that were quivering. "So I pushed. You guys do it all the time."

"We also train constantly and prep for those days we need to push. All you did was prove you can't use willpower to overcome lack of training."

Cougar returned with the water. The silent question asked as he handed over the two bottles had Joe shaking his head. Kelly wouldn't appreciate more direct intervention. With a nod Cougar returned to his run.

Joe made sure Kelly drank more than she thought she needed. She was angry but also embarrassed. "Come on," he said softly. "I'll walk you home."

She shot him a look of annoyance. "I don't need the company."

"Come on."

It was a long, silent walk. "What were you trying to prove?" Joe finally asked.

"Nothing."

"Kelly —" he didn't know how to handle

her — "please answer me."

"I used to run four miles every day with Nick."

She wanted to reclaim her past all in a day. What had brought this on? "Start running regularly, and you'll do four miles again easily."

She didn't answer him.

They eventually reached her home. "I'll pick you up, same time tomorrow."

"No thanks."

"I didn't ask. Be ready. You'll thank me for it in a few weeks." He sighed when the patio door quietly closed. Whatever had been bothering her this morning, it had just left a very bad taste for both of them. What had he done? This wasn't like Kelly. Everything had been fine when he first picked her up. It made him miserable to know something he had done must have caused the change. As he ran along the shoreline back toward base, he was the one others glanced at and tried to keep up with.

"All right, Ryan!" Kelly cheered from the water's edge as he made another successful ride. She had taken her lunch break early so she could surf with him for half an hour.

She was trying her best to forget that morning. How was she supposed to tell Joe it bugged her that he wasn't Nick? Joe was quiet when he ran. By the end of that first mile, Kelly had begun to resent getting up early and being out of shape, and the silence grated on her nerves. Nick told her jokes. He told her jokes when she groused about getting up, when she warmed up, and during their run he made sure she had more to think about than the fact she was running.

She teased Joe about being a bear in the mornings, but she had been worse. A grouch. She owed him an apology and she didn't know how to explain her behavior. Tomorrow. She would learn her lesson and be the one to start the conversation. He had been running on his own or with Boomer for the last three years. He wasn't accustomed to just chatting. When he ran, he thought about running. She had always liked that about him before, his attention to what he was doing. Well, it only made sense that there would be a few times when that same trait would irritate her.

Ryan planted his board next to hers in the sand. "Was that one better?"

"Great. You made the adjustments beautifully." Ryan had great balance, but he tended to oversteer and crash when the wave momentum began to push him. This time he rode the wave until it diminished.

"When I keep my weight on my back foot, I can feel the board responding to the wave."

"That's the biggest part of being a great surfer. You have to feel what the wave is doing." She picked up her surfboard and headed back into the water. "Can we make this our last ride? I'm freezing."

"Sure."

They swam out on their boards until the swells were beginning to show their form. "Which wave?"

Ryan chose well. Kelly watched to make sure he got up on the board, then picked up the wave behind him. He rode the wave into the shore. She heard the applause as he finished and turned her attention as she finished her own ride, dropping into the water when her wave ran out.

Charles. Ryan was recounting his morning as Kelly carried her board to the beach and pulled on her sweat-suit jacket. She towel-dried her hair as she walked toward them.

"I saw that last ride. Ryan is improving."

Kelly put her arm across the boy's shoulders and gave him a hug. "Ryan is a great student. I'm proud of him. Another few weeks, and he'll be riding the waves like that every time." Ryan was blushing. She ruffled his hair and laughed as she stepped away, having made sure he both heard and felt the praise. "What about you, Charles? Ryan didn't tell me if you surf."

"I can wipe out with the best of them."

She grinned at the self-directed humor. "Really?"

"I'm athletic enough to know I prefer my feet on the ground."

The fact he didn't mind admitting it to a lifeguard made her like him all the more. There was no attempt to impress.

"You looked pretty good out there too."

"Lots of practice."

"I hear a dodge there, but I'll let you off the hook."

He could pay a compliment and not mind if it was gently deflected. She appreciated that.

"Nice tie, Dad."

Ryan shrieked with laughter as his dad wrapped him up in a hug. "You bought it."

The yellow silk was out of place with the otherwise conservative dark suit. Charles definitely looked out of place on the beach, but apparently was not worried about what the saltwater and sand would do to his suit and shoes.

"What's the medallion, Kelly? It's pretty."

She lifted her hand to close around it. "Nick's eagle. My husband's call sign in the SEALs was Eagle because he walked point, was the spotter for the group. He wore this medallion for years."

"A good memory."

She nodded, pleased that he seemed to understand the importance of having it.

"I promised Ryan dinner out tonight. Would you care to join us?"

She looked from father to son and was startled to realize she wished she could accept. She really liked these two; they so easily conveyed an exclusive club. The invitation to be a friend was there to be accepted. "I'll have to pass, but thanks. Joe is coming by when he gets off work."

"Are you sure?"

"Yes. Maybe another time."

"I'll remind you someday you said that."

She laughed softly. "Do that."

Twenty

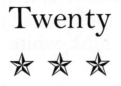

Masking tape covered the woodwork, the countertops were covered in newspapers, the floor had a drop cloth laid out, and the smell of paint hung heavily in the air. Joe almost had the ceiling in the kitchen finished.

"Ready to take a break?" Kelly asked, studying his work. He was fast. He had already given most of the ceiling a second coat.

"A few more minutes should do it."

She was grateful he had apparently dismissed this morning and her unexplainable behavior. He had appeared after work bringing Misha with him, ready to help her paint and wallpaper, and in the last hour hadn't brought the subject up. She owed him for that kindness.

Kelly set down the roller she had been using on the east wall, and with a rueful smile looked at her paint-splattered T-shirt. She was glad now she had taken off Nick's medallion before she began painting. "This is a memorable second date."

Joe glanced down and quirked an eyebrow. "You did look better dressed Sunday night. I don't think white freckles are in this year."

"You should see your hair. You're going gray."

He touched it, amused. "Really?"

"Rather salt and pepper at the moment."

Kelly pulled out the pitcher of lemonade she had mixed earlier that day and retrieved glasses. She filled two as Joe finished up. When he was done, she handed him a glass. Since all the chairs were now stacked in the living room and she had used her couch for the breakable items she had moved from the kitchen counters, they sat on the floor using the cabinets as backrests.

"I like the wallpaper you found."

"Do you?"

"It looks like something you would choose. Very . . . floral."

She chuckled and knew the compliment was sincere but also knew it was way outside something Joe would normally comment on. He was trying. It was not a busy pattern, the design was subtle, but it was an improvement over white walls. She planned to use it to set off the area around the table from the rest of the kitchen. She had a matching border to go above the cabinets as well. "Since the house is overflowing with flowers right now, I thought the pattern would fit right in."

"I've noticed all the flowers."

"And here I thought you were never going to mention them," she teased.

"Charles has good taste, in flowers as well as his choice of lady to shower them on."

"I hear a compliment in there somewhere."

"Probably. I'm glad you didn't say we had to keep our dating quiet. If he keeps hovering, I'll have to shoo him off you one of these days."

She laughed at that image. "He's just a friend, Joe. You've got nothing to worry about on that front. Besides, I like Ryan. I don't want you shooing them away."

Joe sighed and reached over for her right hand. "Then how about a ring — right here? I can give you my Annapolis graduation ring. Just like when we were back in high school."

"I couldn't wear it when I was on duty for fear I would lose it, and I'm already wearing Nick's eagle medallion on a chain." She rested her glass against her jeans. "But it was nice of you to offer. How about a bracelet that says *She's Mine?*"

"Just remember that."

She sneezed at the stirred-up dust and wiped the back of her hand across her face, then abruptly sneezed again. Joe rescued her drink from her hand with a laugh as she dropped her head down and her hair swung forward as she tried to stop another one.

"Okay?"

She did her best to nod and wipe at her eyes only to blink like crazy when paint transferred and her eyes began to burn. Joe reached up to the counter and retrieved a clean rag. "Thanks." She dried her wet eyes and blinked away the rest of the stinging irritation. It was almost as bad as when she touched her eyes when there was salt on her fingers.

Joe set aside their drinks and took the rag from her hand. "Come here. You're wearing more paint than you got on the walls."

He tugged her closer. Her heart fluttered, and her hands came to rest firmly against his forearm. This was being close with no safety net — the equivalent of lighting a fuse — only he didn't seem to notice the way every one of her senses had just gone haywire. He calmly wiped at the white freckles on her nose, apparently unperturbed by the contact. She wanted to slide her hands through his hair and compel him to kiss her. The thought of their first kiss had been clouding her mind for days, and she wanted to experience it, wanted to know.

The corded muscles of his upper arm were firm. She wanted to wrap her hand around his arm and rub that muscle with her thumb, trace its definition. She swallowed and closed her eyes. She was going to look foolish doing so, but she had no choice but to pull away before he finished removing the paint. He was too observant to miss how she was reacting. She eased back an inch.

"Kelly."

She opened her eyes to find him watching her, and the intensity in his eyes made her quiver. He was absorbing her, his gaze so intense, no amusement now. She had known his eyes were blue, but as she looked into them, the rest of the world around her faded. There were only those blue eyes and the mystery of what he was thinking . . .

His hand slid under her hair and cradled the back of her neck. "Kelly —" he whispered her name as he lowered his head.

It was bliss. His mouth was warm and firm as it settled on hers. Her raging emotions settled, and then burst back to life again. It was a relief that the suspense was over and surprised delight at what she found.

Someone had taught Joe how to kiss. She came to rest firmly against his chest and the kiss deepened. He was holding back, but what he was letting her share was enough to make her wonder how she had endured without this. She felt who he was come across in his kiss. The power and the control. He was taking exquisite care of her even as he explored.

Her hand settled on his chest. All her senses were drinking him in. She could feel his heartbeat under her hand.

He ended the kiss with obvious reluctance. The hand cradling her neck slid over to her shoulder and then eased down her back. She buried her head against his shoulder, hiding, catching her breath.

The tension was gone. She wanted to laugh. She could feel her body relaxing now, starting with her toes and working up through her muscles — a deep relaxation that came from being totally absorbed with someone.

He was idly stroking his hand over her hair, repairing the damage he'd done.

"That could get addictive," she finally said.

His warm laugh set everything right again. "That is a very safe conclusion." He coiled a strand of her hair around his finger. "I'm going to dream about that kiss."

His hand tipped up her chin. He was smiling, and it was an intimate one she hadn't seen before, and certainly never directed toward her. "You taste like honey with just a little tartness, but I'm guessing that's the lemonade."

Feeling a comfortableness with him she didn't expect, she propped her elbow on his arm and considered him. "You were like . . . dark chocolate icing that you put on top of cupcakes. Rich. Not too sweet. Full of surprises. Who taught you to kiss?"

"Oh, now you want me to kiss and tell."

"Yep. You're good."

She swore he actually blushed.

He looked at her for a moment, then ever so slightly nodded. "The East Coast, a long time ago, before the stripes of command settled me down. I used to like to spend Friday nights on a date."

"I bet you broke a few hearts."

"Not intentionally." He pushed back the hair that had fallen across her forehead and smiled. "We've got paint drying on rollers and it's not going to get done on its own. We were supposed to be painting tonight, not getting permanently sidetracked."

"You're changing the subject."

"You bet I am."

She laughed and leaned over and retrieved her lemonade glass; the ice had melted and the drink was watered down. "Okay, we'll get back to work. If we must." Their first kiss had knocked any sense of proportion out of her. It had exceeded both her expectations and her dreams. She needed a few moments doing something safe.

She got to her feet. "What do you want to tackle next?"

Joe watched her for a few moments, then reluctantly got up and turned his attention to studying the ceiling. "Another coat should finish this. We'll need to move the refrigerator out."

Kelly nodded and moved to shift the drop cloth in front of it out of the way. The top of the refrigerator was dusty. She grimaced at that as she moved the newspaper spread over it aside. Reaching over, she pushed open the patio door a little wider to help with the smell of paint. Misha, relegated to the back patio, sat outside the screen and whimpered. "Sorry, girl, not while the paint is open."

Joe wrestled the appliance away from the wall. "You have quite a collection back here." He picked up items that had fallen between the refrigerator and the countertop. Notes, to-do lists, coupons, and a snapshot of Nick from years ago.

"I don't think it's been moved in a few years."

Joe put aside what he had found for her to glance through later. "Can you still get around?" The kitchen was small, and with the two of them working with the refrigerator pulled out, it was tight.

"Yes. I'm fine." She turned her attention to taking down the remaining light fixture about the sink.

"Joe, how do you get paint out of Misha's fur?"

He spun around, alarmed.

"Gotcha."

He sent her a look that made her laugh. "Misha and paint are a dangerous combination."

"I remember the stories from when you painted the boat." The light fixture came loose. "Yuck." She shook out dead bugs from the globe of the light fixture into the trash can. "Next time you get to do light fixtures."

"Everything is small and dead."

"Exactly."

"Tell your men to back off. There is no reason to be watching Kelly." Charles told the general, trying to control his anger. He'd spotted the men when he left the beach.

"The next few days are critical. You need to keep your focus," the general replied. "You should not be worrying about a woman when there are higher priorities on your plate."

"And I'm telling you to back off. You would be wise to listen."

"Make a threat like that and I'll just have to remove the problem from the scene. Would you be paying closer attention to my shipment if she disappeared? If your son disappeared?"

A day ago the threat would have stung, but the stakes were climbing and there was no time for emotion. "Your weapon would never arrive," Charles replied coolly. If he was going to get them out of this situation safely, he had to have some maneuvering room, and pushing those guys back in their coverage was crucial. He should have just arranged an accident for the men following him. He still might have to. "Tell your men to stay out of sight. Even my son has mentioned seeing them watching." His point had been made. Charles hung up the phone.

Kelly arched her back to loosen her muscles. She was sitting on the floor finishing the last of the patio door trim. Out of paint in her small can, she turned to pour more. She froze. "Joe, Misha is inside," she said softly in warning.

Joe, finishing the trim along the ceiling, didn't bother to look around. "I'm not falling for that one again."

Kelly didn't dare laugh.

Misha had come in and lay down beside her water dish to watch them work and was lying on the newspaper. And right beside her was the lid of the open paint can. So far she had white paint under her chin, and, from what Kelly could remember of the newspaper, also on her belly.

If Misha got up to come this way, not only would she come right through the worst of the paint, but she'd also hit the open box of wallpaper paste powder. All it would take for her to move was a glimmer of encouragement. Her tail was already wagging as she hoped for an invitation. Kelly averted her eyes to try to discourage Misha from coming over. "Joe, she is three feet behind you, just hoping for one of us to play with her. She brought her chew bone with her and has it resting on her front paws."

His paintbrush stopped moving. "You're serious. How did she get in?"

"The garage? The doorknob doesn't latch well, and when I went out for more tape, I must not have flipped the deadbolt. More important, how do we get her cleaned up without leaving paint footprints across the carpet?"

"Let her come this way; then I'll pick her up."

"Are you sure?"

"Got a better idea?" He set down his paintbrush, came off the ladder, and slowly turned. "Hi, girl. Come here."

It was all the encouragement Misha needed. She managed to get paint on her feet, belly, tail, and muzzle. Joe securely got a hold of her and a lot of the paint transferred to him.

"We might as well give her a bath." Kelly stifled a laugh as he tried to hold the squirming dog. "We've got to do something pretty major to clean her up."

Joe looked from his dog to her. "This isn't cute." His look — she couldn't contain her laughter and it bubbled from her. What she would give for a camera right now. He braced himself and picked Misha up.

She hurried down the hall to the bathroom to get the shower curtain and the bathroom rugs out of the way, then moved aside so Joe could set Misha down in the tub. Misha was quivering and whimpering — she hated getting a bath.

"Let me do this, Joe, if you wouldn't mind tackling the path of disaster she left?" Joe looked at his dog, then glanced back at her. "She's all yours."

Kissing Kelly could most certainly get addictive. Joe tried to shake off the bemused state of mind that had him crossing the kitchen twice to do the same task. He was cleaning up while Kelly dealt with his dog.

She kissed like a dream. She was a little out of practice, and that reality only made it more intoxicating. He had not wanted to let that first kiss end.

He rubbed the heels of his hands over

his face. Second date, and she could make him crazy without trying. So much for the vague idea that he could take this slow and give her plenty of time to figure out what she really wanted. He was beginning to figure out exactly what he wanted. It was definitely Kelly and something very permanent. He just had to figure out how to make it work.

They were in the shallow waters. The fact they had been friends for years was helping with two issues: the comparisons with Nick and her uneasy acceptance of the fact he was on active duty status, but deeper waters were ahead. Kelly was going to want children.

Providing leadership on that question was going to be an interesting challenge of honoring her dream while also doing what was best for them both. God was going to have to figure this one out and let him know what was right because it didn't look like there was a simple solution. Joe loved children. But he was not going to be an absentee father. A child deserved to have a father around. And a SEAL on active duty traveled on average 180 days a year. Last year, faced with special circumstances, he had been deployed for 232 days. That was tough on a wife, but for a young child —

Joe wasn't ready to rush into that situation. But asking Kelly to wait several years was not exactly the right answer either . . .

He pushed aside the problem for the moment. It was going to take time to figure out. And prayer. He turned his concentration to finishing the kitchen. He had to give Misha credit for smarts; she had managed to get inside and make a real mess. He closed paint cans, cleaned brushes, folded the drop cloth, took out the trash, and put back light fixtures and outlet covers. They would have to deal with wallpaper another night.

When he was done he pulled out a chair at the table and sat down. He could hear a hair dryer from the bathroom. Misha was getting the full treatment tonight.

After a few minutes the dryer shut off and the bathroom door opened. Misha came racing down the hall, thrilled to be free again. She came skidding to a halt beside him. Joe caught her to him. Kelly had done a good job; Misha's coat gleamed and she smelled like baby shampoo.

"She's as good as new. No more paint."

Joe glanced up and had to smile. "You look like you've been in a battle." There was soap drying on Kelly's shirt and her hair had dropped down from the clips she had used to keep it back. She looked cute when she was a mess.

"It was, but I won." She ruffled Misha's fur. "It was worth it." She glanced around the kitchen. "Hey, it looks almost normal."

She sounded so surprised that he laughed. "We'll do the wallpaper tomorrow night?"

"Please." She pulled out a chair and spun it around. "I really appreciate this."

"I enjoyed it."

"Sure you did. I suckered you into working on your evening off."

"Better to spend the time with you than watching some baseball game on TV," he countered.

"Liar."

"The kiss was adequate compensation."

She blushed, just a little. "The wallpaper will be a challenge. The walls aren't straight."

He quirked an eyebrow at her for ducking his comment but let it pass. "I remember Nick once threatened to raise one corner of the house. I'll figure it out." He was reluctant to end the evening, but if he stayed much longer . . . Things were already getting out of control; to stay would just insure they ended up over their heads. "I'd better get this dog home before she gets herself into any more mischief."

"Probably wise."

Kelly walked with him to the patio door. A hug right now would be a match to dry tinder. He put three feet of distance between them and tried to ignore the awkwardness that was present. "G'night, Kelly."

"Good night, Joe. I'll see you on the beach in the morning."

"Early."

"I'll be awake long before you get here."

She wouldn't understand if he said he sincerely hoped she overslept. The anticipation of seeing tussled hair and sleepy eyes was going to keep him company tonight. "Tomorrow." He called his dog and wisely went home.

Joe's pager went off at 0200. He saw the number and immediately picked up the phone. He called the duty officer to report he was on his way in and eleven minutes later pulled into the parking lot at NAB. This place felt different tonight, no longer peaceful but rather gearing up for action.

He headed to the administration building, passing staff officers moving through the halls. Joe nodded to the security officer controlling access to the senior staff wing and passed the communications officer for the day shift. They were calling back the full complement of staff. His boss waved him into the conference room.

"Sir."

There were four officers present, two of his counterparts from other platoons and a civilian Joe had never met before. The maps on the long table were of the South China Sea.

"We've got another shipment," his boss said simply. "Raider's back, and he's traveling with this one."

Twenty-one

★ ★ ★

Joe stopped breathing for a moment before his eyes narrowed, the intensity burning. His confidence spiked. Raider was back. He had been prepping for this day for three years. "What do you have?"

"Mr. Harnley, fill him in."

Accustomed to Lincoln's brusque tone, Joe wasn't surprised when the civilian jumped a bit and fumbled the folder in his hand. Joe had seen a lot of folders like it over the years. The top-secret stamp was nothing new, nor was the code word clearance stamped boldly on the front. Defense Intelligence Agency? Central Intelligence Agency? National Security Agency? The guy had the look of someone from the analyst side of the house, not the operations side.

"We don't have much. Our contact in Hong Kong just got this information out to us. A boat will be leaving Hong Kong with a destination of Maytiko Island, southwest of Taiwan. The island has a decent harbor, an overgrown airstrip, and has been deserted since World War II. The device is nuclear, but we don't have specifications. It's apparently being flown from there on to Taiwan."

If the shipment got through, it would create a conflagration in the China–Taiwan relationship. China would never tolerate Taiwan having a nuke. "When is it moving?" Joe asked.

"The plane arrives at dawn, Monday the twenty-second, island time."

Joe scanned the maps. With the date line and time zones, that meant Sunday morning — four days from now. He nodded. They had worked with worse. "Who's the buyer?"

"We picked up a fragment of a conversation on an encrypted Taiwan military channel," Mr. Harnley replied. Joe raised an eyebrow at that. A rogue in their military — how high up, how well organized? He accepted the piece of paper he was handed, surprised at being given raw data.

[Subject 1] Your device has been
    found.
[Subject 2] How soon can it be
    delivered?

[Subject 1] Eight days.
[Subject 2] No sooner?
[Subject 1] Patience. There is more
  paperwork with this one.

"That's all we got of the conversation. The transmission date, the reference to eight days, it matches this shipment information."

"So the plane landing on Maytiko Island may well be from the Taiwan military."

"Yes."

It was going to be touchy. Trying to intercept the device in Hong Kong was out — it was now Chinese soil. Tracking the plane into Taiwan and taking it there on the runway would be difficult — they didn't know who the buyer was or whom they could trust. That left an intercept on open water or the island. "Lincoln said Raider was traveling with this shipment."

Mr. Harnley nodded. "That's all the contact knew — that the man you call Raider was personally delivering this device. We don't know if that means he is on the boat leaving Hong Kong, flying in on another plane to meet up with the shipment, or coming in on the same plane taking the device to Taiwan."

"Why break his pattern on this one? He's

always remained far from the actual shipments."

"He's been in hiding for the last three years; his buyers may be a little jittery to work with him. Or possibly it's the same buyer as three years ago, only this time they want a personal guarantee the shipment gets made."

It was still a troubling departure from everything Joe knew about the man. And he wanted Raider to be there, meaning his evaluation of the risks was far from impartial. If the intelligence was good . . . "Is there any way to get confirmation of this data?"

"We're trying. We've got nothing so far."

Joe glanced at his boss. "Platoons Echo and Foxtrot are in the area. Can they shift to intercept?"

"They've already got their hands full. We'll have to deploy resources from here," Lincoln replied. "Joe, I want you to work up a plan to take the shipment at Maytiko Island. Grant, you've got stopping the boat in international waters. Larry, you get the nasty one — assume we have to snatch it off a runway in Taiwan. I need plans by 1800 hours. Wake up your men, gentlemen."

Joe felt the adrenaline, the focus, could

taste the anticipation. He wanted this mission, was confident by 1800 hours his platoon would not only have a workable plan to present, but that it would be the best option.

Four days was enough. They could use today to plan, tomorrow to train, then pack and deploy on Friday. It would be an eleven- to thirteen-hour flight, depending on the jet stream, to get them into the area.

"Bear, stick around a minute," Lincoln said.

Not liking the implications of that terse directive, Joe waited for his boss to finish talking to one of the officers as the other platoon leaders left with copies of the maps. He followed his boss back into his private office and accepted the seat he was waved to.

"The fact that this is Raider — is this going to be so personal I should put another platoon in your place?" His boss had always been blunt.

"No, sir." He practically growled the words. It would be personal, but it would only sharpen his men's focus, not detract from it. It had sharpened his.

His boss had a way of looking through a man to his soul. He eventually nodded.

"That's what I wanted to hear."

"Sir, the informant in Hong Kong — a lot can change in three years. How trustworthy is this data? It goes against everything we know about how Raider operates."

"The fact he is supposedly traveling with the shipment bothers me too, but a more interesting question — how is Raider still able to work through Hong Kong now that it's under Chinese control?"

"Someone is being paid to look the other way."

His boss nodded. "Probably."

"What if China knows about the shipment and is still letting it proceed out of Hong Kong?" Joe asked. "Could this shipment be a Chinese attempt to create a provocation within Taiwan?"

"If the shipment succeeds, China has an excuse to act militarily before the device can be deployed. If it fails, it still splits Taiwan's military more sharply between those trying to force independence and the government's position. China wins either way," Lincoln said. "We want Raider, Bear, but we have to stop that device."

Joe thought about the implications of that as he walked down to see the duty officer to have his men paged. The profile on

Raider showed he stole for money not ideology. But stepping into the China–Taiwan quicksand? It was a political escalation from his point of view. A change in his approach, or did the conflict simply create the best market price? So much misery was created because of this one man's greed. Were they going to lose another SEAL trying to stop this shipment?

Nick.

The grief was back like a wave. He had never been able to tell Kelly the truth. It was one thing to hide the truth of what had happened from Kelly when he was her friend, another to bear that burden now that they were dating. She knew he accepted responsibility for what happened, for Nick's death. But that wasn't the same as her knowing how he died. She didn't know Joe's shoulder injury had come first. That Nick died saving him.

He needed Raider to be there, needed to be able to put the past to rest. If he couldn't tell her, at least he could stop the man responsible. He owed that to Nick. And to Kelly.

"What do we know about the ship?" Boomer asked.

Joe sat back and listened as his men

worked the problem. Dawn was still only a tinge of pink in the sky, and the fifteen men had already transformed the conference room they had appropriated for planning the mission into a small war room with relief maps of Maytiko Island showing elevations, satellite images of the old runway, weather data, logistical data. Questions were being asked and answered all around the room, and out of them was coming a powerful, workable plan.

Cougar had been prowling for data about the boat. "It's old, Russian in design, a discarded supply ship once used to service their patrol boats. It was converted to civilian use five years ago and now flies a Norwegian flag. Its deep cargo wells are divided into four holds by metal plating; the holds are only accessible from above. The ship's central hub is two levels: Above deck is the control room, and below deck it's divided down the center into staterooms on one side, engine room on the other. We can assume the device will be in one of the four holds. The normal crew complement is five."

"There is no access from the engine room or staterooms into the holds?" Wolf asked.

Cougar shook his head.

"So if we control the deck, we control the device," Wolf concluded.

"Exactly."

"They have to lift it out by crane?"

Cougar nodded. "There are two, built into the ship structure."

"That's the ship. What about the island?" Boomer asked. "Where's the best terrain for a strike?"

"The satellite pictures show we've got a lot of thick tree cover," Wolf mentioned.

"The forest has grown up to touch the old runway. We can take the shipment at the pier, in transit to the runway, or once it is loaded on the plane. As long as we keep that plane on the ground, the terrain means we can make our move anywhere we desire."

"The plane is scheduled to arrive at sunrise," Boomer cautioned. No SEAL wanted a mission run in the daylight if they had the option of attacking in the dead of night.

Wolf pulled over the latest images of the runway. "I doubt they'll try to bring the plane in early, while it's still dark. This runway shows signs of having been cleaned up, but I don't think they can risk the plane being damaged by trying to arrive at night."

"If they have been working on the runway, we have to assume they have a number of people already on the island, that we will be dealing with more than the men on the boat," Cougar pointed out.

"Then we should let Grant's platoon hit the boat while it's still in international waters. That would limit the number of tangos to the men on the boat," Boomer decided.

Joe stepped in. "Having Grant take the boat at sea best limits the opportunity for casualties, but it would also alert Raider very early on that we know his plans, and we'd miss the first opportunity we've ever had to grab him. The guys in Washington may want to take a little more risk if there is a chance we can get Raider too," Bear assessed. "For now, let's assume Grant's platoon is not available. Assume there are an unknown number of men on the island we'll have to deal with. What's the best option? The harbor?"

David, the platoon's radioman, pulled over the nautical map. "One option: We wait here, outside the coral reef, for the ship to enter the harbor. We come in behind it and hit while they are moving to unload the device. That leaves all the threat in front of us."

"But it could be a nasty threat," Wolf assessed. "Until the time the plane arrives, the harbor will be the center of attention for any men on the island. There is not a lot of cover to work with; it's a wide beach, and they would have the advantage of being above us from these rocks."

Boomer ran his finger across the map. "What if we wait? Let them unload the device? Because of the terrain they would have to bring it to the airfield along this route. We ambush them here at this choke point, take the device, and return back up this ridgeline and call in a helo to take us out. We would have the cliffs at our backs, and they would have to come uphill toward us to attack."

"How do we get there unseen?" Wolf asked.

"I doubt they would be expecting a threat to come from the cliffs. We climb, set up on the trail, and we wait," Boomer replied.

Joe watched the reaction, saw the nods around the room. It was an interesting option even if it meant a steep rock climb in the dark to pull it off. It could get them in position without being detected.

"We don't know for certain what time the boat will arrive. What if they haven't moved the device from the boat and it's getting close to dawn?" Cougar asked.

Boomer studied the terrain. "We could sweep down this way and hit the boat, then secure the device there. We put men into the water to come up behind the boat; others use the boathouse for cover and cut off anyone on the beach from coming back up the pier. We can control the decks and seal anyone on the boat below deck; we can control the pier and cut off anyone on-shore. If possible, we then steal their own boat and take the device out that way. If they have sabotaged the engine room or the control room, we get the device out over the side for pickup."

"Complex," Bear remarked. "Tell me about the runway options."

"Assume the plane lands shortly after dawn. We could disable the plane, seize the device, and retreat back to the far end of the runway, then call in a helicopter to extract us," Wolf offered.

"We could wait until the device is aboard and then steal the plane," Cougar added. There was laughter at that option, but it was actually worth considering.

Joe looked around the room. "Let's switch objectives for a moment. Raider. How do we identify and capture him?"

"The problem is getting him to the island," Boomer replied. "If we move on the device before the plane lands, assuming he's coming in by air, the odds are he would get a message alerting him to our attack, and the plane would divert."

"The plane has a point of no return when the fuel on board requires it to land," Wolf noted. "If it can't turn around because of bingo fuel, they may have no choice but to come onto the island."

"If they plan their flight right, it could probably divert to the Philippines," David suggested.

"We could track it and intercept it on the runway there if it diverts," Wolf replied.

Boomer got up to pace. "What about this? We take it in two stages. Stage one is the urgent reality — the device. The best odds are if we hit in the dark, when the device is in transit from the harbor to the runway. It gives us the element of surprise and better terrain. So we do that first and get the device out of the equation. Stage two: Raider. He is either on the boat or coming in by plane. We bottle him up. We remove the urgency on us to engage. We sabotage the boat, and we disable the plane when it lands. If they divert the plane, we follow and take the plane when it lands.

We then have a group of men stuck on an island with no way off and no particular urgency on our side. A Naval exercise run out of Okinawa could effectively blockade the island until they were all arrested."

Joe liked the idea. He wanted a mission that had a reasonable expectation of no casualties. Bottling Raider up would be as effective as a capture. They had enough general details of a plan to begin working specifics. "Let's split into three groups. Boomer, work up snatching the device in transit from the harbor to the runway. Cougar, look at the fallback of taking the device at the boat if for some reason they don't start to move it and we are running short of time. Wolf, assume we can get the device out of there — what's the cleanest way to bottle them up? Everyone pay special attention to asset logistics. Equipment has to already be in Okinawa or able to fly out with us Friday."

The men moved into teams to begin working on the details. Joe watched Cougar and Wolf tackle the assignments he had given them. He was confident the plans they developed would be comprehensive. They were the two who would someday take his and Boomer's places in leading the platoon. It would be in good hands.

Someday. Joe wasn't ready to give up his role yet. While the teams worked on the details, he turned his attention to the device they would be transporting. There would have to be more than a few precautions taken. Raider had shown his preference for compartmentalizing information. The odds were good this device was going to get moved around by men who had no idea what they were moving. He had to plan to deal with a device in less than stable condition.

Joe glanced at his watch and knew something was wrong. 0710.

He closed his eyes.

He had just blown off Kelly.

Twenty-two

★ ★ ★

Kelly waited until almost 7 a.m. before accepting Joe was not going to meet her or call. He had forgotten they were going to run this morning. The disappointment was sharp. It would have been better if he had joined her and growled at her for the pace she set during the run than to realize he had forgotten her.

She was tempted to pull off her tennis shoes and go back inside and not run, but it would be an admission that she was running because of him. She had done that yesterday, had made a total fool of herself by trying to run his pace and not embarrass him.

Kelly locked the door, pushed her keys into her pocket, and set out for the sand. She needed to run for herself. The workout would give her time to think.

No one had ever said dating would be easy. She had forgotten how hard it was on the ego to wonder what someone else thought of you.

Had she ever been this uncertain about Nick?

She was surprised to realize she never really had been. Nick had chosen her, and she had known early on that she was his girl. When they had gotten engaged then married, it was wonderful and exactly what she expected.

She was out of step with Joe. She was the one who had said I love you. Trying to impress him was a good way to get her heart broken. She let her shoes kick up sand and forgot about the fact she was running while she thought about Joe.

She loved him. More now than ever before. She had let herself begin to dream about a future with him, let herself believe it might come true. Maybe tonight after they did the wallpaper, she could talk him into driving up to Sunset Cliffs to watch the moon rise. That would be so romantic.

Did Joe know Nick had proposed there? It probably wasn't fair to duplicate locations she had gone to with Nick, but having lived all her life in Coronado, it was impossible to avoid them. At least she had that in her favor; Joe wasn't jealous of Nick.

He *was* jealous of Charles.

If she knew she would be dating Joe, she would have returned the dress. But what was done was done. While she wished the situation with Charles had not evolved as it had, it was providing an interesting contrast. Charles was what she could've had if she wasn't choosing Joe, and she found herself relieved that she wasn't even interested in pursuing the civilian choice. She wanted Joe, even with the risk of being involved with a military man again.

She was still thinking about the kiss from last night. She hadn't had her toes curl like that since the last time Nick had come home from deployment. She hadn't imagined it would be like this dating Joe. They had been friends for so long she had never thought that dating would so easily ignite a firestorm inside. He wasn't just Joe anymore. He was her Joe, and being close to him was becoming the center of what she was thinking.

She would fix him dinner tonight. It was easy not to think about the fact she was running as she planned the evening.

As the evening wore on, Kelly told herself to stop watching the phone, but it did no good.

"I'm sorry, Kelly. I didn't mean to blow you off without a phone call this morning." Joe's voice on the answering machine earlier

that day had sounded frustrated. *"I won't be able to run with you tomorrow either. Listen, I'll call you back later, after you get home from work. I hate talking to a machine."*

He hated talking to a machine; she hated *listening* to a machine.

The day was practically over and Joe still hadn't called back. Kelly couldn't get herself occupied, and trying to work on her finances simply added to her frustration. She got up and paced. Joe was like Nick, not one to forget to call. That meant Joe was occupied and couldn't call.

The roses were beginning to droop just a bit. She took twenty minutes to refill water in all the flower vases. Ryan and Lynnette had stopped by earlier to say hi on their way to a movie, Lynnette's mom playing chauffeur for the early part of the evening. Kelly wondered how their evening was going, wondered what Charles had thought of Lynnette.

She finally chose to retreat outside and curl up on a lounge chair.

The phone rang inside and she jumped up, afraid she would miss the call. It had to be Joe.

"Hello?"

"Kelly, it's Charles."

She felt disappointment and was

ashamed at her reaction. "Hi, Charles."

"Are you busy?"

She glanced at the kitchen table. "Working on my finances." She wove the telephone cord around her finger. "Thanks for interrupting."

"I'm just up the street at North Island. I've got a few minutes to kill before I pick up Ryan and Lynnette from the movie. Can I invite myself over for coffee?"

She was surprised and she hesitated. She owed it to Joe to remove any question of where her loyalties were. "Sure. Need directions?"

"I'll find you. Thanks, Kelly."

She started the coffee. Charles arrived, and she was surprised to see him in jeans and a casual shirt. His hair was wet.

"Racquetball tonight. I got trounced," he explained as he stepped inside.

"Intentionally?"

"No, tonight I was trying my best. The admiral will sign off on a hundred million dollar joint project with Her Majesty's Navy regardless; I shouldn't be disappointed with losing a simple game."

"But you are."

"I like to win."

"I wondered how you'd spend your evening with Ryan off on a date," she said.

"They stopped by here."

"Did they? I like Lynnette. And yes, I noticed you were playing matchmaker for my son. Thanks."

"I wasn't sure you would react that way."

"Give me some credit. You've got good taste." He followed her into the kitchen. "You've been painting."

"Joe and I started last night. Wallpaper on that wall is next."

"It looks really nice."

"Thanks. You should have seen Joe's dog — she managed to sneak inside the house and get paint all over her coat. We ended up throwing her in the bath."

"I'm sure she loved that."

"Hated every moment." Kelly got down the mugs. "How do you take it?"

"Black is fine."

She nodded and brought him a mug.

The phone rang. "Excuse me a minute." She took it in the living room. "Hello?"

"I'm sorry, Kelly. I didn't mean to call this late."

"Joe." She was relieved to hear his voice. In the back of her mind had been the small suspicion that he was hurt. "I knew you would call if you could. Are you home?"

"Not for another hour or so. I just wanted to say again I'm sorry for not touching base this morning."

"It's okay," she said slowly, knowing what all those pieces meant. She felt cold. It was as close as Joe would ever come to telling her something was being planned. "Do you need me to get Misha?"

"Not at the moment."

That was a temporary reprieve. He wasn't getting on a plane tonight. Of course that could change with a beeper message, and often did. "If that changes, let me know."

"Thanks, Kelly. Can I call you back later? It would be late, and I don't want to wake you up —"

"Call," Kelly cut in. "It doesn't matter what time it is."

She heard the relief in his voice. "Thanks. I want to talk to you." She heard muffled voices in the background. "I've got to go."

"I'll be expecting your call." She hung up slowly, feeling the distance. She had always felt it with Nick when a mission was happening, that his attention was only partially on her even when they were having a conversation. With Joe — being involved with a platoon leader was going to have its own unique stresses.

"Everything okay?" Charles had stepped into the living room.

"Fine," she replied, needing to dismiss the call. It wasn't something she could talk about. She gestured to the roses. "You have brightened my whole house."

"That was the intention."

He had carried in her coffee mug. "Ryan mentioned a wilderness camping trip being planned for next week. He sounded interested."

She settled on the couch. "The church youth group is going. It's a true wilderness camping trip: white-water rafting, rock climbing, sleeping in tents, even twenty-four hours with a compass and a map to get back to base. It can be a life-changing experience. They leave Tuesday morning and get back Saturday night. The sign-up sheet had nine teens and four adults going."

"I can see why Ryan was intrigued. It's not too late to add him?"

"As long as they know this week, they'll be able to plan food accordingly."

"I'll ask him when he gets home and give you a call." Charles set aside his coffee, then paused when he saw a picture. "Is that your husband?"

Kelly glanced over. "Yes, that's Nick."

Charles studied the picture and frowned. "How long ago was he killed?"

"Three years."

"How did he die?"

"A training accident."

Charles glanced over at her, apparently recognizing the evasion. "I'm sorry, Kelly. SEALs and their secrets can be difficult."

She neither confirmed nor denied his assumption. "Your wife — what happened?"

"Cancer. You would have liked her. She grew up in the church, was a bright light to everyone she met. I've never understood why God let her die when she was so young."

"I've asked the same question about Nick."

"Have you figured out anything?"

Kelly shook her head. "What about you?"

"God stole my wife from me — that was the answer for so long. Now —" he purposely lightened his tone — "the grief fades. I've stopped trying to answer the question. There isn't an answer."

She heard the honesty in his words, his emotion. *"God stole my wife from me . . ."* She was surprised at how close it was to her own reaction of *God doesn't care about me anymore.* How long had it taken Charles to come back from that anger, to once again put together a relationship with God? He was in the church, was bringing his son up in it; the hurt must have passed.

It took three years for you to face the problem, yet you stayed in the church and covered up the anger that entire time. Would you really know if Charles had faced his anger?

Kelly wanted to ask him, to find out if the decision point she had reached was also a common occurrence for those who lost someone close, but she didn't feel like she should ask such a probing question, not when he was already being much more open than she would have expected for a new friend. Maybe when she had known him a while longer she would ask him about it.

Charles stayed for twenty minutes, then went to pick up Ryan and Lynnette from the movie. Kelly watched at the door as he pulled out of the drive; then she turned off the front porch light.

She carried their coffee cups into the kitchen. Charles was looking for a friend, might even be interested in something more under different circumstances. But he had accepted a friendship, and that was what she was willing to offer. He was the one who had casually mentioned Joe a couple times, accepting that he was Kelly's choice.

Who did she know who would be a good match for Charles? She could play matchmaker for the son. Why not the father too?

She put away the bills. She would go ahead and curl up in bed, let herself catch a nap rather than wait up for Joe to call. It was the routine she wanted to establish. She didn't want him worrying about what time he called her; anytime night or day was fine, whenever he had a moment free. And she didn't want to get in the habit of waiting up for him and adding to his sense of pressure when he couldn't call.

Kelly shut off the lights behind her and went to get ready for bed. She brushed out her hair, set down her hairbrush on the dresser, stopped, and frowned. Nick's medallion was not in its usual spot. She always left it beside her jewelry box on the few days she didn't wear it. Closing her eyes, she tried to remember where she had put it.

Of course. She had taken it off yesterday before she began to paint and had put it down on the counter next to the stove. Turning the lights back on, she went to get it.

Nick's eagle medallion was not where she remembered placing it. It was not on any of the kitchen counters, under papers, or under the mail. It wasn't in any of the kitchen drawers it might have fallen into.

Had she even seen it today?

Ryan and Lynnette had been over — she had gotten out a plate for the cookies. Then Charles had come over — she'd fixed coffee. She had been around the kitchen tonight fixing dinner. She simply couldn't remember having seen the medallion.

Kelly started searching the kitchen again, moving deliberately around the room, looking everywhere. It wasn't here. If she had moved it, if Joe had moved it, where would it be? She checked the basket where mail landed, checked the table in the hall, looked again around her jewelry box and across her dresser. Back again in the living room, she pulled up cushions, looked under furniture. It had to have dropped somewhere. Tears started to fall when she had looked everywhere she could think of.

Lord, I've lost Nick's eagle. I have to find it. It's the most precious possession I have next to my wedding ring.

At eleven, she finally did what she never did — she paged Joe.

"Kelly, what's wrong? I got your page."

She heard the sharp concern. She had bothered him at work, in the middle of something important. She regretted that and yet felt like she was losing Nick all over again and couldn't help but ask. "Do you remember seeing Nick's medallion last night when you picked up the kitchen?"

He was slow to answer. "I think so — yes, it was on the counter by the stove. I remember setting my drink down on the newspaper, and the medallion beneath it almost made my glass tip over."

"I can't find it. I've looked everywhere."

He was quiet for several moments. "I don't remember moving it," his voice had dropped, recognizing what she would be feeling.

"Could it have fallen between the counter and the stove? We found things by the refrigerator."

"It's possible. You're sure you haven't seen it today?"

"No."

"The trash."

She whirled, feeling her stomach sink. It was empty, and she had taken the barrels out that morning for the weekly pickup. She closed her eyes. "It's already gone."

"I'll come help you look as soon as I can get away," Joe promised. "It has to still be in the house somewhere."

"You're sure? I know you're busy."

"I'll be there."

She put down the phone and started

looking again, forcing aside the emotion. It was here somewhere. She went back to her bedroom knowing she would have put it away there. Her search gave the same result. Nothing. She went back to the kitchen again, frustrated. She pulled out kitchen drawers, nearly pulling them off their tracks, churning through the contents.

Forty minutes had passed and she was thinking about trying to move the refrigerator out when the doorbell rang.

"Joe." It helped just seeing him.

"We'll find it, Kelly." It was close to midnight. Joe should be home. Instead, he was here because she needed him. "Thank you."

His hand on her shoulder gave a reassuring squeeze. "Show me where you last saw it."

Half an hour later, Kelly sank onto one the kitchen chairs. Joe had done everything from pulling out the stove and refrigerator to looking through all the painting supplies he had packed away while she gave Misha a bath. They had both looked everywhere they could think of. The medallion was simply gone.

"I'm sorry, Kelly."

She looked at him, weary. "If it went out

319

with the trash, it's gone for good. If it's been misplaced in this house, I'll find it." She forced herself not to dump her pain on him. "Thanks for coming by to help." What went unsaid was what they both feared. Joe had accidentally thrown away Nick's medallion.

He squeezed her folded hands. "I wish I could hand it to you."

"I'll keep looking. You need to go. You've had a long day. I know I interrupted you." She wanted to ask what was happening but knew he couldn't answer, and it would only add to her worry.

"I do need to get into work early," he said with great reluctance.

If he had a mission coming, the last thing she needed was him tired and distracted. She forced herself to smile. "Go home, Joe. I'll find it." She hugged him at the door and held on tight. "Take care of yourself."

He rubbed her back. "I would give anything to change this."

"I know you would. It's okay."

She watched him leave. Even though she was in the process of putting Nick into the past, she didn't want a treasured memento wrenched away from her like this. It stung. It really stung.

Twenty-three

★ ★ ★

"Wolf, let's do it again," Joe ordered. The men throughout the mock-up of the ship, pier, and boathouse stepped out to regroup. Wolf's group had the device; Cougar's group had control of the ship deck; Boomer and the men with him had control of the pier. They were working on the most complex situation they might have to deal with — taking the device from the boat. Lincoln had approved their plans last night. Joe had been right: The need to capture Raider was considered worth the higher risk of taking the device on the island and not on the open sea.

The three groups were beginning to move in sync. They were rehearsing to determine lines of fire, progression of movement, pausing at each step along the way to refine the plan. If they had to go to this fallback plan and take the device at the boat, they would have to be fast. They had to take control of the device, steal the ship, and get it moving out to sea before the men on the beach could coordinate an attack and overrun them.

They had taken over a corner of the SEAL training grounds on San Clemente Island for the work. The mock-up wasn't pretty, but it was a good replica of the boat deck, from the railings they had to climb over to the position of the cranes. Special attention had been paid inside the boat's central hub so they could practice going through the doors and controlling the corridors. Doing the assault at night, on a rocking boat, possibly in the rain — all the past training and missions would be used to translate this exercise into the actual mission. They didn't have a plan yet that satisfied Joe. Time was an enemy once the first shot was fired.

This afternoon they would shift gears and work on their primary assault plan — taking the device while it was in transit from the boat to the runway. They would have the helicopter pilot who was deploying with them available then.

The helicopter. That was one part of these plans that Joe found the most troubling. If something went seriously wrong, they were still depending on air to get the device out. They had to look at that part of the operation again. Still, control of the device was key. They had even figured out a backup plan to sabotage the device — rip out the circuit board guts, take the plutonium core, and get out.

They would hopefully not need the fallback plans. If everything went right, this mission would go like clockwork. They would climb the cliffs, grab the device as it was in transit, and extract it by helicopter. Then two SEALs would slip down to the harbor and sabotage the boat, while three of them — Cougar, Boomer, and himself — would wait at the runway, sabotage the plane, and try to grab Raider.

Joe let himself relax; the men would be ready. They would be running through these mission work-ups again tonight, swimming in from the sea.

Where was Nick's medallion? The urgent question came back center stage without being prompted.

He felt like he had betrayed a friend. There was no way to replace it. He was afraid he had accidentally thrown it away; he simply couldn't remember. He had folded up the paint-splattered newspapers, washed paintbrushes, carried the drop cloth outside, but he was still convinced the medallion had been there on the counter when he was done. He didn't have the time to help Kelly look today, couldn't even tell her why he wasn't helping her. If it had been lost in the trash — it had been an accident, but he was responsible.

When he told her tomorrow he was deploying . . . he didn't want to see the suppressed fear he knew would be there.

He understood it, felt for her, but he needed her to get past it for his sake. He didn't need her fear rubbing off on him, didn't need to carry the burden of knowing she was back home, afraid. He could only imagine her reaction if she knew he was going to confront the man who had ultimately been responsible for Nick's death.

Boomer got in his face and quietly hissed, "Get your act together."

It was like getting slapped by your mom for not listening. It stung. The men were ready, waiting on him, and his attention was not on the task at hand. His jaw tightened and he strode over to the stern of the ship mock-up where his men would climb over the side. They were taking their cues from him on how to treat the fact this was Raider they were going after, and he was letting them down. Big time. "Cougar, call the mark."

He wasn't designed to handle a relationship, not if he couldn't keep it out of his work life. Wherever he had gotten the impression Kelly and Nick had an easy time of it, he had been seriously mistaken. If he didn't forget about Kelly while he was doing his job, the next time his attention strayed off focus he might be dead. Worse, someone else would be.

I'm sorry, Kelly. I love you, but from now on, you don't exist while I am at work.

The small-group Bible study at Christi's that night was crowded. They were studying Luke, going through a chapter a week. *God is my refuge* . . . when I feel hurt. Kelly tried it out for size as she parked and walked up the drive, deciding it would do for tonight. The medallion was gone. Joe hadn't called today, but she knew he was getting ready for something big and probably didn't have a moment free to call. It didn't take Christi telling her Boomer was likewise busy to know that.

Kelly settled into a chair beside the couch and found herself drawn into a conversation with Ashley and Linda. They had both married in the last year, one to a banker and the other to a schoolteacher. She wished she could have the kinds of ups and downs they did. Trying to adapt to Joe was going to be harder than she had anticipated.

"Joe isn't coming?" Ashley asked.

The habit of saying nothing was too ingrained to break. "I'm not sure what his schedule is tonight."

She found herself assigned to be the scribe as the evening began and Christi asked, "Are there any prayer requests tonight?"

Tell them about what you decided in the water. Ask for their help with your quest.

She couldn't do it. The prompt burned in her heart, and yet she didn't have the courage to tell these friends what she had talked to Mrs. Michaels about on Sunday. "I have one. I've lost Nick's eagle medallion." It was a compromise, but it at least admitted she was hurting.

"Kelly, where? What happened?" Liz looked hurt she hadn't mentioned it already.

"Joe and I were painting the kitchen Tuesday night. I remember taking off the medallion and putting it on the counter before I went to get the paint supplies. Neither one of us remembers moving it, and we've looked everywhere. There's a possibility when we were folding up the newspapers and drop cloth that it somehow got into the trash. We don't know." The fact it had been Joe who folded

the newspapers, picked up the kitchen —
She didn't say it, for she knew how miserable he felt about it.

Christi and Liz both volunteered to help her look for it. It was a balm to Kelly's heart to know they understood how she felt.

The evening eventually drew to a close with coffee and ice cream for those interested. Kelly got up to help Christi and was stopped several times by friends as she crossed the room. She finally faced one last question, and it wasn't as friendly as it sounded.

"I heard Joe took you to the Grill. Did you have a nice time?"

Kelly didn't know how to answer Veronica. She knew Veronica had been trying to get Joe's attention for months, had talked openly about wanting Joe to take her out. The question had an edge to it. "I found the restaurant beautiful and the food very good." Not talking about Joe seemed like the best thing she could do under the circumstances. Veronica wanted to ask another question, but Kelly managed to sidestep her with a smile.

I can tell I'm dating again. The comments have started. She didn't want to admit how good it felt, despite the comments.

The wind chimes were stirring. Joe sat on the one chair that fit on the balcony off his second floor bedroom and listened to them, listened to the sea as well. The mission was ready. The men were ready. Tomorrow they would deploy.

As the man responsible for the outcome, Joe felt the burden.

Raider.

Lord, I'm ready to kill, but it's for the wrong reasons, and that bothers me more than the fact it might be necessary. He killed my best friend. This is personal. I can't let this opportunity for justice pass by. I can't afford to fail. Help me get my distance back, please.

He did his best to avoid getting drawn into one of Kelly's theological questions beginning with the word *why*. Tonight she would be surprised at the turmoil the ethics of war were creating in his soul.

In a morally just cause, he could kill. The Old Testament was full of warriors whom God called his own: Gideon, Joshua. David was a man of war, and he was called a man after God's own heart. Jesus Himself was called a man of war. At the end of the world, Jesus was pictured returning on a white horse carrying a sword and making war. There was a place for laws and justice, for men who waged war to uphold duty, honor, and country. Joe believed that. Nick had believed that and had died defending it. They protected the world from men like Raider.

If he had to make a split-second decision between trying to take Raider alive or killing him, would he fire?

All the factors that went into the decision played out in his mind: the risk to his own men to try to capture Raider, the absolute necessity that he be stopped, Joe's personal need to see justice done.

God, when the time comes, help me make the right decision.

He prayed for the success of the mission.

He prayed for the safety of his men.

He prayed that God would help Kelly while she waited.

Joe finally felt at peace with what was coming.

Kelly. He let himself think about her for the first time that day. In one respect dating was proving to be a harder transition than he had thought. He was thinking about her at times when he couldn't afford to be distracted.

He was ashamed of the irritation he had felt earlier knowing she would likely be afraid when he deployed. It was selfish of him to ask her not to worry simply because he didn't want to carry that burden of feeling responsible. He knew it wasn't easy for her to date another active duty SEAL. Waiting was going to be hard on her, and if something happened — he didn't want her to be hurt again as she had after Nick's death.

He wanted to call her but it was late.

He went back into his bedroom, found a pad of paper and pen, and took a seat on the bed, leaning back against the headboard. He picked up his Bible. He was a new Christian compared to Kelly, and he didn't know what to write, what to say to her if something should happen. But he had to leave her something. If she read this letter, he had to find the right words.

Lord, what words of comfort will she need?

He began the letter, *Kelly, I love you.*

An hour later, he folded the two pages, closed his Bible, and carried both of them downstairs. He left the letter in his Bible on the dining room table and beside it placed an item he prized the way Nick had his eagle. It was a grizzly bear, carved decades before, in burnished wood. His father had given it to him.

As soon as she opened the patio door

Friday evening, she knew he was leaving. Joe was in woodland green cammies, not the desert cammies he normally wore at NAB.

"Kelly, I'm going to be gone for a while."

Simple words. They put her facing her biggest fear less than a week after she agreed to start dating him. Saying yes had been so easy and dealing with the reality of this was so hard. The emotions went through her in an instant.

I love you, Joe. I wish I were free to say that again.

Her hand tightened on the door handle behind her. She absorbed every nuance of his face, memorizing it, knowing she had once before said good-bye to a man she loved and never had the opportunity to see him again. "I'll get Misha for you and your mail," she said softly, not willing to put her emotions into words. She didn't want Joe thinking about her. She wanted — needed — him to have the distance, that mission face, as Nick had called it, the focus on what he had to do.

"I would appreciate it."

He ran his hand gently down her cheek and she instinctively pressed against it. "I'm going to miss you."

"I'll miss you too."

"Can I kiss you good-bye?"

She wasn't expecting the soft question. A good-bye kiss wasn't like just another kiss. It carried so many resonating memories with the past and that last kiss she had shared with Nick. If something went wrong, it might be her last kiss with Joe, and she didn't want to have bittersweet sadness tinge the memory. Did he understand any of that? Was that why he had asked first? Her nod was so imperceptible she wondered if her muscles had frozen.

His fingers tipped her chin up as he lowered his head. He tasted like coffee, his lips firm, smooth, and warm against hers. The kiss was soft and gentle, definitely checked. The passion she could feel enveloping her was being tempered and held back. He didn't want this one to get out of control, and she both regretted and was grateful for that fact. Stirring passion would eat them both alive with frustration. He raised his head with reluctance, caressing her lips with his thumb. "Kissing you is . . . very nice."

"Come back, so we can do it again," she whispered.

"You give a man a good reason to hurry back." He eased back a step. "I've got to go."

"Be careful, Joe."

"Kelly —" His confidence came through

in the direct gaze — "trust me."

He left as suddenly as he had come.

The C-130 was loaded with equipment. Joe moved among the men, doing one final check before the plane went wheels up. It was coming up on 2000 hours, Friday night. It would be a long, noisy, rough flight. Thirteen hours in the plane without the benefit of an in-flight movie or even windows to enjoy the view. The C-130 carrying the other two platoons had lifted off earlier in the day.

With "good-to-go" replies among all the men, Joe moved back to his seat beside his second-in-command.

Boomer had brought along a thick thriller. Joe slipped on his headphones to add Mozart to the noise and opened a commentary he had brought along. Heavy reading, but it required his undivided attention, and that was the best way to handle an upcoming mission — to stop thinking about it.

Kelly, I'll be back soon. Then you and I need to talk. I already miss you.

The plane moved with a heavy reluctance, used an incredible amount of runway, and lifted into the sky bound for the Far East.

Twenty-four

★ ★ ★

Joe's home was quiet, still. Misha met her at
the door, whined softly, and Kelly knew the
animal sensed the fact Joe was gone. Misha
looked sad, had no spring to her step. Rather
than pass her by to do the chores that
needed to be done, Kelly sat down beside
her and wrapped her arm around the dog. "I
know you miss him, Misha. I do too."

She rubbed the golden coat. "I love him.
He leaves and the energy in my day disap-
pears." She tipped up the dog's face.
"Would you like to come keep me company while he's away?"

The question earned her a wet nose in
the face. Kelly buried her face in Misha's
warm fur. She loved this dog. And while
Joe was gone, Misha would be more comfortable at her home.

Kelly forced herself to get to her feet.
There were chores to do since Joe would
be gone an indefinite period of time. Kelly
found plastic bags and tackled his refriger-

ator to remove anything that would spoil in the next few days. A glance showed he had already carried out his trash. There were two messages on his answering machine, and she wrote down a dentist appointment reminder and a note that the library book he had requested had come in.

The house felt empty without Joe. She could stay for a while, surrounded by his things, but it would only make the loneliness more acute. If Joe didn't come home — the idea made her feel slightly sick. She knew he was good at his job, was well prepared, had good men with him. She had been here before. But the last time God hadn't protected Nick, and the returning fear tasted sour.

Lord, don't let me doubt Your love and Your power. Not when I'm working my way back to a relationship with You. Please keep Joe safe.

She needed to assume the best and not the worst. Kelly forced a smile as she looked down at Joe's dog. "Come on, Misha. Let's go home."

Kelly woke Saturday morning, glanced sleepily at the clock, and came abruptly awake. The team would have arrived wherever it was going by now. The blankets had bunched to one side of the bed, and the pillows had dropped between the bed and the side table. She tugged them back up.

She had faced many mornings like this when Nick was alive, the first day she woke up with him somewhere unknown. And despite how new and more intense this one felt, she had gone through days like this with Joe during the last three years. Waiting was hard. But it was not knowing that was the hardest. Until a page came from the dispatcher saying he was back or to say an e-mail had arrived for her, she was on her own.

Lord, I promised I would bring You my troubles. Here I am, facing the tough challenge I knew would come when I considered Joe instead of a civilian. Keep the men safe. Give them success. And bring them home.

Misha had curled up on the blanket Kelly had put down beside the bed. She reached over the edge of the bed and rubbed her head. The dog yawned. Kelly leaned her chin on her hand. "You look comfortable." It was nice having Misha here. She could take her down to the beach later and throw a Frisbee around — it would kill a few hours of her day. She knew how long the days would stretch, and filling the hours was a major part of the challenge.

Boomer was gone for an indefinite period of time as well. Maybe Christi would like to have a ladies' night. If Liz was free, they could make an evening of it. In the old days when Nick had left on deployments, the platoon wives had a standing arrangement to get together that first night. They would come and go from either Kelly's or Christi's home, coordinating baby-sitting and errands so that no one in the group would be left in the lurch by the sudden deployment. Kelly missed that part of the routine. She reached for the phone and found that Liz was delighted with the idea. She had no more than hung up the phone when Christi called her with the same idea.

With the evening plans settled, Kelly rolled out of bed, weighing options as she dressed for how to spend the day. When Joe got home, she'd like to have a special evening planned. She wanted to let him know she was glad to see him without overdoing it. She'd have to dig out her cookbooks and see if anything looked exceptional.

She read the San Diego paper from cover to cover as she ate breakfast, looking for any clue as to where Joe might have gone, what problem he might have been

337

sent to solve. The full platoon had been deployed. Sixteen SEALs was a pretty heavy arsenal being brought to bear on a problem. There was nothing in the newspaper she found that helped her figure out what was going on.

She could get the wallpapering done today. It would be a distraction and she needed that. Joe would've helped her with it when he got back, but she suddenly decided it would be better if she did it herself, showed she was capable of staying busy and productive while he was away. It wasn't like she had pressing items on her schedule today; she could take her time. Kelly went to get the wallpaper and supplies feeling much more cheerful about the day.

Kelly studied the wallpaper pattern to figure out how to match one strip with the next. She had bought a complex design. This wasn't going to be easy. She was glad now she had bought an extra roll. She set out the supplies, prepared the paste, and got to work.

"Slide over Misha."

The dog was curious about this project and was right under her heels. Misha moved aside and Kelly carried the first strip over and stepped up on the stool. Kelly sealed and smoothed the top half of the strip, then carefully slipped free the portion she had folded. She stepped off the stool and smoothed her rag over the full strip down to the floor.

She worked steadily for three hours to complete the main wall. Doing the border above the soffits — maybe she had best wait for Joe. Working over her head would be difficult enough, and the strip had to be held out to the side when it was put up.

The doorbell rang.

Liz was early. She had said she would pick Kelly up at 4 p.m. or thereabouts. Kelly wiped at the paste drying on her hands as she walked through the house.

"Charles, hi." She was surprised to see him.

She held open the door, but he declined with a smile. "Ryan wants to take Lynnette fishing, so we were just running over to pick her up. I've got the wilderness camp registration forms completed if you wouldn't mind taking them with you to church tomorrow."

Kelly accepted the envelope with a nod. "I'd be glad to."

Misha tried to push past her and go outside, but Kelly blocked her path with a practiced foot. "Stay inside, Misha."

Charles looked down at the animal. "Joe's dog?"

Kelly was surprised by the question; Misha had been with them when they went sailing, and Charles had seen the dog before. "Yes. She's managed to get wallpaper paste on her coat this time," she remarked ruefully.

Charles leaned down and held out his hand to greet the dog. "I mistakenly thought she was yours. Going to have her for a while?"

"I'm baby-sitting for a few days." His question made her uneasy but she wasn't sure why.

"Ryan wants a dog just like her."

Kelly relaxed at the easy comment. "She's good company, a good breed for kids."

"I'll remember that." He nodded to the envelope. "Thanks for this, Kelly. Ryan is looking forward to going."

"I'm sure he'll have a great time. Good luck fishing today."

Charles looked amused. "We'll see if Ryan realizes that part of being a good date is baiting Lynnette's hooks and cleaning her fish."

"He's smitten. I think he'll catch on."

She watched Charles leave, waved at Ryan in the car, then looked down at Misha. "Paint, now paste. Are you just attracted to stuff that is bad for you? This is going to be your second bath in a week."

Laughter with friends — it was the best antidote for worry there could be. Kelly knew Bear had left for a live op, not a training mission. Christi knew the same about Boomer, but they both found a way to accept it and leave it aside for a few hours. Liz had brought the movies and she had chosen several that kept them in stitches.

Liz's son Christopher stirred, taking Kelly's attention momentarily from the movie. The infant had been asleep in her lap for the last half hour. She watched his eyes to see if he was waking up or simply changing positions. Liz didn't ask her to baby-sit nearly enough. Kelly didn't mind the bottles and the diapers and the constant attention required to know how he was doing. She loved babies. Liked older kids too, especially teens like Ryan and Lynnette, but babies were special.

Liz was a mom, Christi about to become one, and Kelly wanted to join the club. It wasn't just that they were leaving her behind, sharing an experience she could only observe. It was the fact that being a mom had been her dream. To get married again, have a family, would restore what had been robbed from her three years ago. She stroked her hand over Christopher's soft hair. Joe would make a wonderful dad.

The movie credits began to scroll by.

"Kelly, you never did tell us. How was the first week seeing Joe?" Liz asked.

Kelly didn't know what to tell her friends. She didn't know how to put perspective on the week — too much had happened. She finally shrugged. "It was fine."

"Just fine? Come on, you can do better than that," Christi teased. "Has he kissed you yet?"

She blushed.

"He has," Liz exclaimed.

Their happiness for her was real. "A couple times."

"You make our lives look boring. First there was Charles; then you and Joe startle us all by dating. I can't wait for your encore," Christi remarked.

Kelly knew her friends were happy for her, and that helped cushion the fact she went home after the girls' night lonely for Joe, wishing he was around instead of somewhere overseas.

The house was quiet and Misha trailing her around didn't begin to make up for the fact Joe was somewhere beyond the reach of a late-night phone call.

She eventually curled up in bed thinking about him. On impulse she pulled open her nightstand drawer and got out her stationery.

Joe, tonight finds you far away from me, and I am thinking about you.

If you were here, I would tell you about my attempt at wallpapering the kitchen (it looks good if I do say so myself), about Misha getting her second bath in a week, and finally about my evening visiting with Liz and Christi, who, of course, asked about you.

It is hard to convey in that small prism of events how life is so different now with you a part of it. When I was wallpapering, I was thinking about your home and mine and what our home might look like someday. And when I was talking with Liz and Christi, I was thinking it would be nice if we could make friends with a new couple at church who would know us as a couple, not as individuals — I want us to have common friends.

I wish we could walk the beach together tonight.

Kelly sighed and stopped writing, finally putting away the letter, knowing already she would not give it to him. It was unfair of her to bring those kinds of topics up when they had just begun to date.

I love you, Joe. That's what I want to tell you tonight. And it's the one thing I have to wait to say.

2230 hours. The platoon moved into the surf zone of Maytiko Island and crept from the water like crabs under the watchful eyes of the two men who had gone ashore thirty minutes before. The platoon regrouped at the base of the cliff.

It was going to be a hard climb.

Joe scanned the sheer cliff with his night vision goggles. The wind and saltwater of the sea had pounded this cliff for decades. Anything loose had been swept away long ago. They would have to take it in stages, using multiple anchor points and setting men at each stage to lift the heavy equipment up the cliff's face. Joe nodded. They had made harder climbs.

From the equipment brought ashore came the long black ropes. The swim gear was hidden. Weapons slung over their backs, equipment vests snugged tight, the first men began to climb.

Rock climbing was a matter of patience, balance, and focus. It was an indication of how ready his men were that the first stage of the mission was accomplished with barely more than a dozen words over the mikes as information passed between them during the climb. The first men to the top fanned out to secure a perimeter in the tropical foliage, the equipment and explosives were brought to the top, and then the rest of the men finished the climb.

Joe knelt at the top of the cliff and made a careful sweep of the area to ensure they had left nothing to mark their arrival. Good. The most vulnerable part of the mission was past. He moved into the tropical cover.

"Nothing disturbing the wildlife," Cougar whispered over the mike.

Bear nodded. Nothing disturbing the wildlife meant there was no one in the area making noise — either no one was there, they were asleep, or they were quietly watching. It was the last option Bear worried about — the SEALs hadn't disturbed the wildlife either.

"Lead us through slow and steady." He glanced down the platoon of men. "Remember — no one shoot the wildlife. A pair of glowing eyes is not necessarily a threat." He received back a series of clicks through his earpiece as men signaled their acknowledgment. Joe thought a few of the clicks sounded like men silently chuckling. The night vision goggles gave an unfair advantage in a fight at night, sometimes too much of one. Two years ago, another platoon had had a mission come apart because someone reacted too quickly to the wildlife creeping in to check out who was walking silently by.

They had the benefit of a nearly moonless night and cloud cover. From this point, they had to cover just under half a mile through the tropical forest to reach the choke point in the path from the harbor to the airstrip.

The platoon moved out in single file through the heavy foliage, moving downhill as they went. Joe had to listen hard to hear even the movement of the man behind him. The cliffs had been the right entry point; no one on the island would expect the threat to come from above. For the first time since they had entered the water, Joe felt himself relax. They were on the island. They wouldn't be leaving until the mission was done.

If it went perfectly, they would have Raider. Joe's three-year prayer for justice would finally be answered.

"Cougar, any change?" Bear whispered.
Bear had sent Cougar and a sniper to watch the beach. "Still five men walking around on the boat, three inside the boat-house, and six on the beach. They still haven't opened any of the four hold covers, and the men are settling in for the night. A couple of them on the beach have stretched out on blankets. No one appears to be in a hurry to do anything. And the only men present have come from off the boat."
Why had no one come down to meet the boat when it arrived? Where were the men who were expected to already be on the is-land? Why weren't they moving the device toward the runway for the pickup at dawn?
The questions with no answers were frustrating. This mission wasn't happening as planned. The platoon was settled into position ready to hit the shipment in transit, but the other side wasn't cooper-ating. "Apparently they aren't going to move the device off the boat until the plane arrives, and we are out of time. We're going to plan Bravo — we're hitting the boat."

The men appeared from the earth and the tree line, movement revealing their shapes and breaking their camouflaged cover. It was a silent transition.

"Stay ready," Bear cautioned. "I'm not entirely convinced the only men we'll have to deal with came in on that boat."

They set off for the harbor moving silently.

Fourteen men on the boat, maybe as many as twenty, as some may not have come up to the deck. Where were the other men who should be on this island? Someone had cleared up that runway recently. They could not have all left. There should've been at least someone left with a radio to wave off the boat should anything unforeseen happen. Someone should have come down to meet the boat when it arrived.

They joined Cougar. The boat, the pier, the boathouse, the men on the beach — all were less than four hundred yards away around the rocks. Joe moved onto the boulders and inched his way forward on his belly to join the sniper and see the situation for himself. The mock-up of the boat had been much better than expected. He scanned for any changes that would have to be made to the assault plan and found only minor ones. For minutes he studied the men. *No sentries?* Considering what they were smuggling, it was hard to believe they didn't take a precaution of having one man looking for trouble, even if they didn't expect any.

They think they are the only people on the island.

They've been at sea at least the last fourteen hours.

It's the middle of the night.

They want to wait until the plane arrives to move the device.

Joe still found it troubling. What was he missing? He scanned the tree line at the back of the beach. "All the men down there came off the boat?" he asked Cougar again.

"Yes."

Joe eventually nodded, then moved back to the men.

0422, Joe silently signaled, setting the time of the attack. They acknowledged and moved into the water.

It was a slow, deep swim to get into position.

At 0422, six of his men appeared silently from the water to surge up the sides of the boat, seven appeared on the dock. Joe was the second man to the dock, positioned at the corner of the boathouse for line of sight down the pier to the beach. He counted the seconds by his heartbeats as he watched in his peripheral vision his men sweep through an assault they had planned and rehearsed until it was instinctive.

They got eight seconds before the first return fire came. Joe was startled at the ferocity of it. Fourteen men, most of them already down, could not hit the dock like this.

"It's coming from the tree line!"

Joe looked around and saw men rushing across the sand toward the pier. Too many men.

Joe dropped his forehead against his arm as another bunch of wood splinters tore from the dock. With forty to forty-five men coming at them to try and overwhelm the pier, they couldn't knock them down fast enough. Even the two snipers left on the rocks were finding it a challenge to slow them down. And somewhere in that tree line were two machine-gun nests determined not to give them a chance to try.

Boomer raced around the boathouse to the front line they had established, bringing more ammo, spreading the clips between them as he ran. He dropped in beside Bear. "I'm glad we brought more ammo than even I thought we would need."

"The boat?" They would lose the pier soon if they couldn't stop the machine-gun nests.

"Cougar's almost got it."

Shredded corrugated steel from the boathouse came raining down around them.

Boomer leaned against him as he began pulling grenades from his vest pockets. "Do you get the feeling we were expected?"

Twenty-five

⋆ ⋆ ⋆

Kelly felt uneasy with no reason for it. When she would have normally stopped to chat, she by-passed friends in the church lobby to instead slip into the sanctuary, seeking the quietness there. She found an empty bench and took a seat, set aside her purse and her Bible. The sanctuary was cool. The organist had begun to play a background chorus to prepare for the service.

She gripped the back of the bench before her and rested her chin on her hands. Something was wrong.

Lord, I don't know why I am feeling such a burden to pray for Joe right this minute, but You understand the need if there is one. Give them courage. Keep them focused. Keep them safe.

God is my refuge . . . Please be their refuge at this moment.

The burden lifted but not the sense of disquiet. It was like this when the team was deployed, the lack of news foretelling the worst. She repeated her prayer and the unease finally changed to calm trust. Even if they didn't need the prayer, she did. She needed to let go of the worry. God was her refuge too. What if Joe didn't come home? She let herself consider her worst fear. Would she change what she had decided regarding Joe?

No. If anything she would waffle less and instead show more courage. She had let Joe see her afraid and worried. Instead of going to God and being honest — *I'm worried; help me know You are my refuge* — she had asked Joe to accept her worry as normal, to carry that pressure she put on him.

Her eyes were beginning to open. She hadn't escaped those three years of wandering unharmed — she was back but the restoration was still going on. Three years of going her own way had taught her to worry about life. Right now her worry was a good benchmark for how far from "God is my refuge" she had come. If something happened . . . She had survived before; she would survive again.

She owed Joe an apology.

God, I'm sorry. When Joe gets back, I want a chance to talk with him. I owe him that.

★ ★ ★

"We control the boat. We'll cover while you come across!" Cougar yelled.

Under this kind of fire the time for the four of them still on the far side of the boathouse to get safely around the dock, climb over the boat railing onto the open deck, and get into the central hub was too great. The device had to come first. "Get that boat out of the harbor!" Bear hollered into the mike. "Swing around the reef to meet up with the snipers. We'll take to the water and extract at point Charlie."

"Roger, L-T!"

The engine was throttled hard, surging the diesel boat away from the dock and back to sea under SEAL control, most of the platoon already aboard.

Joe could see history repeating itself — the platoon taking the device to safety, he and a few others holding off the men who were trying to stop that from happening. It was his and Nick's final actions all over again. He had just repeated the exact same decision. It was the right move. Logic told him that.

There was a time to be illogical.

He wasn't repeating history, logical move or not. "Boomer, Franklin, Wolf, scrub point Charlie. We are heading to point Alpha on top of that ridge. We're going out by air."

It was a decade of sand, sweat, and trust that turned the three of them toward the new objective he gave without even a question. He chose going into the gunfire in front of them instead of back into the safety of the sea behind them.

"I'm going to slide into that crevice at the end of the pier and drop a few grenade rounds on those gunners; then we're going to move like lightning up to the right around those rocks and come around above them. Franklin, Wolf, get ready to run. Boomer, stay put until I fire; then keep them off my back until I can reach that first step. As soon as I'm there, go for the rocks."

He had to fire uphill into the gunners. The only way to get shells into those nests was to be in the tip of the V. Get to the end of the pier, and he could literally send them each a fastball down their throats. Six steps. He saw each one in his mind; six steps exposed before he could dive off the pier to the sand and be back under cover. He could do it in five. Kelly would appreciate him doing it in five. *I love you, Kelly, but you're still a distraction.* "I'm going now!" Joe rushed forward, low, exposed to the gunfire as he lost the shelter of the boathouse and sprinted along the pier.

The symphony of covering fire drowned out the fire coming toward him. Joe knew it was providence not skill that slammed him into the sand, bruised but unhurt. "Get ready to run!" He racked the tube, took a breath, and pivoted up. "Run!" The blast cratered the right machine-gun nest even as his words echoed through the earpiece.

He was rolling to put two down the throat of the left machine-gun nest even as he heard Boomer yell, "Bear, roll right! We've got company behind us!"

Joe rolled right and got slammed on the back with debris as the end of the pier took a mortar round. Where had they gotten mortars?

He got a glimpse and felt the world twist. Another boat. It must have been anchored in some cove, camouflaged and waiting. It was small, maneuverable — it couldn't stop another boat, but it could spray everything in its path with gunfire.

Had he and the other SEALs gone to the water to exit the cove, the four of them would be dead. The realization was like a fist in the gut. *Lord, thank You!*

If that boat pulled to the pier and unloaded the men on board, they might still end up dead. It wasn't the odds; it was the ammo. His vest was way too light for another firefight.

"Boomer, get off that dock!" Boomer saw the threat, should have broken for the rocks moments ago. Joe could see him flat on his belly on the dock, lying between the boathouse and the empty diesel barrels.

"I'm right behind you," Boomer yelled back.

Wolf and Franklin had the lines of retreat protected, could hold back the men on the beach from moving forward but could do nothing about the boat now reversing engines to close with the dock. Joe dashed from his exposed position to the first boulder where he could give Boomer some cover, then heard his friend close to a step behind him. "Keep going! It's going to be hot!"

The dock and pier shredded behind them in a powerful explosion, a wall of fire and heat reaching out to envelop the boat, and moments later the mortars on board lit all at once. "One problem solved," Boomer remarked as they ran.

They disappeared into the rocks along the ridge with Franklin and Wolf, leaving confusion behind.

Moving fast, ready to fire, they cut north. Franklin was calling in the extraction helicopter as Joe and Boomer split directions to circle and ensure the landing zone stayed clear.

The race up the ridge had his heart pounding in his ears, the gunfire absorbing his hearing. Only as they slowed at the extraction site did the static-meshed voices distinguish themselves into discernible words. "Say again, Cougar. Say again."

"The holds are empty! There never was a device on board!"

Joe got the news the mission had failed as fire erupted from the beach below tracing up into the sky toward the incoming helicopter.

He had almost gotten his men killed. For no device, no Raider, he had almost gotten his men killed. Joe leaned his head back against the cold metal of the helicopter gunner's rack and closed his eyes, let it sink in that they were safely racing out to sea, and felt the nausea slowly fade. His body was taking pleasure in reminding him what he had just endured. The adrenaline had been so powerful it had nearly stopped his heart.

"You'll get a medal for taking that kind of risk."

Joe didn't bother to open his eyes as Boomer moved from manning the side gun to the floor beside him. "Getting a medal for failing is hardly something I want on my record."

"You saved my life, not to mention that of Franklin and Wolf by getting us off that pier when you did. If they don't award you the Navy Cross, I will."

"I notice you blew apart the pier about two seconds away from perfect," Bear replied.

"It seemed like a prudent thing to do under the circumstances."

Joe smiled. "We hadn't even thought about that one when we what-if'd what we might need to do."

"That dock was a classic World War II Seabee design, and goodness knows my dad built enough of them. Use a small charge to blow a hole in the center pillar, then put a brick of C-4 inside the pillar's hollow core and blow that. It's literally like blowing a chimney apart. You just have to know the metal beam is hollow. If dad built it, he wanted to know how I would blow it up. It was one of his favorite Saturday afternoon questions. I've done that dock before, just never live."

"We owe the medal to your dad."

"I just wish I could tell him the story."

They shared a smile. They both knew this mission would never declassify in their lifetimes. Joe returned to the problem. "We should have known the mission was blown."

"How?"

"None of the tangos came out to meet the boat. I knew it was wrong. We should have taken the time to send a reconnaissance team around behind the beach." They had considered it during the mission work-up but in the end ruled it out. It took time, split their men, and ran a high risk of an accidental encounter destroying the surprise factor.

"We would have still gone to get the device."

"The other side not only knew we were coming, but they also knew it far enough in advance to set up that reception committee. I want to know where the leak is," Bear replied grimly.

"Do you think Raider deliberately fed us false information through that contact in Hong Kong?"

"After that mission three years ago, he had to know that he had a mole somewhere in his organization or we would never have been able to intercept that K-42. Why not feed out bad information at a critical time and watch us react? It's what I would do." They were getting outmaneuvered by the man and it was time for it to stop. Past time.

"He picked the wrong platoon to mess with."

Bear nodded. Somebody had just punched a grizzly bear, and he could feel the fury. "I want this man, Boomer."

Twenty-six

★ ★ ★

Their flight arrived back on Naval Air Station North Island at 1400 hours, Monday. Joe stood at the base of the ramp as the men filed off the cargo plane in pairs, carrying their personal gear. He watched faces, reading eyes, seeing what he had expected in the grim expressions. Getting shot at when it was a setup did not sit well with any of them. This was a mission they would debrief in earnest. They would learn from it.

He saw Boomer and Christi meet each other, Boomer's long hug that did not let go. His friend had almost gotten himself killed taking those extra few seconds to blow up the dock. Boomer had done it without hesitation to protect the rest of the team, but it had been a decision that had ramifications. Boomer had come close to never seeing his wife again. Joe could feel that emotion across the tarmac and understood its depths. If he had been forced to face Christi and tell her Boomer was not coming home as he had once been forced to face Kelly — Joe knew it would have destroyed Christi.

The last of the men came down the ramp. Joe thanked the pilot who had expedited their return home. The supply crews came in to begin unloading the heavy equipment. Joe picked up his own gear.

Kelly waved to get his attention. Joe hesitated and then moved toward her. He could see she had been worried, had spent a hard weekend waiting, wondering. Her smile now was broad, full of relief. What would she think if she knew how close it had really been? If it had turned out differently, could she have handled a second time having someone tell her a SEAL in her life was dead?

He could hide behind the secrecy that was part of his profession and deny to himself just how close it had been; he could forget this mission. He wanted to do that for selfish reasons. He didn't want to have to deal with the implications. But he had to. He loved this lady.

"I'm so glad you're home."

Joe returned Kelly's hug but didn't let himself draw her close, didn't let himself do anything more than accept it and then step away. He wanted to wrap his arms around her waist, hug her tight, and kiss her breathless. He loved her so very much. *Lord, what have I done? It would destroy Kelly if she came to meet a return flight and I wasn't on it.* The real risk he was asking her to accept was suddenly clear. If something happened, it would destroy that smile. Raider had set him up once; there was no guarantee it wouldn't happen again. *What am I supposed to do?* The question was agonizing to answer, for the truth cut into the happiness he longed to have with her.

He saw some of the happiness in her expression turn to wariness. He brushed his fingers through her hair, forced himself to smile. "Thanks, Kelly. I'm going to be busy here until late tonight. Could you keep Misha for me another night?" He was shutting her out but didn't know how else to respond. He had to think this through, fast.

"Of course." She took a half step back. "Are you okay?"

"Not even a sprained ankle. Everyone on the team is fine." He wanted to add "it's been a very long plane ride" to give her an excuse for his behavior, this distance, but couldn't do it. It would be hiding behind a convenient excuse. "Call you later?"

"Sure." Her disappointment was obvious, but she covered it quickly. "Whenever you're free."

He nodded and reached down for his equipment bag, hating the situation. "Thanks."

Joe had been so distant.

Kelly stretched out on the couch, the house around her silent, the time passing slowly as she waited for his call. When she had hugged Joe she wanted to reach up and kiss him, to truly welcome him home. Seeing him had been such a relief, but then she had felt the distance. He was there with her, but not in spirit. His attention was still elsewhere. Had something happened? Something gone wrong? She wished she could ask.

Lord, I don't know what's wrong. I only know something is. I can feel it.

She hoped for the phone to ring. *Please let him call. We can talk and clear this up. The silence is disquieting.*

The dinner she had planned was slowly turning into something fit for Misha. At least she had left the steaks in the refrigerator and changed at the last minute to lasagna. The page had come, letting her know the men were on their way home. She had felt enormous relief, much larger than she had ever expected. Joe was back safe. She was going to hold onto that even as the situation roiled with uncertainty.

She forced herself not to call him. Maybe she had read the situation wrong. He wasn't Nick. He couldn't walk home from a mission and let someone else deal with its wrap-up. Joe had a different burden to bear after a mission; he was still working.

When he was done, he would turn his attention back to her; then she would find out if there really was anything wrong. She didn't like this delay, but she had to get used to it. Joe wasn't Nick. She couldn't expect the same response from him.

How was she supposed to respond when she saw him next? With Nick it had been simple: launch herself at him and trust him to catch her. Those welcome home hugs had been wonderful. Maybe by the next mission she would have figured out with Joe how this was supposed to work. She buried her head in a pillow at the idea of repeating this night.

"Lincoln, they knew we were coming. The cargo wasn't on board, so they got word while we were still some distance away. Someone tipped them off." Joe felt like tearing up the summary as he dropped it to the stack on the desk. His notes written during the return trip were extensive, but they didn't come close to figuring out how it had happened.

"We're looking into it, Bear. When your men have been debriefed, give them a few days liberty, but tell them to stay close. You are unofficially on short notice. Make sure they know that. I can't put you back into rotation until we get a handle on what happened, make sure the leak didn't come from our end."

Bear was surprised at that. "Sir?"

"We think Raider is manipulating what is happening from here. Echo and Foxtrot were sent chasing a ghost. Your platoon was set up. And in the middle of it we have Iris Wells turning up dead. Coincidences don't run in threes."

"You think a shipment got through." It became clear where Lincoln was heading, and it was something Joe had wondered about. The setup they had walked into had been elaborate.

"I do. I think all too soon we are going to be reacting to something in the world. This Taiwan–China–Hong Kong triangle didn't appear out of the blue. I want your men rested and ready to go — and on the assumption Raider does have a contact inside, it won't hurt if he thinks the platoon is standing down for a few days of R and R."

"Yes, sir."

"Have the equipment repacked and reloaded. We're going to put a C-130 on thirty-minute standby until I get a better feel for what's going on."

Joe nodded at the order, accepting the precaution as wise. He did hope they would get a second chance. He needed one. His men needed one.

"How are the men taking it?" Lincoln had the same perspective he did.

Joe smiled slightly at the question. "They don't like getting set up."

"Any enemies, Bear?"

"What?"

"You got shot; Nick was killed. Three years later it's your platoon that gets set up. Any reason to believe this is personal? Did you know Iris Wells, by any chance?"

Joe blinked at the question, at the reach back in time, and was startled to realize he had never connected them that way. The thought shook him that this might be personal. "I didn't know Iris other than by sight, to walk paperwork over. She was good at her job, didn't mind sorting out the red tape for us." His thoughts were racing. Iris. Nick. This setup of his men. Was there a link that ran through *him?*

He thought about his trips to personnel, trying to remember where Iris sat, who was around her. "Boomer has a cousin in the personnel department who sits somewhere near Iris. I took her out to the symphony once when Kelly was unavailable. But that's a reach." But he had known her. His men had twice faced danger attributed to Raider. If the man was able to follow their movements, manipulate them . . . the possibilities exploded in the back of his mind.

"Pass that on to the investigators. Pass on any glimmer of a connection between Iris and your platoon. Ask your men to do the same."

"Yes, sir." He'd start his own aggressive search for any such connection. He'd found Iris washed up on the shore and her death was now a critical unknown to solve. "Have they determined what happened? How she died?"

"There was heavy oil found in her lungs that she could have swallowed only if she had been pretty far out to sea when she went into the water. She had to have gone off a boat, been swimming for quite a while, then couldn't make it back to shore."

"There's still been no indication of what boat she was on?"

"Her car was found at a parking lot down at the harbor launch. No one has come forward indicating they saw her. They are checking every boat in the San Diego and Catalina areas that was out of its slip Sunday."

"A needle in a haystack."

Lincoln nodded. "They need a break. Desperately."

He should go get Misha. Joe thought about it but didn't move from where he sat at the dining room table. He didn't want to face Kelly yet, didn't want to look at her and have to deal with the fact he had let the man responsible for killing Nick get away. Tonight he wished he still drank. He sat at the dining room table pushing around the little carved bear with his finger, drinking a 7-Up that tasted stale and wishing another five hours had passed so he would have an excuse to go to bed. He would call Kelly tomorrow. When he figured out what he was going to say.

"Bear."

Joe went to the door, surprised to find his second-in-command here on the night he would've expected him to be solely focused on Christi. Joe pushed it open. "Come on in, Boomer."

"Got a minute?"

"Got a year. You want something?"

"Whatever you're drinking."

Joe scowled at the can. "You don't want it. This case must have cooked in a truck somewhere. Hold on; I'll be back with something passable for both of us."

He found two root beers and brought them back with glasses of ice, too tired to wonder why Boomer was here. With anyone else he would have covered his own comedown from the failed mission — Boomer understood it without putting it into words. Joe had led the mission; the mission had failed. The fact it had been a setup, the fact he had brought all his men out alive, didn't cover his fatigue of what might have happened.

"Joe, I'm getting out. I'm not going to re-sign when my tour is complete. My son needs a father, and this one was too close to seeing mortality for me to want to risk it again."

Boomer said it simple, straight, and Joe felt the numbness like he had when he had been shot. His friend was quitting. In place of words, there was only silence. Yesterday he would not have understood; today — he understood.

For Boomer to quit — he bled Navy. This was not a quick decision. He was a lifer, and for him to make this decision . . .

Joe didn't even try to talk him out of it. "The team will miss you. You're the best AOIC in the SEALs." Joe wouldn't have the team he did without Boomer's leadership through the years. Boomer had been close, not as close as Nick, but when he was gone — "I'm personally going to more than just miss you."

"I'll miss the action, Joe. When I'm in the middle of it, I love it. When I come home and look at Christi, my perspective changes."

"You're sure this is what you want to do?"

"It's time. I have Christi to think about, and soon a son. Some younger man is going to try to fill my shoes only to find out it isn't as easy as it looks."

"Very true." Joe sighed and studied the boots he had not yet taken off. "How are the men doing?"

"Blowing off stress like they usually do. Angry. Frustrated. I passed word along to their favorite hangouts if trouble brews to give you a call."

"I appreciate that."

"They want to find the person responsible for the foul-up and convey their disappointment in person. The men who knew Nick are taking it the hardest. They wanted Raider. It's personal."

Joe nodded. "Raider is the worst kind of enemy. The kind you can't seem to catch. He does make mistakes. He does bleed like everyone else. He isn't this perfect criminal who leaves no trail, but he's eluded us so many times . . . And this time he set us up."

"Almost got a lot of people killed," Boomer agreed. "He steals. That's the problem. He doesn't want glory, power, recognition. He simply steals for money."

"It can't be just for money, not after all these deals he's pulled off. If even half the deals attributed to him were his, he became self-sufficient for several lifetimes over many years ago. He doesn't need the money."

"Is it ego? An oversized ego that can never say enough is enough?"

"I think he's doing it just because he can," Joe replied. "And the hard thing to accept is that he may just get away with it for longer than we will be around to hunt him. He's going to be the prize that got away." Joe looked at his second-in-command and didn't say the obvious. Raider had just taken his second casualty. Boomer was leaving the SEALs. "What will you do when you get out?"

"There have been a few people asking if I would work construction demolition. I know how to take a building down — there's getting to be more demand for it all across California."

"If you quit, you will never have blown your safe."

Boomer smiled. "A child's dream, never to come true. But you have to admit, it was a nice one to hang onto."

"The guys are going to want to plan a send-off."

"I've been to those farewell wakes. No thanks. I'll tell them when it's official and do a small farewell."

Joe shook his head. "You can try. But it will never happen."

"Are you going to tell?"

"Christi will tell Kelly. Sorry, Boomer — as soon as Kelly knows, your party is a given. You'll just have to wade into the fray and survive it."

"Thanks a lot, Bear. Now that I'm feeling maudlin, I'd best get home to Christi and remember why I'm doing this.

I'll see you at the base in the morning."

Their handshake was firm. "Anytime you need someone to cover your back, I expect you to call."

"That's a given."

As Boomer walked down the steps and Joe closed the screen door, he felt a sense of void creeping in and longed to no longer be alone. He needed Kelly to turn to at this moment, someone who would understand what it meant for a platoon leader to lose his assistant officer in charge. Boomer was closer than family.

Remind me You are here in this quiet empty place, Lord.

He wanted to turn to Kelly, and she was the one person he could not turn to. In a week, he had managed to lose the freedom to turn to the one person he would have sought comfort from in the past. She didn't need to know the mission had almost been fatal.

Boomer was leaving the SEALs because he wanted to be around to raise his son. If Boomer didn't see how to make marriage, children, and the SEALs work, Joe knew the obstacles were larger than they appeared.

Joe couldn't leave the SEALs for Kelly. It wasn't in his makeup to walk away from the place he truly felt he belonged. And she wanted children. There were men in the SEALs with families, but there was an equal number, if not more, who had left the Teams when they got married or their marriages had come apart.

He couldn't hurt Kelly by misleading her. He would rather choose not to have children than put himself in the position Boomer was in — feeling like the best option he had was to quit. Joe knew he was in for the duration of his career.

To her credit Kelly had never asked him to change that. But he was back to what was reasonable to ask. She was dealing with the risk of marrying an active duty SEAL again. If he told her no children while he was on an active team, he would take away her dream, and there was no way he could do that to her.

He could let her go free. Let her find a civilian who could love her and give her a family.

The thought tore at him. He knew who was waiting in the wings.

Joe walked back into the dining room to retrieve his Bible, then remembered the letter. He drew out a chair at the table, sat down, and slowly reached over to extract the pages.

As he read the letter, he realized the words of comfort he had written for Kelly could now equally apply to him.

The Lord is good.
The Lord is merciful.
The Lord never changes.
Hold on to the character of God, Kelly. Why this happened, I do not know. But I stand in the presence of this God today. Allow me to tell you what I know as I see Him face-to-face: The Lord is good; the Lord is merciful; the Lord loves you.

He loves you even more than I do, and I love you deep in my heart, where I hold those things I treasure close. Remember me with laughter, Kelly, as you remember Nick. You honored us both with your open heart. Nick and I will be waiting to see your smile again soon. It will be a good reunion. Remember that.

Your best friend,
Joe

He realized as he was folding the letter that he was crying. He wiped the tears away feeling sadness deep in his soul.

Lord, I have to tell her I made a mistake

rather than say what's in this letter. I chose the wrong time to try and reach for a dream. To continue the course we're on, knowing what I would have to ask her to accept . . . I can't hurt her like that.

He felt the sadness press in. It was the right decision but not an easy one. He took the letter upstairs to his dresser and placed it in his keepsake box with his reminders of his parents.

Joe got the phone call at 2300 hours and was still up, having expected it. He got the keys to his Jeep and headed to Mick's Pub. At least no cop cars were in the parking lot. He made his way through the restaurant area and followed the sound of the commotion to the back bar. Joe wasn't surprised to find his men blowing off steam. He was surprised to find they had done their best to put a dent into the decor.

The sailors who had apparently made the mistake of saying the wrong thing were on the floor in a tangle of limbs. "Back off, Franklin." The man had his back to the door and didn't realize the fight was now over. Joe had already lost one man from his platoon because of this failed mission, he didn't need another ending up in the brig.

"L-T —"

He stopped the explanation with a look. "Cougar, help him out of here. The rest of you, go cool off."

Joe scanned the mess.

"Your men didn't start it, Bear."

He glanced at the owner, who stood at the end of the bar. "But it looks like they finished it." The ongoing beef between SEALs and regular Navy liked to flare when men lost common sense. Joe understood it, didn't appreciate it now, but understood it — he would have once been at the center of it. Mick was the one who had called him. "Send me the bill, Mick. They'll pay it, along with giving a formal apology."

"Not a problem," Mick agreed. The apology was worse than paying for the damages, and Joe and Mick both knew it. The room was beginning to sort itself out, tables and stools being righted. Joe felt some satisfaction at noticing no SEALs were on the floor. At least they hadn't forgotten how to fight. Anger was good. It was better than bailing out like Boomer had just done. That wasn't fair to Boomer, but the result was the same. Raider had just cost him a good AOIC.

"You haven't been by much," Mick commented.

"No, I haven't." Joe sent a smile of apology to his old friend. "Another time. Thanks for the call, Mick. I owe you."

"On the house, Bear. I'm just glad it wasn't in commemoration of a wake."

Twenty-seven

★ ★ ★

Joe didn't want to see her for some reason, and Kelly felt the sting of that. It made no sense. The platoon had been back almost a full day and Joe still hadn't made the effort to call. What was going on? It hurt to be treated this way — it was rude and she deserved better. If nothing else, he should have called because she was still watching his dog. She would call him when she got home.

She focused her attention back on Ryan coming across the church parking lot, now carrying a packet with him. "Did Dad give me a medical release? I can't leave without one."

"Right here." She retrieved the envelope Charles had given her. She had turned in the registration form Sunday but kept the rest of the papers for today. "Are you sure you have everything you'll need? Your sleeping bag? Bible? Soap? A good watch?"

"All forty things on the checklist. I'm

set, Kelly. I'm supposed to store my stuff in the blue van."

"I wish your dad was here to see you off."

"That's okay. I appreciate the fact you brought me." He folded the medical release with his other papers and slid them into his duffel bag.

"Don't take too many chances out there in the wilderness. I've got a vested interest in you being alive and well," she teased, finding herself reluctant to see him leave.

He laughed. "Yes, Mother."

She blinked, smiled, and knuckled his hair. "Someone has to take away your fun."

"Did you know Lynnette is going?"

"I had heard that." A whistle blew. "There's your cue."

He hugged her, surprising her, and then grabbed his duffel bag and sleeping bag and headed for the van Lynnette was getting into.

"Thanks, Ryan," she whispered quietly. That boy was going to steal her heart if she wasn't careful. She was at loose ends for the rest of the day, though she didn't move immediately. She waited until the group was ready to leave, then sighed and got out her car keys.

Joe was waiting on the other side of the parking lot, standing beside his Jeep. Kelly slowed her pace once she saw him, surprised he was here, surprised he had tracked her down in the middle of the day. She drew closer and she could see the tension in his stance. With the dark sunglasses he had on, she couldn't tell what he was thinking, but she could see he was wound tight, had probably never wound down, she realized with some dismay.

"Can you give me a couple hours? Alex told me you were off for the rest of the day," he asked.

"Sure."

"Would Silver be pretty empty this time of day?"

The beach sprawled for miles. Midafternoon on a weekday, visitors would be sparse. What was wrong? She didn't ask because she was afraid of the answer. "Yes."

He walked around to open the Jeep door for her.

"No, let me follow you." She wanted them to talk, but not while his attention was on his driving. She wanted him facing her where she could see his eyes and read what he wasn't saying. It sounded rude to decline to ride with him, and she tried to soften that insistence with a smile. "Stop and get us a couple cold drinks from a drive-thru, and we'll find a picnic table."

Joe parked the Jeep, then waited for Kelly to park her car beside him. He reached over and picked up the cold drinks he had bought. Kelly locked her car and joined him. He gestured to a table nearby.

She accepted the drink he handed her. She didn't say anything to open the conversation and Joe didn't know what to do — chitchat and then drop his bombshell or simply tell her. She had been his friend for a long time. He was going to hurt her, and he hated what he was about to do.

"Kelly, we made a mistake to date."

He saw the disbelief, and then her eyes shuttered, wiping away any indication of what she was feeling.

"Why?"

"Boomer made the decision not to reenlist when his rotation comes up."

"I can't say I'm totally surprised because of the baby." She looked at him, then looked away. "I'm sorry for you. I know he will be hard to replace."

"Yes." Joe looked at her, wishing he didn't have to do this. "We have the same decision in front of us. You want children."

She appeared to stop breathing. "Yes, I do."

"I can't see leaving the SEALs. And it isn't right to hold up your dreams by asking you to wait for an indefinite period of time, probably years."

"Joe, we're not Boomer and Christi. You can be a SEAL and we can have kids. I've seen you with Christopher. You would make a good dad. And I know you like kids."

"It's not that easy, Kelly. I don't want to be an absent father. I'm away almost half the year. That's not fair to my children, and it's not fair to me. I want to be part of their lives. Simply put: I can't afford to get distracted on a mission, and being married, having children, you would be there in the back of my mind. That's natural. But an instant of hesitation — it puts those under me at risk."

"You're serious."

"Just dating you has been a distraction. It really is best if we go back to just being best friends."

She lowered her eyes, didn't look at him, didn't answer him. The sweat began to trickle down his back. "What are you thinking? Please say something."

"You've made the decision."

"Kelly —" he could feel the pain inside at what he had done — "do you understand why?"

"Yes." She glanced up and smiled — it was quick, forced, but a smile. "I do understand. We made a mistake." Her voice grew tight. "I want our friendship back, Joe. Our real friendship, not a polite how-are-you-doing shell like most couples that break up settle for. Not the quiet, what's-going-on silence of the last week."

He blinked at her intensity. "So do I, Kelly."

She nodded, got up, and gathered up her purse. "I won't be home until late. I can either bring Misha by in the morning or you can swing by and use your key."

"Kelly —"

"Not now, Joe, okay?"

She didn't wait for his nod, simply turned to head across the grass to the parking lot. She was walking away from him, and it felt like his heart was getting torn out. He got up to follow her, not liking this unfolding reaction he had triggered. "Kelly."

She turned at her car.

What should he say? What could he say? He never intended what he did say. "Did you ever find Nick's eagle?"

Any remaining emotion left her face. "No," she replied starkly. "It's gone."

She had made a fool of herself. Kelly walked down the rocky shoreline at the distant end of Silver Strand Beach and wished she could at least feel angry about it, but all she felt was hurt.

Joe didn't want her.

It ached to put it that baldly, but it was the simple reality. He didn't want someone to come home to at the end of a day at work. He didn't want someone to come home to when a mission was complete. He was content with his silent house, his dog, and his boat.

Why did she have to love a man who had no place for her in his life?

Why had he ever asked her to date in the first place?

Lord, did I do something wrong?

She took a deep breath and tried to think. Joe had said he didn't want to date her because she wanted children, and she was a distraction. She had assumed he wanted children. Had she been wrong? No, he had implied the problem was when.

A distraction — what was she supposed to do about that?

God, I can't solve these two problems. They are legitimate, but they're not the real problem. The real problem is Joe doesn't want me in his life enough to figure out a way to deal with the changes that would mean.

Why didn't You protect me from getting hurt? I don't understand. I love him, and he wants to walk away.

She walked across the sand, staying close to the water, relieved to have the beach to herself. As she walked, she wiped away tears that silently streaked down her face.

She had made a profound mistake. She had been projecting her own emotions on him.

What did Joe want? She had tried to see him as wanting what she did, and he finally had to say it didn't fit. But what did Joe want? He had said yes, had asked her out for a reason. She had just been too absorbed in herself to understand what it was.

She drove around Coronado that evening, taking a private journey through her past, grieving over Nick, but also Joe. No matter what he wanted for the future, things had changed between them now for good. She had never guarded her heart with him before, never second-guessed her words, and in the future she would have to.

Their friendship would never be the same, for this history between them, those three unfortunate words she had said — I love you — would always sit there.

She felt like part of her life had just been shattered and she didn't know how to pick up the pieces.

She finally forced herself to go home, to seek out relief for her headache.

Misha did not greet her at the door when she unlocked it. Kelly gave a sad smile. At least Joe wanted his dog with him, even if he didn't want her.

Her answering machine was blinking with a solitary message. She hesitated before touching the blue button to replay the message. "Kelly, please, call me when you get home. We need to talk."

Her finger on the delete button erased it and the sound of his voice.

If Kelly was trying to avoid him, she couldn't have done it better. Joe set down the equipment summaries he had been trying his best to focus on. He had the office to himself as Boomer just left to check on the C-130 pallet loads.

Joe had told Kelly they needed to go back to just being friends because he couldn't handle the distractions with his work, and all Kelly had managed to do today with her silence was totally distract him.

He had handled it all wrong. He couldn't blame her for not wanting to talk to him, but he didn't like the idea of her crawling away to lick her wounds in private. Up until this disaster, she had turned to him when things went wrong.

He hadn't slept, and even the house felt wrong this morning.

Joe reached for the phone.

"Marsha, I need a favor. You said you do apologies."

The bouquet of daisies was delivered as Kelly was reading the special section of the newspaper devoted to the upcoming Memorial Day events. Monday was going to be a hard day to get through, and she had counted on Joe being beside her. There would be an honors service at Nick's graveside. She knew Joe would come to the ceremony and she almost wished he wouldn't.

Kelly opened the card that came with the flowers.

Please accept my apology. I never intended to hurt you. Joe.

She sighed and wished she had the courage to call him. "Joe, you didn't hurt me. I let my expectations hurt me. I assumed you wanted the same thing I did. I'm the one who said the three words that got us into this mess."

Rather than have to deal with letting the phone ring, listening again to the answering machine take his call, for she knew he would call again, Kelly reached for her keys and went to the hallway closet to get the camera bag. Nick had been the photographer, but he had taught her enough to get by. She would drive up the coast and take photos rather than stay here and try to pretend nothing was wrong.

She was a coward not to want to talk to him, but it simply hurt too much. Joe had made his decision. Now she had to find a way to live with it and find a way to do it with grace. Joe didn't need to be worried about her. But she couldn't turn the emotions and dreams off in an instant. She needed this weekend to adapt. She would because she had no choice. God had promised to be her refuge. And she needed one.

The invitation to drive out to the wilderness camp came from one of the parents as Joe was debating how to spend what looked like a long Thursday. He had the rest of the week off, Kelly still wasn't talking to him, and he didn't think it was fair to track her down and force the issue.

He might have just lost his best friend, and the pain was acute. He deserved it for breaking her heart; he'd seen what a blow his words had been. If only he could undo his rush into saying *I want to date.* He had seen the problems even then, yet had ignored them and gone ahead, thinking they would disappear.

Lord, I hurt Kelly. I need to talk with You.

He left Misha with Boomer and drove over to meet Henry. He had a backpack with him on the chance he decided to stay out at the base camp until the group came back on Saturday.

Joe needed time in the wilderness with God. He was in a wilderness now of his own making. There had to be a place of peace for both him and Kelly. He hadn't meant to hurt her. He owed her so much. He would find a way to get them both to that place.

Twenty-eight

⭐ ⭐ ⭐

Charles opened the lower drawer of his desk, his memory drawer. The precious memories of a lifetime were stored there, from pictures of Ryan as an infant to the diaries and letters his wife had written. He retrieved with care the small box he had recently added to the drawer. Closing the drawer, he placed the box on his desk next to the letter he had spent days drafting. He opened it and picked up what rested on a cushion of cotton batting. Nick's eagle.

He knew Kelly had to be searching for the medallion by now, and he regretted having found it necessary to take something so personal to her. He knew of no better way to make sure Joe understood the danger Kelly was in than to deliver the medallion to Joe at the same time he sent a note signed as Raider. He needed the message to be blunt and direct. Protecting Kelly had become as important to him as protecting his own son. The men trailing him had killed Iris; he was not going to let them get to Kelly.

The misdirection had worked. The device was arriving tomorrow in Taiwan via a grain barge passing through Hong Kong.

He was relieved the SEAL team was home unharmed. He had known when he set up the ruse that the odds were high that someone would not return alive. There had been no choice. The ruse had allowed him to focus the general on what was happening with the SEAL team, had pulled the general's men from watching Ryan, watching Kelly, to instead watching the training and deployment of the SEAL team. He'd been able to get Ryan safely away.

The men were back watching him today. Charles had seen the car pass his, but at least Ryan was now far from here. The men shadowing him couldn't watch Ryan in the wilderness and also watch him.

The plan was working. Ryan was safe. He'd bought Kelly a few more days of safety. The device was being delivered. For the next few days he simply had to stall everyone.

Once the device was in the general's hands and the setup clock for making it active began to tick, he would deliver the medallion to Joe with the warning that Kelly was at risk and also pass along what information he could in the message describing the general's location. He would then run with his son as fast and as far as he could before the general realized he had been betrayed.

Charles still had the activation codes in his possession, and although he had thought about corrupting them or stalling on sending them, it wasn't worth the risk. He'd pass on the codes as agreed upon. The skirmish at the island had certainly been a good move. The general had actually tried a joke during the last phone call.

The activation codes weren't absolutely needed anyway, so it wouldn't be worth the danger to withhold them. The codes allowed the software in the weapon to be modified directly without going through layers of security. The codes changed daily. Charles had the master key, but on the day the assembly was complete he'd have to put in a request to a contact in Russia and get that day's permutation to pass on to the general.

The fifteen-digit activation code would allow the men working on the weapon to connect and take full control of the device source code. From that point they would have to modify its targeting and firing algorithms. Charles was guessing even the most brilliant men couldn't reverse engineer that part of the software in less than three days. That would give the SEALs time to move in.

By then he hoped to be with his son on a private island in the Caribbean owned by an old friend.

The plan time line worked, but it still left Kelly in a lot more risk than he was comfortable with. He couldn't afford to warn Joe too early, but if he left it too late . . . Charles sighed as he turned over the medallion Nick had worn. The eagle was farsighted and flying free. He needed to get Kelly away from here. Just as he had seen in the circumstances a way to get Ryan away from the trouble for a few days, he had to figure out a way to get Kelly somewhere else as well.

He put the medallion away, considered moving it to his private safe, but instead put it back in the memory drawer with the picture and diary of his wife. It was something precious to Kelly, and he would keep it safe. He would make sure she got it back. He folded the draft of the note and returned it to the safe along with the folder of activation codes and the last details on the money transfers. Everything else regarding this deal had been shredded.

He was going to have to steer Kelly as he had the SEALs with a mix of truth and fiction that would at least keep her safe. He didn't want to do it. What Kelly thought of him really mattered. He didn't want to see that distrust enter her eyes, that wounded look as she realized the truth.

He was crazy to assume he could keep the reality of the role he had played in her husband's death buried forever. He wished he could. Kelly liked him. She had no idea how much balm was in that quiet fact. She liked him. He hadn't liked himself for so many years that it was a comfort to have her look at him and still see something admirable.

He'd keep her safe. He owed her that at all costs. Enough innocent people had paid a price for his actions. No more. He wouldn't be able to live with himself if something happened.

Twenty-nine

★ ★ ★

"Slide your hand to the right and you'll find a crevice you can grip," Joe instructed Ryan, bracing his feet and pulling the rope around the back of his waist to keep it taut between them.

Ryan reached out where Joe directed and slipped his fingers in. The boy was improving with each climb. This was their second attempt to scale this particular rock face, and it looked like Ryan would make it this time. "That's the way. Good. Shift your weight in closer to the face of the rock. Work with what it gives you."

Joe was glad he had come out to join the wilderness camp. He was able to offer another expert hand at rock climbing and map reading. The boys had kept him busy, but for the first time Joe also found himself able to decompress and unwind. He liked to teach, always had, and the boys were motivated to learn.

Ryan was a good kid. It was the longest

stretch of time Joe had been able to spend with him and he liked what he found. The boy was smart and had that hard-to-teach quality of being a cautious thinker while also having an innate confidence that he could do whatever was before him. Rock climbing was the latest challenge.

The twenty-four-hour adventure alone with their Bibles, sleeping bags, maps, and compasses would begin this afternoon. Joe planned to silently move between them during the night, make sure none managed to get lost. He found himself wishing Kelly were here. She would have enjoyed this.

"What's wrong with Kelly? She looked sad when she took me to the church Tuesday."

Ryan's question startled Joe. Tuesday seemed like a lifetime ago. It was before he had given Kelly another reason to be sad. "She lost Nick's eagle."

The boy nearly fell. "The medallion?"

"Yes. It's important to her and we can't find it."

Joe thought Ryan would change the subject as he climbed several more feet without saying anything, but he eventually asked, "Does she have any idea what happened to it?"

"I may have accidentally thrown it into the trash."

Ryan risked a look down. "You? No way."

"We all make mistakes." And he had managed to make a couple glaring ones in the last week.

"She wore that medallion everywhere."

"Yes, she did."

Ryan slipped and Joe instinctively moved his arm down and out to set the rope. Ryan dangled in the air. "Want me to lower you down?"

The teen shook his head. "I'm getting to the top of this rock. Hold on; I'm swinging back in to try again." The teen swung his legs and pushed off the rock once, then used his momentum to come back and grab hold the next time he got near the rock face.

"Good job."

"SEALs finish what they start. Including wanna-be SEALs," Ryan replied, finding his footing again. "What did I do wrong?"

"Reached out too far. Keep your hands in close so your body mass can help you."

If he hadn't been such a jerk, someday he could have been doing this with his own son. The reality of what he had given up was huge. Joe was enjoying this, passing on what he knew, sharing his passion. Ryan was serious about someday trying for the SEALs, and Joe thought he might actually have what it takes. The teen had a growing, strong faith, courage, and the right desire to excel. He was soaking in the basics, including the core one: *never quit.*

Ryan reached the top and gave a triumphant laugh. "Joe, can I rappel down?"

He smiled, knowing it was the reason Ryan loved to climb. "Sure. Come on down."

"Kelly, you can wear the blue dress, we won't stay long, and I guarantee you will have a good time. Come on, say yes."

Somehow Charles had found out she and Joe had broken up, and Kelly would love to know who had told him. He was being charmingly persistent in seeing that she didn't have a reason to mope around on a Friday night. An art gallery showing — not a normal event for her, but it did sound interesting.

Would Joe even care if he knew?

She coiled the telephone cord around her finger. She would enjoy the time with Charles, but it didn't seem right. She wasn't going to be great company tonight. But her option was to stay home, and that was an even worse option. "Yes, and thanks for asking."

"I'll pick you up at seven. We'll eat afterward."

She would be scrambling to make it in time, but she could do it. "I'll be ready."

She hung up the phone and lightly traced a finger over it. She was going to take the people in her life as they came to her, on their terms. No more projecting what she wanted in life onto those around her. Charles was a friend, and tonight she could use one. Tonight she could really use a friend.

Charles picked her up right on time. Kelly couldn't help but remember the excitement she had felt only a short time ago when it had been Joe coming to pick her up.

The art gallery showing was by invitation only. It was obvious at a glance that this was not her normal crowd, but for an evening Kelly decided she could pretend she fit in. It was a little like being Cinderella for a night.

"Let's wander," Charles suggested.

Kelly slipped her hand under his arm, content to take his advice. "Let's."

An hour later Kelly was confident Charles was more interested in her impression of the art than he was in studying it. She also knew from his occasional comments that she had good taste. They circled through the second floor galleries. "I like this one."

Charles studied the painting. "Do you? Why?"

"The painter understood solitude."

"Solitude? The lady looks lonely."

"She has her memories."

Charles looked at the painting, then back at her. "Would you like it?"

She laughed. It wasn't the first time he had asked her that question tonight. "The only thing you are buying me tonight is one of those hot pretzels you told me about from the shop around the corner."

"Come on, we can have dinner first."

He took her to a small restaurant near the gallery and told her stories about the Orient, London, Paris, and Rome. He made a life spent traveling come alive. When he suggested his home for coffee, Kelly was comfortable enough to want to go.

His home was a surprise. Not just the baseball glove dropped on the stairs or the stack of library books on the side table, but the trophies on the fireplace mantel and the snapshots on the tables. It looked like a lived-in, comfortable home. A wealthy man's home. The wall of windows overlooking the crashing surf below made Kelly appreciate why Charles had chosen this house.

"You have a beautiful home. And quite an art gallery of your own." Kelly paused by a painting in the living room, a small work of flowers. "This is exquisite."

"Your taste is excellent." He handed her the coffee. "Wander around; I'm curious what you think."

"Do you collect intentionally or because something strikes you at the moment?"

"I'm choosy, but more because I have limited room to display pieces than lack of those which capture my interest."

Kelly wandered through the room, absorbing the breadth of what he had acquired over the years. "I have to admit, it would be a hard choice between the horses and the flowers as to which is my favorite." When she finally settled on the sofa, she smiled across at him. "Thank you. I can't remember the last time I had a night of art. It has been a pleasure."

Charles unwrapped a piece of hard candy. "That painting you were admiring? The flowers? I stole it when I was nineteen."

The hurt in her expression he had expected, but it still hit him hard. "You see me as a rich man you're not quite sure how to deal with. I don't see myself the same way. I was a thief when my wife met me." He tried to put some perspective on it as he tried to put it in the past. "A charming thief, but still a thief. She knew and she still thought I could be reformed."

She said nothing for such a long time. Her animation had ended. "You told me you grew up poor."

"Trying to excuse my behavior? Thank you, but it's okay. Being a thief is like being a reformed alcoholic, Kelly. You're a reformed thief, but still a thief."

"Why are you telling me this? Why tonight?"

"Because I would rather have you know me for some of who I really am than feel a distance over what I have and what that allows me to do."

"I still like you, Charles. I understand having to redeem a past."

He gestured around him. "You'll get used to all the stuff, Kelly. It's just stuff."

"You don't look like a thief."

"I was quite a good one, actually. It started when I was a child: Being a thief was how I could fit in a world that laughed at me because of the poverty. I stole to have what I needed to fit in, but after a while I did it because I could.

"Amy said I stole her heart, and it was quite apropos. She stole mine. It came down to a choice — between that passage in 1 Corinthians that says no thief will enter heaven or the thief on the cross next to Jesus who repented. Amy asked me which kind of thief I was going to be. It cut. And I changed. I became her reformed thief.

"I bought the painting by the way. I tracked down the original owners and said it had come into my possession. I offered to give it back or buy it. Amy considered that painting my reminder of how far God could bring someone. It's the only thing I've ever stolen that I've kept."

Kelly found he was right; the information changed everything she assumed about him. "How did you ever get to be working with security matters with that in your background?"

"Actually, it turned out to be quite useful. I could sneak around the less savory side of Hong Kong gathering information, and when anyone got suspicious and checked me out, they found out I was a thief because I really was. Amy's father pulled the initial strings to get me clearance, and after I had a track record, it evolved from there."

"Your candor about this is surprising."

"Then let me grant you another surprise. I was sad to hear that you and Joe parted ways. It's obvious you two are close."

Kelly relaxed at those words. "Who told you?"

"Someone who noticed Joe was growling. If you ever find yourself at a loose end while you're waiting for him to get his head on straight, call me. I can at least make sure he has something to be jealous about."

His offer was unexpected. Charles was having a good time with the situation, even if he was taking care to let her know he understood where she was at. "We've just hit a bump in the road. But thanks for the offer. I may take you up on it someday."

"Do. I want you happy, Kelly. And I enjoy your company."

When he took her home at the end of the evening and walked her to her door, she was surprised at how much she didn't want to say good night. "Thank you, Charles. I had a wonderful evening."

"So did I." He didn't try to make it anything more than a smile when he said good night.

Kelly closed the door after him, deep in thought. Charles was a very charming man, and his patience coupled with that were a potent combination. A thief. She smiled at the realization that he could be so honest about his own secrets. She really had to find a friend to introduce him to. She liked him too much not to have him with someone who would appreciate how special he was.

Kelly carefully hung up the dress.

When she slipped into bed that night, she looked at the phone. As lovely as the evening had been, Charles and the fun she had slid easily aside while Joe was an ache inside that didn't fade.

She missed Joe.

She really missed Joe.

She reached over, picked up the phone, and dialed familiar numbers. Joe's phone rang until the answering machine picked up.

Joe, I'm ready to talk and you aren't there. Where are you?

Kelly bit her lip and set down the phone without leaving a message.

He had to tell Kelly about how Nick died.

The stars were shining overhead late Friday night. Joe had done as the wilderness campers did, left to take twenty-four hours alone in the wilderness with God. He was bringing his relationship with Kelly to the One who could help him figure out what to do.

The grief will hit her hard, Lord, and I'm dreading the change that will be in her eyes when she looks at me. Nick died because I got hurt. It's time Kelly knows the truth, but it is going to be so hard to tell her.

Did he want to lose her? That was what he was risking. Charles was waiting in the wings, ready and willing to step forward and offer Kelly not only a future but also a ready-made family. Joe couldn't blame her for liking Charles and Ryan.

What do I do?

The only way to square things with Kelly was to tell her all of it. She needed to know. Nick had died saving his life. Even if that meant he risked her thinking his interest now and over the years had been from survivor's guilt. He owed her the truth.

And he needed to repay that debt — to one day get Raider and bring him to justice. Leaving the SEALs wasn't an option for him. And Kelly deserved a husband and a family. She shouldn't be alone. Either he stepped forward and made that final commitment or he let her go.

He didn't want to lose her.

There was no way out of this conflict. He would be asking her to delay children, asking her to live with the risk of him possibly not coming home from a mission. He loved her. It was time to tell her that and let her make the decision.

Thirty

The church was packed, and most men and a few of the women were in uniform, prepared for the Memorial Day weekend Sunday service. Joe walked quietly among friends, touching base, checking in with his men, many who called this church their home, to see how they were coping after a few days off.

He had returned from the wilderness trip with a resolve deep inside to deal with the situation as he found it. What he wanted and what might now be possible were different things. He had yet to find Kelly although he knew she was here somewhere. Joe made his way through the commons area looking for her in the crowd.

"Joe, could I talk to you for a minute?" Ryan asked. The teen looked unusually serious for someone who a few minutes ago had been talking with Lynnette and the others from the wilderness camp.

"Of course."

"Maybe outside?"

Joe raised an eyebrow but nodded his head toward the side door. What was going on? He followed the boy outside. The parking lot was full. On Kelly's behalf, he was grateful for that show of support. "What's up, Ry?"

The teen pulled a folded cloth from his jacket pocket. "Would you give this back to Kelly?"

Joe was stunned when Ryan unwrapped a cloth and handed him Nick's eagle. "Ryan —"

"Please. Don't tell Dad."

Joe suddenly had to face the fact the teen he thought he knew he didn't know at all. His anger flared because of what Ryan had done to Kelly, at all the time that had been spent searching to find that medallion, at all the pain Kelly had felt knowing it was lost. "You need to give this to her yourself."

"I can't."

"Look at me." Joe waited until the boy raised his head. "You took it; you have to give it back."

Ryan dropped his eyes, but not before Joe saw the tears. "I can't. I'm sorry I let you down," he whispered.

Joe needed the kid to grow up and face what he had done, yet at the same time he knew the contrition was real. "Why did you take it?"

The boy straightened his back and took a deep breath. "It was there."

It had the ring of truth.

"I'll give it back to her," Joe finally replied. "If you tell your father."

Ryan slowly nodded. "Okay." The boy turned back toward the church.

"Ryan."

The boy turned.

"A SEAL doesn't steal," Joe said quietly.

The rebuke hit the boy hard. "Yes, sir. I know."

The memorial service had already begun, and Joe saw Kelly sitting with Liz near the front of the sanctuary. He had hoped to be beside her, but she had not saved a place for him as usual. That hurt. Didn't she want him to come? Had he messed up things between them that badly?

He felt the medallion in his pocket. It was going to be a tough day for her, in more ways than she realized. He found a place in the back.

It was a service that focused on the call of duty, of the call God placed on Christians to follow Him no matter what the

413

cost. His friend in the pulpit delivering the message could have no idea how close that message came to his reality. Joe couldn't see Kelly from where he sat and he really wished he could. Was his first duty to his country or to his friend? There were times the truth was not all that clear. Saying I'm sorry wasn't sufficient to convey what he felt.

He moved toward Kelly at the end of the service as she stood surrounded by friends.

"Joe." She turned toward him, her smile somewhat sad, and reached for a hug. This was a day of memories like no other.

"Hi, friend," he whispered. "I've missed you." He was incredibly relieved at the hug she offered. "I didn't mean to hurt you."

"I know." She reached for his hand and gave it a squeeze. "Friends?"

In one quiet word, she set aside days of hurt and uncertainty. It felt so good to have her hand once again in his. "Always."

Joe took a chance and interlaced their fingers rather than release her hand. He didn't want their relationship to revert all the way back to just friends, but at the moment he was relieved she was offering at least that. He had missed her. And the thought of how much he had lost settled on him like a heavy weight. There wasn't a relaxed openness anymore; her face was strained and tired. He wished he could wipe that away.

"Walk with me down to the graveside service?"

Joe nodded. The cemetery was covered with small flags honoring the fallen heroes, placed there by servicemen that morning. She carried another one for Nick's grave.

It was a short, simple service, given greater impact by the fact they had to walk past almost a hundred SEALs in full dress uniform assembling to pay their respects.

When it concluded, Kelly placed her flag. She stood for a moment before the simple white headstone. His own memories made tears burn behind his eyes.

She stepped back from the grave and her shoulders squared. When she joined him, her eyes were bright and clear. "Let's go."

Only after she had passed by did the men begin to disperse.

"Come back to my place, Kelly. We need to talk."

She looked at him and he was afraid for one moment that she would refuse, and he couldn't blame her if she did. He was relieved when she nodded and didn't ask him what it was about.

She was quiet on the drive to his home,

and he looked over at her several times. The sadness was there, and the quiet resolve to get through the day.

When she was seated in the living room, he took a seat beside her and slipped his hand in his pocket. "I was asked to return something to you." He handed her Nick's eagle.

She looked stunned. "I thought it was gone for good." She looked over at him, obviously struggling to understand.

"Someone asked me to return it, Kelly. That's all I can tell you."

Her hand closed around it. Her eyes closed, she swallowed hard, and looked incredibly troubled. "Charles?"

Joe was startled by the name, at why she would even think it. He shook his head before he realized it was better if he didn't answer any questions. "No. But I'm not going to play names."

She looked sick. "Ryan."

Joe closed his hand around her fist. "I'm not going to say."

"I won't ask," she agreed softly but already seemed to have curled in on herself, wounded.

"I'm sorry."

She tried to smile. "It's okay. You said we needed to talk. Was it this?"

Joe shook his head. "I need to tell you something that's been tearing my heart out. Something that SEAL security has kept me from telling you . . . but it's too important for us. I've got to tell you. It's about Nick, how he died."

She looked over at him, stunned.

He hesitated, uncertain where to begin. "We were on a mission to retrieve something that was being smuggled. It was a success, but as we were leaving I was shot in the shoulder. Nick came back for me, got me into the water, and as we were swimming out to be picked up —" Joe found it difficult to put into words — "Nick was also shot. Once, in the chest. We tried so hard to keep him alive, and he fought so hard. He died, Kelly, despite everything the doctors could do. He died because he came back to save my life."

What greater love does a man have than he lay down his life for his friend? He had repeated that honor silently to Nick as he stood at the graveside and knew there was much he would do to make himself worthy of that sacrifice. He watched Kelly, afraid of how she would react.

"You were his best friend, Joe," she finally whispered. "Did you expect him to do something else?"

"No. But I feel guilty about it every day — that God let me live and not him. Nick had you, talked about having children. Nick died and it nearly destroyed you."

"I'm glad God sent you home. Had the situation been reversed and Nick came home hurt and you died, he would never have been the same. The grief he felt over losing you would have robbed me of the husband I knew." She looked over at him and there was pain in her eyes. "You wanted to go out with me to replace what you felt I had been robbed of — a husband, children."

That she would react this way was his worst fear. "No, Kelly. I admit I was afraid that would be your reaction so I hesitated to tell you. But, please, believe me when I say that has no bearing on my asking you to date." He got up to pace the room and shoved his hands into his pockets. "The man who arranged that shipment we were after had arranged several others before then. He was never captured; he disappeared after Nick died. Until last week. He reappeared. We should have caught him last weekend."

She looked shocked. "You went after the man who killed Nick?"

"And another smuggled shipment."

"Why are you telling me this?"

"Because I need you to understand why I won't leave the SEALs like Boomer did. I owe Nick."

"I would never want you to leave the SEALs. It's who you are."

"I can't ask you to risk losing someone else." He sighed. "I don't even know what I am asking of you. I was going to see if you would give me another chance, if you would accept the risk I represent, be willing to delay children. But now — I'm not even sure I dare."

"Joe, I love you."

He looked over at her, saw the pain and the hope in her eyes. He crossed the room and sat down beside her. "Give me time, Kelly. I really do want a future with you." He wrapped her in his arms and felt relief when she slid her arms around his waist. "I love you," he whispered. "I don't want to break your heart, and I've come miserably close to it once. I won't do that to you again."

Her hand slipped around his neck and tugged his head down. Joe lingered close even after the kiss ended, resting his forehead against hers. He wanted this, needed this.

"So what do we do now?" His smile was rueful. Her hands were coiled in his shirt and he didn't want to talk. Talking only got him into trouble. "We take this slow." He rubbed the backs of her hands, enjoying the softness, until she sighed and opened them. He caught them in his.

"We can work out the problems," she reassured him.

He wished he could give her all her dreams now rather than ask her to accept uncertainty. "I'm not sure what the best answers are."

"Then we'll find them together with God's help." She leaned her head back to look at him. "Did you really mean it when you said you loved me?"

He slowly smiled. "Yes."

"Say it again."

"With pleasure." His kiss left them both breathless. "Shall I say it again?"

She giggled. "Please."

Memorial Day on Monday dawned bright and clear.

Kelly opened the glass-encased cabinet and took out the flag that had once draped Nick's casket. It was still folded tight, no red showing. The grief this year for a fallen hero was different. She knew he had given his life to save Joe's. She was proud of her husband in more ways than she could put into words.

You saved his life once, Nick. I'm going to save it again. She loved Joe. The man had carried his burden long enough. She wanted to be his wife, give them a life together. She wanted it, and in the same way "I'm going to marry Nick" had once resonated within her, she made the same decision about Joe.

Children. She had heard Joe's reservations, felt for him. He didn't want to be an absentee father, to miss large stretches of his children's lives while on deployment. It was hard for her to accept waiting years, knowing her age, but she really did understand his position.

She could wait. Joe clearly needed that time, and she would give it. She wouldn't mind a few years focused just on him. The man deserved that. They would have a family when he was ready. Even if that meant they had to adopt someday in the future. She chose Joe. She loved him.

Her hand closed around Nick's eagle.

She slipped it off. *Nick, I'm not saying good-bye, but it is time to let go.* She set the medallion on the flag and returned them to the cabinet. Joe would understand the significance. Kelly turned her wedding ring, considered it, and then slowly slipped it off as well. Her hand felt bare. She slipped the ring back on.

With a sigh she pulled the ring off again and reached inside the cabinet and put her wedding ring with the flag and the medallion. Her life with Nick in three emblems — their marriage, his career, and his death. It was time to leave it behind.

Lord, it's been a three-year journey to this point. Joe and I need to find a footing for the future that is stable and comfortable for both of us. Nick and I had a wonderful life. Let me bring the best of what I learned forward and leave the rest behind.

The man Joe had gone to try and capture — she had always assumed the person responsible for Nick's "training accident" was dead. Now she knew there was someone still at large, not yet brought to justice. The entire sense of closure she had was ripped away.

Don't I deserve to have the man responsible for Nick's death brought to justice? Please, Lord, honor what Nick did with his life. Find this man. Bring him to justice.

She closed the cabinet on the flag, the medallion, and her ring.

She looked again at the medallion.

Somehow she was going to have to tell Charles she suspected Ryan was stealing. It was going to shatter her friend. He spoke about his past as something he was proud to have overcome, but she knew it was his soft spot, the place that would hurt him most.

There had only been four people in her house who could have taken the medallion — Joe, Lynnette, Ryan, and Charles. Joe had told her it wasn't Charles who gave him the medallion to return. No way was it Joe. Lynnette had a cop for a father and one of the strongest moral senses of right and wrong Kelly had seen in a teen. That left Ryan.

Charles had probably told Ryan the same story he had told her about his past — he was the type of father who would want his son to learn from his mistakes. Instead, Ryan must have decided stealing was something cool to do. And if it was Ryan, he wasn't new to stealing — not when he could steal from her and act perfectly normal around her when he saw her next.

Joe worried that he had almost broken her heart.

Ryan had.

She would have to talk to Charles today.

Thirty-one

★ ★ ★

F-16s were breaking overhead in the missing man formation, part of the Memorial Day ceremonies at the Naval Air Base North Island, when the call came in. Charles answered the phone after taking a deep breath.

"Retrieve today's permutation of the codes; we'll be ready for it later today. It is quiet there?"

"No one is moving. They heard only about the diversion," Charles replied, relieved to have this deal almost concluded. "Transfer my money in twelve hours and I'll send the codes." He worked hard to keep the tension out of his voice. This was a deal and he was going to treat it as one. It was the one thing the general expected from him. "Then I expect you to call off your shadows. I'm leaving here with my son before you state your intentions to the world."

"You will enjoy Egypt."

"Or Paris," he replied coolly. "I won't

pass along the authorization codes until the money is received."

"And I won't call off my shadows until I have them," the general countered. "We understand each other, you and I. Besides, it is not profitable to harm someone you anticipate doing future business with." The general laughed. "Twelve hours, my friend, and our deal is done."

Charles hung up the phone. Twelve hours. It was an eternity. He hoped his plans to get out of this safely worked.

He slid the envelope out of his pocket and tapped it against his palm.

There had been no sleep last night. He thought about the medallion in the drawer and the completed note in the safe. His original plan was ready to go. He'd pass on the activation codes and then leave town. He would take Ryan by boat to a private airfield north of here, and they would fly to Houston to catch their flight to the Caribbean. The medallion and letter he'd leave with a courier to deliver to Joe about the time he and Ryan boarded the plane.

It was all set. It was all thought through. And instead he was ready to throw it to the wind and act before then. Kelly was in too much danger. It ate at him as a nagging fear, the realization there was a hole in the time line where he would be gone and Joe wouldn't know about the problem.

Charles couldn't approach Joe directly. But maybe he could directly approach Kelly. She understood security. She'd been married to a SEAL. She would accept information without asking that he give her all the facts behind his statements. He'd finessed harder problems.

He had to get her away from here as close to when he and Ryan left as he could. And he may have already made that necessity not optional just by requesting the contents of this envelope.

Kelly was surprised at the message from Charles, not that he had called — she had expected that on this Memorial Day holiday — but at his request. He had moved his boat to the dock near Joe's.

The ceremonies were over and the rest of Memorial Day stretched out ahead of her. She had turned down Joe's offer to join him, thinking she would rather get in a nap and forget the day, only to lay down and not be able to sleep. Charles's request had been a good excuse to get out.

"Kelly — over here," Charles called. "I'm so glad you could come down on such short notice."

"I wanted to talk to you for a moment too, so I'm glad you phoned." She walked down the pier to the guest slip he was using. "Your boat is beautiful." It was a large vessel, beautifully crafted, chrome gleaming with a hull painted a deep blue with white trim.

"Isn't she? There is a cabin, small office, and a galley below."

"Is Ryan here?"

"Down at the far end of the pier talking with friends. Listen, the reason I wanted to see you — some time ago I remember you telling me that you had never been outside of California."

"That's true."

"Have you ever thought about it?"

She was puzzled at the question. "Sure, occasionally."

"Come aboard and sit down for a minute. I need to talk with you."

Something in his expression made her step down onto the boat and do as he asked. "What is it?"

He looked over at her and sighed. "I've got something for you." He reached into his pocket and pulled out an envelope, then handed it to her.

She opened the envelope and was stunned to find there were plane tickets inside. To Paris. "What's this?"

"A vacation. No strings attached. If I thought you would accept, I would invite you to go with Ryan and me, but I already know that answer. So I'm asking you to go on your own vacation, or better yet convince Joe to go along. There are two tickets there. It's time for you to take that vacation."

"I don't understand. Why?"

He ran his hand through his hair. "You're not safe here."

She felt cold suddenly. "What do you mean?"

"I hear things. You know, that's my job. Please, I can't explain, but it's important. You need to take a vacation for a couple weeks."

"You're going to have to tell me what you heard." She understood restricted information, but his request made no sense.

He finally nodded. "The men who killed Iris may try to kill you."

"What?"

"Trust me on this, Kelly. If Joe had the information I do, he would be telling you the same thing. You need to get out of the area for a couple weeks."

"Have you talked to the police?"

"The wrong thing to say, lady." She barely had time to turn before one of the men she had passed on the pier, one of the crewman she assumed, stepped down on the boat and grasped her arm, too tightly for comfort. "He really was trying to do you a favor."

"Let her go." Charles tried to step between them, then stopped when a second man came to his side, a gun in his hand.

"Who are they?" Kelly asked Charles, instinct telling her he knew.

"My shadows," Charles replied bitterly. He looked at the first man. "This is a mistake. Let me talk to your boss."

"You can call him from the open waters with the item you owe him. Go below with your friend and just be glad it's not your son we decided to grab. We're going for a boat ride."

Joe was trying to work on his boat and not making much headway. He was determined to take Kelly sailing in the near future, maybe out to Catalina Island. It was a chance to share not only his passion for sailing but also some uninterrupted time with her. They needed that time together. They were back together, but it was still uncertain ground.

Joe smiled as he remembered her giggle. He had missed that lighthearted Kelly, the one who had been swallowed up by three years of recovering from grief. She was back and he wasn't going to let anything mess it up.

She had passed on joining him today, but he understood. Her sleep the last few days had been very broken, and it made sense that she would try and get a nap. She said she would call around five o'clock and they'd look at going to dinner.

"Joe!"

He looked up and saw Ryan on the pier looking like he had run a fair distance. Joe's feelings were mixed at seeing him. Ryan was one of the reasons Kelly liked Charles so much. Ryan had also hurt her by taking that medallion, betrayed that trust she showed in him. But the boy had been trying to make amends.

"Hello, Ryan."

"Dad and Kelly —"

Joe's eyes narrowed. "Slow down. Put your hands on your knees; get your breath back."

"They took the boat out."

"Okay . . ." Joe said slowly, not sure what the problem was other than his feeling jealous of their friendship and the fact Kelly had said yes to Charles when she had said no to him.

"Dad was waiting for the guy who normally does our boat maintenance, to let him know a seal had cracked on the diesel engine. There's no way he would risk taking that boat out on the open sea today. And he just left me at the pier." Ryan shook his head, as if realizing he wasn't making sense. "There were two men on the boat."

"Ever seen them before?"

Ryan shook his head.

"The men you saw are probably the mechanics taking the boat out after they fixed the problem," Joe said calmly. "Are you sure your dad and Kelly were aboard?"

"I saw them going down into the cabin. I hollered but Dad didn't hear me."

"Would he be carrying his cellular phone?"

"He never goes anywhere without it."

Joe handed the boy his. When Ryan got no answer, Joe was not entirely surprised. Shutting off the phone when you were with Kelly was what he would do.

He pointed to the ship radio. "Try to raise him on that."

Ryan tried repeatedly but got no answer.

That was odd. The Coast Guard frowned on boats not having their radios powered on. "Come on, we'll take a sail, confirm everything is okay. I need to check out the latest repairs I've made anyway."

"Thanks, Lieutenant."

"Get a life jacket on, and you can help me get her ready to go."

Joe was about to cast off the mooring lines when his pager went off.

"What is it?"

"The base." Joe reached for his cell phone. The message waiting for him was short. "I'm sorry, Ryan. I have to leave you and go in to the base."

"But something's wrong. I know it."

Joe could tell the boy really believed it. "You can come with me, and as soon as I'm done if they're not back, we'll go out. Or I can call the man who runs the pier and ask him to watch and help you try to get in touch with your dad's boat. They may have been testing the radio and running channels and simply didn't hear you. Your choice."

"Go with you."

"Then we need to move."

They were locked in the small cabin. The bunk was narrow and beside it was a small dresser. The only other door was a small one into the head. Kelly shivered as she sat on the edge of the bunk, her attention focused on that door and the lock she had heard turn. Under her feet she could feel the engines increase in power and the rocking of the boat pick up. The man had had a gun and it had looked lethal in his hand. "Charles, who are they?"

The man she thought she knew was pacing in the small open area of the cabin. "I think one of them killed Iris." He sat on the bunk beside her, staring at the door, thinking. "We'll be okay. They need something I know. At least I hope they still do. It's not that much money that he would risk the delay."

"Ryan was left at the pier."

"He's safe for now, but he won't realize what happened to know he should try and get help. I gave him money to buy his friends lunch. He may not even have realized we're gone." He rubbed his hands across his face. "I knew the man would try something like this; I knew a double-cross was coming. I thought I had more time."

"What man?"

He sighed heavily as he glanced at her. "I stole something, Kelly. I'm not making excuses, but the buyer threatened my son. He didn't leave me much choice in the matter and the deal concludes tonight. The buyer is rather paranoid about something happening to his purchase. I guess you could say grabbing us is insurance."

"But he'll get charged with kidnapping."

Charles gave a rusty laugh. "He's acquiring a weapon, Kelly. I know for a fact he's done worse than kidnapping through the years. The last time we did a deal was three years ago, and Joe and Nick swiped his purchase before he could pick it up."

Three years ago . . . "You stole something and got Nick killed trying to retrieve it?" She recoiled at the realization. *This was the man Joe set out to stop.* She tried to move away from him, and his hand gripped her arm, stopping her movement.

"Kelly, I never intended for Nick to get hurt. He shouldn't have been, for I fed the SEALs precise information on where the shipment would be, all the way down to the railcar numbers. And the smugglers — they thought they were moving guidance system parts. Joe and Nick should never have been hurt; they had done dozens of missions much more dangerous."

"You got Nick killed!" She surged at him, coming at him with fists clenched.

He grabbed her hands to stop her. "Don't, Kelly."

She finally sank down on the bunk, fighting the fury. "I don't understand how you can justify this to yourself. What about God? What about 'thou shalt not steal'? What about 'thou shalt not kill'?"

"I didn't intend it to happen!"

"That doesn't help much."

He looked at her, desperation in his gaze that she would understand and forgive him. "Kelly, God stole my wife from me. He doesn't care about me. At first after her death, I would steal, and then I would go to church the next Sunday to remind God that I had done it just because I could. When the anger faded, I continued to steal because I wanted God to care enough to catch me. Only He never did. He just let me go on stealing because He didn't care what I did. He's the Father you don't want to have, the one who doesn't care to stop His son from being a thief — just like my old man here on earth."

"Charles, that's not true."

"Then why did He steal Amy from me? The one good thing in my life, the one reason I reformed, and He took her. He left me without a wife and my son without a mother."

"You're angry at God because He let your wife die?" She saw herself in Charles. The rebellion, the hypocrisy. She had lashed out at God and denied Him being

Lord in her life because He had allowed Nick to die. She'd felt equally angry with Him because He once let Joe walk away. Charles was doing the same thing, but on a harsher scale — he was deliberately stealing, shaking his fist at God by breaking the commandment not to steal. Though his rebellion was external, hers internal, both were paying the price of their actions. "Who are you?" she asked incredulously.

"If I could give you back Nick, I would, but I can't. So I've been trying to make it up to you in the only way I know how. I let you into my son's life. I trusted you with the most important person to me."

"Making it up to me? Charles, you got my husband killed!"

Thirty-two

★ ★ ★

The security guard at the base cleared him in. Joe thought for a moment and turned toward the administration building, positive that was where he would also find Boomer. He needed to make sure Ryan was supervised while he followed up on the page and got a sense of how long he would be here. If it was going to be a while, he would ask the community relations officer to take Ryan back to the pier and watch for Kelly and Charles to return. He parked and reached for his sunglasses case from the dashboard.

"I saw Dad with the lady who drowned," Ryan remarked.

"You what?"

"I just realized it when you pulled into the base. Dad met her here one evening. It was night. I didn't remember her hair being blond; that's why I didn't recognize her picture. Dad had two tickets to a concert for her. We got here, parked in visitor parking, and she met Dad by that bench.

437

They talked maybe two minutes, and then we went on to a ball game."

Joe looked at the bench Ryan indicated as they walked toward the doors of the administration building. "Why the tickets?"

"Dad gets free ones all the time at work. He gives away most of them."

Joe didn't have time to figure out the implication of Charles and Iris being friends. It was potentially huge, but it was another problem. Inside the building he pointed Ryan to the visitor lounge just off the reception desk. "Sit here and stay put until I come back or send someone to get you. This isn't a place you can wander around."

"Yes, sir."

Joe dug out change for the vending machine in the lobby and handed it to Ryan. "Get a soda. There are several sports magazines in the spin rack."

Joe headed toward the wing of the building his boss called home. The briefing was already underway in the conference room. Joe found he was one of several who were arriving in response to callbacks. The casual dress was a clear giveaway.

"That device we missed a week ago got through by another route," Lincoln said grimly, pacing at the north end of the room beside a large map. "Taiwan has a weapon, and they will get it operational in a matter of days if they've also acquired the codes. We've deployed platoons Echo and Foxtrot in the region to deal with the situation. We don't know how large this faction is in their military. The leader is a General Kerhi, and he's already confident he can take control of the government. We intercepted two transmissions from him with the man he is planning to put forward as the new president. We've got a slim window of time before China learns what's happening, or for that matter, the present government of Taiwan. If Taiwan knew they could get their hands on a nuclear device, they would take it, hide it, and pretend they never saw it. We've got to get it back.

"Which leads me to the next problem: where this general has the weapon. We don't know. Echo and Foxtrot will be in the area in two hours.

"Gentlemen, if that's not enough, we also think Raider is here, that the lady who drowned was one of his contacts. Raider knew we were deploying to stop the shipment and he sent it another route, turning the recovery mission into an ambush. He is our best lead to General Kerhi and where he stored the weapon, what his intentions are. We need to find out who Raider is."

"You think he's still around?" Lincoln's operational officer asked.

"We don't know. We're taking what precautions we can. The only people who know Echo and Foxtrot are responding are in this room; I had the orders cut out of Virginia."

Is Charles Raider? Joe tensed at the thought.

Iris Wells drowned.

Ryan saw Charles with Iris.

Charles appeared in Kelly's life just when Echo and Foxtrot were diverted . . .

Is he Raider? The thought was intense, alarming, and felt all too true. How better to monitor their movements than to be friends with someone very close to the SEALs, the widow of a SEAL? Kelly would never knowingly give any information about them — but to someone who knew her, it would be pretty easy to learn when he was gone.

Joe closed his eyes. Misha.

When someone wanted to know he was gone or when he was back, it would not be that hard. They didn't have to watch him; they could simply watch Kelly.

Charles. The man was Kelly's friend. To think he was Raider was stretching to incongruity. Charles passed top-secret secu-

440

rity clearances, was trusted by the military establishments of two countries. He was wealthy and had no reason to steal.

Kelly would be appalled at what he was considering.

Joe slipped out of the briefing with a question that had to be answered immediately.

He found Ryan in the visitor's lounge where he had left him, the teen paging through a golf magazine. He stopped directly in front of his chair. "Ryan, who took the medallion?"

The teen paled. "I did, sir."

"I don't think so. Where was it?"

"What?"

"When you took it — where was it located?"

"On the table in her hallway."

"Try the kitchen counter by the stove. Did Lynnette take it?"

"No!"

"Then who did?" Joe didn't have time to figure out how to help the teen deal with the truth. "It's very important that I know. Did your dad take it?"

Ryan looked down, obviously miserable. He nodded. "I found it in his office. It was in the drawer with a picture of my mom," he whispered.

Ryan had returned the medallion, accepted the blame for having stolen it, and lied to cover for his dad. Joe had to admire his courage.

It made no sense that Charles had taken the medallion.

Charles was Raider. The implications took his breath away. And Kelly was with him.

"We need to find this boat."

Joe sketched everything he knew to his boss Lincoln. Kelly was with Charles. It scared Joe to death. Iris had apparently been a contact for Charles; she was dead. Kelly had unknowingly been used for the same purpose. They had to find that boat — and fast. But where were they going? Why had Ryan been left behind?

Lincoln looked over at him. "I'll get every asset I can pull looking for that boat. In the meantime, get a few of your men and get to Charles's house. Check his office. Get me anything that might indicate this is our man. Stopping this device is our number-one priority, so use some discretion, but don't let a locked door stop you. He's signed military waivers with those security clearances — and he just became a potential military security risk."

Joe nodded, knowing information this explosive required that they act immediately. He'd get that proof. He was desperate to find some clue as to where Charles was with Kelly. "What about his office downtown?"

"See what you get at the house, and I'll see about getting us into his downtown office. Hopefully, we'll have located the boat by then."

It wasn't the best solution, but in the end Joe took Ryan with him and Boomer. Cougar and Wolf came along in another car following them. He limited his explanation to the basics — that they were going to do what was necessary to find Charles. Ryan had picked up the seriousness of what was going on and was nervous. But there was little Joe could do about that because the truth was even harder to deal with. They had sent base MPs in civilian clothes to watch the pier.

Ryan lead the way once they reached his home, directing them to Charles's office.

Joe was impressed with the room. The man loved fighter aircraft and he knew the men who flew them. The photographs and the signatures on the wall were a Hall of Fame from more than one country.

The picture on the corner of the desk of Ryan in a baseball uniform gave him pause. Joe sat down at the desk and started going through the calendars and appointment books.

"Boomer, there has to be a safe here somewhere."

"It's behind that painting." Ryan pointed to one behind the desk. Boomer lifted down the picture to take a look.

Joe glanced at Ryan. "Do you know the combination?"

Ryan shook his head.

"You said you found Kelly's medallion here in his office. Where?"

Ryan came around the desk and opened the third drawer on the left. "Here."

Joe picked up a letter and recognized Kelly's handwriting on the envelope. He opened it and found a thank-you note for the roses Charles had sent her. He picked up the picture beneath it.

"That's my mom, Amy."

"She's very pretty. Any particular reason he keeps this picture in a drawer? There are other pictures of her here in the office."

"I think it was Dad's favorite."

Joe glanced at the back of the frame and opened it to slip out the photo on the chance something was written on the back of it. It was blank. Figuring out the combination to the safe was going to take more time than they had. "Boomer, we need to get into that safe. Just don't destroy the contents."

Boomer reached for the case he had brought along. "Consider it done."

Joe had come here expecting to prove Charles was behind this. He was still stunned when they found the evidence in the safe to prove it. The cutting charge Boomer had used had sliced into the metal around the lock, and the safe now rested open and accessible. For Kelly's sake, and Ryan's, Joe had been hoping he was wrong. There wasn't much: a telephone number, wire transfer accounts, some handwritten notes, one of which read like a diary page of the deal, and activation codes. Everything else appeared to have been shredded.

He picked up his phone and punched in a code to relay the call through encryption. "Lincoln, we've got enough to prove it's him. The activation codes are here; they may not have been sent yet."

"Information on the buyer?"

Joe scanned the pages. "Enough the intelligence guys may be able to figure out where General Kerhi has the device."

"Get everything back here, fast."

"Sir, the boat." Joe was acutely aware of the time running out.

"We're working on locating it. As soon as it's found, there's a helicopter waiting with your name on it. The rest of your men are already being briefed."

"Thank you, sir."

Thirty-three

✯ ✯ ✯

"There's the boat," Cougar shouted. Joe leaned over to his side of the helicopter to watch the boat as they raced toward it. They were miles from shore; it had taken the relayed call from a spotter plane to send them this way. The boat rocked in the waves, apparently dead in the water. No one was above deck. The boat was hit broadside by a wave pushing it east.

Joe coolly ordered the pilot to take them into a hover. He looked across at Wolf. "Get ready!"

Members of the platoon took positions on the skids. They fast-roped down to the boat, eight of them touching down on deck within seconds of each other, all of them prepared for trouble.

Joe tagged Cougar and pointed to the steps. They moved to check below.

He froze at the bottom step. In the enclosed area of the boat, the smell of blood was sharp enough to be noticed.

The galley was clear. What had once apparently been a small office had been ransacked, but it was also empty. The cabin door was ajar. Cougar slowly pushed it open and it stuck, something blocking it. The blood on the floor was enough to indicate why. Cougar signaled him back and Joe negated it. If it was Kelly —

His hand on the door, he eased through the opening. He wanted to gag.

Charles was dead. A single shot to the heart.

What was he going to tell Ryan? Flawed or not, Charles and Ryan had been very close.

He hesitated, then moved toward the small bathroom. Kelly had last been seen going below with Charles.

Charles was dead.

Kelly was dead. His heart stopped.

It was just a matter of finding her body.

"Get out of there! The ship is rigged to blow!" The warning tore through his earpiece.

"Kelly!"

"It's ticking. Move!" Joe rushed back toward the stairs, up to the deck, obeying Boomer because it was ingrained to trust his men to make the right split-second call.

He barely reached the deck with Cougar

before he heard the first part of a detonation, the primer light. Going deep in the water was instinctive.

When they finally resurfaced, there was nothing left of the boat but burning fuel and shattered pieces of wood.

"Kelly!"

Joe was aboard the Coast Guard cutter *Hanson*, the vessel coordinating the search. He heard a boat come alongside and shortly thereafter his boss came below. "Let's find some privacy, Bear."

Joe followed him. He felt cold . . . and old.

"I'm sorry, Bear."

"My fault, sir. I didn't see the signs in front of me. He was using her, and I never put it together." It destroyed him to put that reality into words. The compassion in Lincoln's eyes didn't help. Joe braced his feet. "What happened with the device?"

"We hit the site in Taiwan. The situation is contained. The device was taken out of Taiwan space roughly twenty minutes before their government tried to seize it from us as being on their sovereign territory."

"Any SEALs hurt?"

"Nothing serious."

"The general?"

"Arrested by his government."

Joe felt at least some relief at that news. "I'm glad it went down the right way."

"We have to suspend this search at sundown and resume in the morning."

Joe looked at his boss, wanted to plead, but saw so much sympathy that he knew it was all his boss could give him. "She's alive. I have to believe that."

"The Coast Guard picked up three men in a speedboat racing for Mexico; the two who were seen near Ryan on Charles's boat are adamant that they left Kelly with Charles."

"They also said Charles was alive. There is no way Kelly would have killed him."

"Even if she found out he was responsible for her husband's death?"

Joe shook his head. "The cabin door was ajar when Cougar first reached it. The men said it was locked. Another lie. Kelly got off that boat. Either because they took her with them or because she got out of that cabin after they left."

"The boat was found drifting at sea seven miles from shore. We'll resume at daybreak. It's the best I can do, Joe."

She wasn't going to be found before nightfall, and this time it was a relief. Kelly locked her hands into the life-vest straps. Her headache was horrible, so horrible it made her nauseous, and the waves made her head bounce against the life jacket when they hit her from behind, adding flaring pain to the equation. Her efforts to swim to shore had ended when she almost hit a jellyfish.

She closed her eyes. She knew she was avoiding the shock of what she had heard, seen, and she wished she could cry.

"We aren't going to be getting off this boat, Kelly. If I give you an opening, can you get to the top of those stairs and over the side?" They had been moving out to sea for hours now, and with it had gone Charles's hope that he could get them out of this situation.

"Charles —"

"I'm serious. I know how long a swim it will be back to shore, but you're going to have to risk it. The odds are better."

"What about you?"

"I got you into this; I'm going to get you out. Will you take care of Ryan for me?"

"You have to —"

"Please, Kelly. Will you take care of Ryan?"

She could feel his fear. "Yes."

"I've owed you a long time for Nick. Trust me and do what I say. There's a life jacket

down here. Get it on."

She slipped it on because she didn't know what else to say, to do.

Charles tightened the straps for her. "Tell Ryan I still remember how to be a reformed thief." He was trying to lighten the moment, but his humor was hollow. "Just don't freeze up, Kelly. There will only be one chance."

Kelly could still hear the sound of the gunshot when she had hit the water. Charles. She didn't dare wonder. She sobbed now at the terror of what had happened, at the terror of what the last two hours had been like. The men were in a speedboat that had come alongside Charles's boat looking for her, trying to find her. Twice she had seen the boat in the distance and prayed the sun would set and give her cover.

The sun was finally dropping below the horizon. Finally.

The long night ahead, alone, out here in the cold ocean — she was so grateful she had the life jacket to keep her head above water. She didn't have enough energy to tread water that long. *Lord, You got me this far. I need You to get me through the next long hours.*

God is my refuge . . . when I'm in trouble. Kelly decided that prayer would be the best one for the long night ahead. God was her refuge. There was no doubt now about that treasured fact. At least one thing had turned out right. She hoped that this was the last time she was tossed into the sea to find that out. On top of the nausea from the headache, the saltwater she was swallowing only made her sicker.

Joe, I need you. Where are you?

She loved him. She wanted a chance to tell him that again. If this hadn't convinced him that danger went equally both directions, she didn't know what would. Joe could be stubborn, but what had he said? She was tenacious? It was a good word. She wasn't going to lose Joe. She only had a very long night to get through first . . . the sea was doing its best to break her will. The water didn't bother to slap at her as it had the last time; instead it did something more dangerous as it rocked her and eased her toward the cold sleep that would kill her.

Thirty-four

★ ★ ★

Dawn was coloring the sky. Joe set the boat on a westerly course, following the morning tides. Boomer was nearby. Cougar and others from Golf Platoon were out in their own crafts. Most had been out on the water throughout the night, none willing to wait for morning. Fog rose from the water, keeping down the speed they could travel. Joe couldn't accept the fact Kelly was gone.

Lord, I love her. Please, I need a miracle.

Life without Kelly would be unbearable. If the worst happened, he almost wished God would let her come back as a ghost to haunt him. It would save him the decades of loneliness that would be the alternative.

He changed hands on the outboard motor and blew on his cold fingers. Kelly being cold he could deal with; her being shot was another matter. He knew the slim odds that she was still alive. Charles had been shot. For Kelly to have gotten out of that situation alive —

He wished Charles were still alive so he could bury his fist in the guy's face.

Condemning Charles for the death of Nick, of Iris, and the danger to Kelly . . . the anger burned hot inside. But Ryan made it impossible to feel only that. Joe had told the teen what had happened rather than have him learn the truth from a stranger. The incredible anger at what Charles had done slammed starkly into the pain Ryan was experiencing. Charles had at least one redeeming trait: He had loved his son. It would have been much easier to deal with this situation if Joe had only known the bad.

If he could reach out and pull the sun up into the sky he would do it. It had been an intolerably long night. So much time had gone by since the explosion. Charles had paid the ultimate price for what he had done, but at least he had been part of what was going on. Kelly had been in the wrong place at the wrong time. The fact Charles had been using her galled him. Maybe if she came out of this alive, forgiveness toward Charles would be easier to find —

He nearly hit her.

From the fog rising on the water's surface there was a splash of orange suddenly in front of him and Joe slammed the boat to starboard as he killed the engine and swiveled his body around in the chair, whatever he had seen disappearing into the fog behind him.

The boat now dead in the water, he grabbed the satchel beside him and went over the side.

Where was she? He had lost her in the fog, and he found her again as much by accident as sight. His hand clenched the life jacket.

Kelly.

Thank You, God!

She didn't stir. He lifted her head carefully from the life jacket and a little more out of the water, worried about the pain etched in her face even as she rested unconscious. *Was she bleeding?* That was his immediate concern.

Her fingers were locked into the life jacket straps so tightly he couldn't get them to open. She was badly dehydrated, very cold. He was relieved to find there was no other obvious sign of injury. "Hold on, Kelly." He brushed a kiss across her forehead feeling the chill of her skin, his arm tightening around her. "I love you. Wake up so I can tell you that."

He began swimming them back to his boat. He lifted her over the side and hauled himself into the boat beside her. He struggled to get the life jacket straps unbuckled. She whimpered, deep in her chest, as he tried to remove it. He froze, hating that he was hurting her. It had to come off. "I'm sorry, honey." As carefully as he could, he cradled her against him and finished working it free. He pitched it toward the other end of the boat.

Hurriedly, he reached for the solar blanket and enveloped her in it, tucking it tight around her. He had nothing to dry her face, and he was dripping on her — but he didn't want to let her go.

Confirming exact coordinates from the GPS, he called the Coast Guard cutter *Hanson*, then Boomer and Wolf. Waiting for the others to arrive was the longest wait of his life. He brought her hands out from the blanket and rubbed his fingers over where the straps had bitten into her skin. She had taken a pounding from the sea, and he was afraid she might have broken a finger.

Where was her wedding ring?

No. Oh no. Of all the things for her to lose in the sea, her wedding ring . . . He kissed her forehead, hugging her tight. He'd replace it with his own.

Nick, I promise I'll take good care of her. I promise you, buddy.

Her eyes began to flutter. "Kelly, can you hear me? Kelly?"

When her eyes eventually opened, she didn't appear to be focusing. "Welcome back," he said softly. *Come on, honey, look at me. Pull out of it enough to look at me.*

She blinked, confused. "It's a pretty dawn," she whispered. Her eyes closed and a sharp look of pain crossed her face.

"Where's it hurt?"

"Headache."

His hand moved carefully through her hair, looking for signs of a blow. He didn't find one. As gently as he could, he cradled her neck in his hand, feeling the fragileness. "I'm sorry."

"Kiss it better."

Her whisper made him smile and he pressed his lips against her cold forehead. "I wish I could."

Her eyes opened abruptly and she winced. "Charles. What happened to Charles?"

He didn't want to tell her but didn't have much choice. "He's dead, Kelly."

She shuddered at that news. "Ryan. Does he know?"

"I told him. We didn't want him to find out from the media."

"How is he doing?"

"Shocked. It's still settling in."

"Charles asked me to take care of him."

Did she know who Charles was? There was something horribly wrong at telling her the truth, that Charles had been responsible for Nick's death. "Ryan is going to need to know you care," he said carefully, knowing she would eventually need to know the truth, but now was not the time to tell her.

She gave a weary smile. "I know about Charles, Joe. I can't reconcile what Charles did with the man I knew."

"I'm sorry I didn't see what was happening."

"Take me home."

"You need to see a doctor."

"Not this time. I want to go home."

"We'll see." It was the best he could promise. He hugged her, loving every bit of her from the dripping hair to the wet tennis shoes. "You'll be okay."

She rested her head against his shoulder. "Just don't let go." She closed her eyes at the sound of a boat nearby, signaling the end of a long night.

Thirty-five

★ ★ ★

Lynnette's father held the screen door open for Joe as he and Kelly came up the walk. Kelly almost fell. Joe tightened his arm around her waist. She was weaving like a young colt on unsteady legs, but he didn't question her decision to be here.

She hesitated at the bottom of the porch stairs, her hand tightening on his arm as she tried to decide if she could do them. Joe waited and she chose to try. He had to give her credit for not being willing to give up. She was going to fold if she didn't sit down soon, but she was marshaling her strength until she was able to talk with Ryan. Joe was grateful that Lynnette's father worked for the department, that Ryan had somewhere other than the police station or social services to stay.

The doctors had fought against releasing her, and the investigators had pushed to get more of a statement before she left. Joe had overruled both on her behalf. He knew what Kelly most wanted and he was determined to give it to her. And then he was going to make very sure she got at least twenty-four hours of uninterrupted sleep.

"Ryan?" Kelly asked as she reached the top of the stairs.

"The living room. Lynnette and I were just fixing breakfast for him. You'll join us?"

"Some coffee would be nice." Kelly glanced up at Joe and he reluctantly nodded. He knew she wanted to see Ryan alone. She rubbed her hand on his arm and smiled at him as she whispered her thanks. She turned toward the living room.

"Ryan?" Kelly sank down onto the couch beside the teen. "I'm so sorry."

All her energy had been focused on getting here. She was glad she hadn't delayed. Ryan . . . she recognized the pain he was feeling, the shock. It was the same look that had hit her when she learned Nick had been killed. Only worse, for this was a boy feeling the pain of losing his father.

"Joe said the two men I saw killed Dad."

She hugged him. It was the only thing she knew to do to convey the fact he wasn't alone. "You're not to blame."

"What happens to me now?"

Charles's second cousin was on his way from Britain, but that would hardly be a great answer for Ryan, a man he had never met before from a country where he had never lived. "Your dad asked me to look out for you. I would like to do that, if you'll let me." She'd given Charles her word and she desperately wanted to be able to keep it. She was worried that he would want nothing to do with her.

"Dad stole your medallion."

"I know. He apologized. He died a reformed thief, Ryan, not a thief. Please believe that."

"Why did he risk everything, get himself killed?" His tears returned. She pulled him toward her and buried the sobbing teen's head against her shoulder. To tell him his dad had been blackmailed, using Ryan as the leverage . . . she couldn't do it.

"A long time ago, when he was angry at God, he stole some things. He got past that point long ago. But the men he once worked for came back. Your dad didn't get involved by choice. He was trying to stop them, Ryan." The explanation didn't change the reality of what had happened. She knew that, and the words felt hollow.

"I don't understand."

"I know. He loved you, Ryan. He was

thinking about you." She leaned back, trying to decide what was best. He needed some sleep and some time. "Are you comfortable staying here for today? Maybe tomorrow we can get things arranged for you to come stay with Joe."

"He's not talking to me."

"Joe? He understands about the medallion."

"I lied to him."

"He'll forgive you. You want to talk to him? He's in the kitchen fixing me breakfast." She tightened her arm around his shoulders. "Come on. I promise you, it will be worth it." She struggled to her feet.

Ryan grabbed her arm to keep her from falling. "What's wrong?"

"I'll be fine. I just went for another long swim and I'm afraid my legs aren't used to solid ground yet."

The comment drew a smile from Ryan. "You can lean against me this time."

"Thank you." She gratefully did just that. Her balance was such she was beginning to suspect it was caused by water in her inner ears.

Joe came to meet them as they entered the kitchen. A batch of biscuits had just come out of the oven and sausage patties were browning. Kelly smiled at Ryan and then glanced at Joe. "Ryan would like to talk to you."

Joe tugged out a chair and pointed her to it. He set a big glass of orange juice in front of her. "Start with that; it will kill some of the saltwater you drank." He glanced at the teen. "Have you started to drink coffee yet?" When the teen nodded, Joe poured the boy a mug, picked up his own, and nodded to the door. "Come on. Let's take a walk."

Joe unlocked Kelly's house, then came back to the car. Kelly was asleep. He eased the seat belt from around her. He carefully lifted her from the car and carried her inside. There was so much relief at having her home. He walked back to the bedroom.

"Thanks, Joe," she awoke enough to whisper the words.

"I promised you would sleep in your own bed."

There was a bear on the bed. She reached down to pick it up so he could pull back the blankets. It was a white bear, worn now, the bear he had given her. It gave Joe hope. "He wears well."

She gave a soft smile. "Just like you."

Joe eased her under the covers, wanting

to follow up on that remark but didn't dare to at this moment. Her eyes had closed with a sigh and she turned her face into the pillow. He brushed her hair back. "Get some sleep. I'll be here when you wake up." It was an unnecessary suggestion; her breathing had already become shallow and slow. He stood there for a moment watching her sleep, then with reluctance stepped from the room and partially closed the door.

She slept through the rest of the day and awoke just before sunset. Joe heard her stirring and set down the book he was reading. "Kelly?" She joined him in the living room several minutes later, wearing a robe over sweats.

"Cold?"

She rubbed her arms. "Yes." She looked around the room, then closed her eyes. "Can we sit outside?"

Surprised at the request, he nodded and rose. "Sure." He reached for the afghan on the sofa to take out with them. The sun was setting over the Pacific. He helped her settle on the lounge chair. "You look more than just sad."

"I am."

He sat down on the chair beside her and brushed back her hair. "Come here. Hug a bear that can hug you back."

She wrapped her arms tightly around him and hung on. The emotion in her actions . . . he wrapped his arms around her and returned the grip, offering all the assurance he could that it would be okay. He wasn't leaving.

"Thanks," she whispered.

He briskly rubbed his hands across her arms. He loved her and somehow he was going to make this better, at least drive the memories back to a manageable proportion. "I wish I could have prevented this."

She shook her head against his chest. "Don't. I didn't see it, and I was closer to Charles than you were."

"I almost lost you. I never want to lose you."

"You didn't."

The night closed in around them. He couldn't have another close call like this, not and have any chance of staying sane. Whatever reassurance she needed from him regarding his career he would figure out some way to give her. He wanted a future with her.

"Will you marry me?" he asked softly. "I love you, Kelly." It wasn't the place and circumstances he had considered when he thought about asking her, but it was the right time, for any delay in those words would haunt him.

She didn't respond. He started to ease her back so he could see her face and she shook her head, not letting him. She turned her head and rubbed her cheek against his shirt. She was wiping away tears against the fabric. The realization caught him by surprise. She leaned back and gave him a smile that came in spite of the tears still falling. "I thought you would never ask. I would be proud to marry you. Very proud."

The joy was overwhelming. He gently kissed her. The celebration would come later when she felt better. "Thank you."

Her gaze held his, searching, and then she looked down and traced the sleeve of his shirt. She slid her hand into his. "What about Ryan?"

He took a deep breath, hearing her worry. He really did like the boy, and he knew where Kelly's heart was. She'd risked her life for that teen. Joe thought about it and then tightened his hand on hers. "He'll have both of us."

"Thank you for that."

"He's a good kid, Kelly."

He tipped up her chin and leaned down, softly kissing her. He felt an overwhelming tenderness that eclipsed even the passion. "Marry me soon?"

"Can you get leave for a honeymoon?"

He smiled at the question. "Watch me. Where would you like to go?"

"I've never been outside California."

"I could probably come up with a warm, private beach where we wouldn't freeze when we went for a swim."

"That idea I love. And I wouldn't mind sailing, if you could find a boat that was in good condition."

"Good condition. I hear a slight against my latest project."

"You have to admit it still needs some work, Bear."

She was teasing him and it felt wonderful. "By the time you get the wedding planned, I'll have the boat ready to sail."

"Two months? After Boomer and Christi have their baby?"

"Done." It was the best deal he had ever made. He lifted her hand and rubbed her ring finger. "I saw your wedding ring put away with Nick's flag. I was afraid you had lost it."

"It was time to take it off."

"What kind of engagement ring would you like in its place?"

"Sapphire and diamond."

He laughed at her immediate reply. "Want to think about it a while first?"

"I already have."

He grew serious. "It was a long night."

"A lot of time to think."

Joe rubbed his hand across her back. "For both of us."

She leaned her head back and smiled to lighten the moment. "I'm hungry."

"Why do I get the feeling that was a suggestion rather than a comment?"

"Steaks are in the refrigerator. I was going to cook out for you last night."

"I'll let you sit here and chat with me while I fire up the grill."

"I hoped you would say that."

He got up and prepared the grill, starting the coals.

She was staring out at the sea. He paused by the lounge chair and rested his hand on her hair to ruffle it gently. "Are you okay?"

"Yes." Her hand reached up and grasped his. "I've fallen in love with the sea."

He squeezed her hand. "I was afraid it would feel threatening after last night."

"No. It was a refuge when I most needed one."

"It's been one for me many times in the past." He listened to the breaking waves.

"It's peaceful tonight."

"Can we always live near the sea?"

"That's probably the only thing I can promise you. You're about to be a military bride again."

"I'm looking forward to it, Bear."

He paused on the way to get the steaks. "Why do I get the feeling my handle is under threat?"

"Well . . . I do have a suggestion."

The gleam in her eyes was enough of a warning. "You wouldn't dare."

"I promise to only call you teddy bear in private."

Her laughter filled the night as he swooped to pick her up with a playful growl.

Dear Reader,

Thank you for reading this book. It was a special honor to write. I absolutely fell in love with Joe and Kelly. And the guys of SEAL Platoon Nine — Cougar and Wolf and Boomer are friends now; I didn't want this story to end!

Those who serve this country in the military are special heroes. They live an adventure, see much of the world, but they also accept demands on their lives most civilians do not understand. I wanted to give a glimpse into that reality with this story — the sweat and blood and dedicated service behind the glamour.

When God calls a warrior, he is molding a man to be one of the pillars of our nation. There are real men like Joe "Bear" Baker wearing the uniform today. This is my tribute and thanks to them.

As always, I love to hear from my readers. Feel free to write me at:

Dee Henderson
c/o Multnomah Fiction
P.O. Box 1720
Sisters, Oregon 97759
E-mail: dee@deehenderson.com
or on-line at: http://
www.deehenderson.com

First chapters of all my books are online, please stop by and check them out. Thanks again for letting me share Joe and Kelly's story.

Sincerely,

Dee Henderson